The day played through Emma's mind.

Her shock at meeting Mason Chandler on Main Street, seeing his two little girls—the silent and troubled Charlotte, the bright and sweet Birdie—and hearing the unguarded words he'd said when he woke after falling from the roof. *You're so good. You could have been mine.*

If only she was young and unmarked by war, she might have reacted differently. But for four years, she had prayed and hoped and kept up her spirits. Trusting that Jonathan, good-natured and honorable, would return whole and they would spend their life together. Instead he'd been buried in Virginia. She stopped her thoughts there.

She did not think of Jonathan often anymore. Mason Chandler returning and the words he'd said to her had brought it all back—all the pain, all the waiting. She would keep her distance from him. But then she remembered Mrs. Ashford's remark about judgment and little Lily's unusual reticence. Those girls, Charlotte and Birdie—how could she help them?

A *USA TODAY* bestselling author of over forty novels, **Lyn Cote** lives in the north woods of Wisconsin with her husband in a lakeside cottage. She knits, loves cats (and dogs), likes to cook (and eat), never misses *Wheel of Fortune* and enjoys hearing from her readers. Email her at l.cote@juno.com. And drop by her website, www.lyncote.com, to learn more about her books that feature "Strong Women, Brave Stories."

Books by Lyn Cote

Love Inspired Historical

Wilderness Brides

Their Frontier Family
The Baby Bequest
Heartland Courtship
Frontier Want Ad Bride
Suddenly a Frontier Father

The Gabriel Sisters

Her Captain's Heart
Her Patchwork Family
Her Healing Ways

Visit the Author Profile page at Harlequin.com for more titles.

LYN COTE

Suddenly a Frontier Father

HARLEQUIN® LOVE INSPIRED® HISTORICAL

 LOVE INSPIRED BOOKS

Recycling programs
for this product may
not exist in your area.

ISBN-13: 978-1-335-36954-3

Suddenly a Frontier Father

Copyright © 2018 by Lyn Cote

www.Harlequin.com

Printed in U.S.A.

And we know that all things work together for good to them that love God, to them who are the called according to his purpose.
—*Romans* 8:28

To my late mother, Catherine Jean Baker.

Chapter One

Wisconsin Wilderness
Early September, 1873

Standing on the sunny riverboat deck, Mason Chandler was painfully aware of the intense curiosity of the other passengers. No doubt it did look odd for a man to be traveling with two little girls yet without a woman. Little Birdie stood on his right and Charlotte on his left in their new matching starched blue calico dresses. The tops of their bonneted heads barely reached his belt. If the girls had resembled each other or him, people might have merely assumed that he was a widowed father with two daughters.

Certainly, Charlotte with her light golden-brown hair and green eyes could pass for his child. But Birdie with skin the shade of dark chocolate could not. And of course, there was the other matter, Charlotte's special problem, that set them apart.

People had stared at them ever since he'd boarded the boat in Illinois. He might as well get used to it. He had no doubt that some of his once-friendly neighbors here in Pepin, Wisconsin, would be shocked and then no doubt cool toward him. What about Miss Jones, the woman who'd answered his newspaper advertisement for a wife?

After corresponding with her for months, he'd proposed to her by letter earlier this year. But he'd been called away to his father's deathbed and could not be in Pepin in March to marry her as they'd planned. Now it was September. He was six months too late. And his circumstances had changed so dramatically that he had sent her a letter months ago releasing her from their agreement. What else could an honorable man do?

He could only hope that he would have time to get settled in again before he finally met Miss Emma Jones. He hoped to be able to mend the situation. But it was a faint hope. So much had changed.

Well, this wasn't the first time in his life he'd swum against the current. He placed one arm around each little girl. These two little ones were his now, and he wouldn't let them down, no matter what.

The crew suddenly began calling to each other and hurrying around, casting the ropes ashore, jumping onto the pier. The steamboat slowed, glided on the sky-blue water and bumped against the dock. Mason picked up his satchel and the small valise that belonged to the girls. And soon they were walking onto the Wisconsin shore.

Though his life had changed, the town looked much the same as it had when he'd left in March. There was a blacksmith, Ashford's General Store, and a few other stores on Main Street, along with a saloon at the end of town. Now, in early autumn, the street was dusty and the trees were still green, though scarlet edged a few high maple leaves. The blacksmith's hammer on the anvil pounded clear in the afternoon air.

The little girls huddled close to him. He caught himself as he began to stride normally, and instead he shortened his steps. Before going to his cabin, he needed to buy a few necessary items at the general store but dreaded facing the inquisitive, talkative Mrs. Ashford. Why put it off, though? He led the little girls across the street and up the two steps to the store.

Plump and grandmotherly, Mrs. Ashford met him on the porch. "Mr. Chandler, you're back."

"Yes, ma'am. I need—"

"And who are these little girls?"

He was saved from replying when the woman looked over his shoulder and exclaimed, "Miss Jones! Here is your intended, Mason Chandler. He's come home at last!"

Mason turned. His heart was thumping suddenly and his mouth dry. Miss Emma Jones, the woman he'd hoped to marry, halted just a few paces in front of him. He drank in her appearance. Tall but not too tall. A trim figure. Bright golden curls atop a face so lovely he thought he might be dreaming. Miss Emma Jones was a beauty. His hope of winning her favor bumped down another notch.

Mason shook himself mentally and, after setting down the baggage, descended the two steps again. He bowed politely. "Miss Jones, I'm happy to meet you face-to-face at long last." An understatement.

"Mr. Chandler." Her voice devoid of welcome, she offered her gloved hand.

He shook it and held it in both of his. Neither her words nor tone encouraged him. "I apologize again," he said, forcing out the words, "for my not being here to meet you in March. I'm afraid I had little choice. Still, I wish things were different."

"The arrangement you made for me to stay with the Ashfords worked out well. They made me very welcome." She paused to smile at Mrs. Ashford. "I'm sorry about the loss of your father." She withdrew her hand from his.

He felt his neck heat with embarrassment for holding her hand too long.

"I was just asking Mr. Chandler," Mrs. Ashford interrupted, "who these little girls are."

At this moment, Charlotte spoke to Birdie with her hands, as was her way. Birdie replied in kind.

"What's that they are doing with their hands?" Mrs. Ashford asked.

Mason replied, "This is Charlotte, my little half-sister, and her friend Birdie. Charlotte cannot hear. They speak in sign language."

"She's deaf?" Mrs. Ashford's voice fell. "Oh, the poor little thing. What a judgment."

"A judgment?" Miss Jones challenged her. "What could a little child have done to deserve being judged?"

Mason looked at his once-intended bride. She'd said what he'd wanted to.

"I didn't mean it like that," Mrs. Ashford apologized. "I'm just sad for the child." Then the woman looked worried. "How long will your sister and her little friend be visiting here with you?"

"I have adopted both girls," Mason said, bracing

himself for the backlash, not looking toward Miss Jones.

Mrs. Ashford's face widened in shock. "How can you take care of two little girls all by yourself?" Before he could answer, she turned to Miss Jones. "You two will have to get married right away."

He couldn't help himself. With a quick glance, he sought Miss Jones's reaction.

She looked as if someone had slapped her.

Mason had not expected her to be pleased with the change in his circumstances, and it was worse to find out here in such a public place where they couldn't talk this through. He closed his eyes in defeat.

"Mrs. Ashford," Miss Jones began, "Mr. Chandler has just returned—"

"Aren't you going to go through with your engagement?" Mrs. Ashford asked.

Here, right here on Main Street—was this where Miss Jones would let him down?

At that moment he heard someone approaching. He turned and saw Levi Comstock, the burly blacksmith and his good friend, coming. Or, he had been a good friend. Would he remain so?

Still in his leather apron and with his soot-blackened face, Levi held out his hand. "Good to see you back. Asa's still got your cow and—also a new heifer—"

"A heifer?" Mason asked with surprise.

"Yes, your cow had a nice little calf in the spring."

Mason couldn't speak. Such good news.

"And those two and your chickens are all in good order with Asa. I still have your horses and wagon at my place. When would you like to come get them?"

In reply to all this warm welcome and news, Mason clasped Levi's large, strong hand and shook it heartily.

"Well, Mr. Chandler," Miss Jones spoke up, "I am happy to have met you and I will see you again soon, I'm sure."

"But Miss Jones," Mrs. Ashford spoke up, "you're on your way to your sister's home today, aren't you? Mr. Chandler's homestead is just up the road from there. You two might as well keep each other company on your way. You can bring Mr. Chandler up to date about all that's happened in our little town while he was away."

Mason did not appreciate the storekeeper's wife's suggestion. The last thing he wanted was to "keep each other company." And it was more than obvious that Miss Jones didn't want to, either. But what could they do here on Main Street but comply?

Emma literally clamped her teeth on her tongue, holding back a sharp retort. She wanted to get away from Mason Chandler. Coming upon him without warning had jumbled her thoughts and emotions in a way she had not expected. But what could she say to Mrs. Ashford? She could not be rude on the main street of town. "Of course," she said politely.

Mason appeared uncomfortable, too.

She liked him better for that.

"You're pretty," one of the little girls said, looking up at her with big brown eyes and chubby brown cheeks.

Emma wished once again that people wouldn't point out her outward appearance. She knew that they meant it in a complimentary way. But she was more than just a pretty face. However, saying this would not be polite, so she merely smiled at the little girl.

Mason asked Mrs. Ashford for the few items he needed to purchase, and then soon the four of them started up Main Street, heading toward her sister's place. Then Mason could go on from there to his homestead.

For the first few minutes while they were walking through town, neither of them said anything. She didn't want to be thrown together with Mason, the man she planned to let down lightly. She wasn't rejecting him personally. After losing Jonathan, she'd never wanted to marry. Only dire need had forced her to accept a proposal from a stranger. But she did not need to marry now as she had in March. So she would be polite and distant.

Soon the four of them were walking a grassy track up a rise from town, thickly guarded on both sides by towering maples, oaks and fir trees. Emma decided talking was better than this awkward, heavy silence. Besides, she wondered how had he come to adopt two little girls. "I don't mean to pry, but I'm interested in your girls." She left the question open for any way he chose to answer it.

He cleared his throat. "My father, a widower, told me about losing Charlotte's mother. When he died, I went to Illinois to find my little sister."

That commanded Emma's attention. Some men might not have been concerned enough about a little sister, especially a little half-sister, to go looking for her. Again, this was to his credit. She wanted to ask about the other little girl, but again her desire to keep her distance and her idea of politeness held her back.

"Birdie also lived at the orphans' home in Illinois," Mason continued as if sensing her unspoken question. "When Charlotte came to live at the orphanage well over a year ago, the woman who runs it, a Mrs. Felicity Gabriel Hawkins, located someone in Chicago who knew sign language and hired her to come teach it to Charlotte. That teacher said that it was better to have two pupils because they could help each other. And Birdie was already Charlotte's best friend."

"I liked Charlotte right away," Birdie said. "And I wanted to learn how to talk with my hands."

At that moment Charlotte looked up to Emma for the first time.

Emma was moved by the lost expression in Charlotte's green eyes. And she was fascinated as she watched how Birdie worked her hands, communicating with the quiet girl walking beside her. Emma suppressed the urge to hug Birdie and silently promised to be a good friend to this little sweetheart. "I'm glad you did, Birdie. I like Charlotte already and I like you, too."

Birdie smiled up at her as she evidently signed to Charlotte what Emma had said. Charlotte almost smiled.

Suddenly Emma realized that somehow Mason was slipping past her carefully constructed defenses. He was kind. Generous. And not hard to look at, either. Blushing, she quickened her step, hurrying them as much as was polite.

Another question niggled at Emma. Should she ask it? Yes, it would distract her from her awareness of him and not give him time to turn the conversation to "them."

"So you were allowed to adopt both girls?"

"That was what caused the further delay in my returning," Mason said. "Mrs. Hawkins questioned me about my qualifications to take charge of my little sister. Which wasn't surprising since she didn't know me."

"Of course," Emma murmured. A blue jay sounded its raucous song as if jeering at her, trapped in this uncomfortable situation, talking politely to a man she had agreed to marry but no longer wished to.

"I told her I was homesteading in Pepin, Wisconsin. That's when she said her childhood friend, Noah Whitmore, was also homesteading in Pepin."

"She knew Noah Whitmore?"

"Yes, they grew up going to the same Quaker meeting in Pennsylvania. And she decided to write to him to gain a character reference for me."

"It's amazing how God orchestrates matters." Emma believed this, yet felt the old tug of disappointment. She'd prayed fervently for her fiancé Jonathan to survive the war. But evidently God had denied her request. Someday she hoped she could accept that with peace. She drew in a slow breath, wishing the brittle feeling around her heart would leave her.

"I suppose," he said.

His uncertain tone caught her attention. What disappointment had he sustained? She brushed away this sudden sympathy and went on. "Since you are here with your girls, Noah Whitmore must've given you a good character reference."

"I am very grateful for my girls." Mason glanced with obvious affection at the two little ones.

The paternal glance softened her resistance again.

She would have to be careful around this man, so as not to mislead him. She'd given all her love to Jonathan and she had nothing more to give.

"Some man kilt Charlotte's mama and she couldn't hear no more," Birdie said. "The doctor say she 'sterical deaf."

Shocked, Emma glanced at Mason. Was this true?

His jawline had tightened.

Emma could tell he did not like this being spoken of. And she didn't blame him. "Bad things happen in this world," she commented, trying to bring the uncomfortable topic to an end.

The little girl nodded solemnly and began to sign to Charlotte.

Without looking at Emma, Mason said, "Birdie, please don't sign what I'm going to say now to Charlotte. It upsets her when people talk about it." Then he did look at Emma. "The doctor called Charlotte's condition hysterical deafness. He said he couldn't find anything wrong with the structure of her ears, inside or out. We fear that Charlotte's mother was murdered and perhaps Charlotte witnessed it. That's what Mrs. Hawkins was told by the person who brought Charlotte to the orphanage." He appeared to want to say more but he didn't.

The hair on the nape of Emma's neck prickled at the horror this sweet little girl might have witnessed. Emma completed his thought. "I will not speak of this."

"I think it's best for the girls if we don't. People somehow transfer what a person's family has suffered to them—as if they have been judged, as Mrs.

Ashford said." He glanced downward. "Will you remember that, Birdie?" he asked gently.

"Yes, sir!" Birdie said. "I only said it 'cause I can see Miss Emma is a fine lady."

This uncomfortable conversation ended as they turned the bend and ahead lay her sister's farm. Judith was doing laundry in the shade of an old oak tree beside the cabin.

"Judith!" Emma called out with sincere relief. "You'll never guess who this is!" Emma made an attempt at teasing, trying to lighten the moment. She hoped Judith's husband, Asa, would appear and relieve her of Mason Chandler. She wanted to be alone to sort out her unexpected reactions to him. Or better yet, talk it over with Judith in private.

Hoping to distance himself from Emma, Mason wished Asa Brant would appear and he could claim his livestock and then head on to his place. He wanted to be alone to sort out his unforeseen response to Miss Emma Jones. But he glued a smile onto his face and pulled up all his reserves of courtesy.

Emma led him toward Asa's wife, who appeared flustered at his finding her in the midst of the weekly chore. Of course, he knew she was Emma's twin sister, but they did not favor one another. Judith had brown hair and eyes to match, and possessed none of Emma's startling beauty.

Then blessedly, the familiar tall and tanned, darkhaired Asa Brant stepped out of his barn. His face lifted into a welcoming smile and he hurried forward, his hand outstretched.

Emma continued on toward her sister.

Dropping the baggage, Mason gripped Asa's hand, once again grateful to find another person who remained a friend—so far. "I'm just on my way home and wanted to stop and get my cattle. I hear I have a calf."

"Yes, both of us increased our cattle this spring." Asa beamed.

"Asa, I can't thank you enough for taking care of them. I'll pay you back—"

"Not a word about that." Asa forestalled him with an upraised hand. "What are friends for?"

Out of the corner of his eye, Mason glimpsed another little girl, a blonde about Charlotte's age, who had come out of Asa's cabin and who was staring at his two little girls. Then he noted a boy with shaggy brown hair around eight or nine years old standing near the barn door.

Mason paused, wondering who they were.

"Before we take care of the cows, I need to introduce you to my wife. Or, I should say, my family," Asa said with obvious pride. Asa led Mason to the woman who was now his wife, standing near the little girl. And the little boy hurried to Asa's side. Asa rested a hand on the boy's shoulder.

Acute envy caught around Mason's heart. If he hadn't been called away, he would be settled now with Emma as his wife. He wouldn't have spent the whole growing season away. Leave it to his father to interrupt and bring disaster to his only son. Mason forced himself to relax his face, tightened by regret. He tried to focus as Asa introduced him to Judith and to the two children, Lily and Colton, whom they had evidently taken in.

He noted that Lily continued to stare at Charlotte and Birdie. Perhaps the little girl was just shy. He hoped that explained her lack of welcome.

Emma stooped to eye level with Asa's girl. "Lily, say hello to Charlotte and Birdie. They will be your new neighbors. You can play with them."

Lily turned her face into Judith's skirt.

"I guess Lily is a bit shy today. But you three will get to know each other over time," Emma said gently.

Mason was grateful for her attempt. It was obvious that Miss Emma Jones was not only beautiful but kind. He needed to go before he revealed even a hint of the sadness that had begun years before when his father had changed for the worse. And his secret now separated him from everyone, not just Emma Jones. "I need to get home, Asa. I want to get the house straightened up and everything settled before evening comes."

"I'd come and help you," Asa apologized, "but I'm right in the middle of something."

"I don't need any help," Mason said.

"Yes, you do," Asa replied. "You have that luggage to carry and the girls and the cattle. I can bring them over later—"

"I don't want to cause you any trouble."

"I would come along," Asa's wife said, motioning toward the laundry tubs, "but I'm right in the middle of this week's clothes."

"I don't expect any help," Mason said again. He held up his hands and stepped backward. "You all have your own work to do."

"I'll come and help," Emma said. "I can drive a few cows."

She surprised Mason into silence. He wanted to study her face to find out why she'd offered help, but of course, he couldn't.

"It's settled, then," Asa said, sounding relieved. "Emma and Colton will lead the cattle, Mason."

"And you'll come back here for supper," Judith said. "We have plenty and would be glad to have your company."

"That's right. We insist," Asa agreed.

After the slights and reflected shame he'd suffered over the past few months, Mason felt humbled by their warm welcome. He only hoped no one here ever discovered the truth about his father, how he'd lived and where he'd died. That might be a bitter pill too big to swallow even by friends.

Soon Mason, still burdened with the baggage, walked beside Emma with Colton.

"I'll box up your chickens and bring them over when I'm done!" Asa called after them.

Mason called back his thanks. The road turned to the north at the beginning of Asa's property, going around it and leading to Mason's homestead.

Emma and Colton carried prodding staffs they barely needed. The cow and young heifer strolled along, pausing occasionally to nibble grass. Mason wished he could hurry them, but no one hurried a milk cow. A contented cow gave more milk, and he would need it. Without a crop, he would depend much on his chickens and cows to keep the girls fed this winter.

"I'm sorry to trouble you," Mason murmured to Emma as they rounded another bend in the road.

"It's no trouble. I was raised on a farm. I like cows."

He didn't know what to say to this. *"You're too pretty to be herding cattle"* didn't seem appropriate. And they were certainly well chaperoned with the silent boy, and Birdie chattering in word and sign, and Charlotte, as always, guarded and silent. All the words he wished to say to Miss Emma must be held back. And she probably didn't want to hear them, anyway.

"That little girl back there didn't like us," Birdie said. "She wouldn't talk to us."

The boy on the other side of the cattle said nothing in explanation.

"Some girls and boys are shy with strangers...people they are just meeting," Emma suggested.

But Mason doubted it.

Birdie considered this. "Maybe," she allowed. "Is this a nice place to live?"

"Yes, it is. I'm the schoolteacher here," Emma said.

Oh, Mason thought. Another indication that this lady's situation had altered. Just like his had. His hopes about her dimmed further. A woman with a paying job would not need a husband.

Birdie's eyes widened. "You're the teacher? Charlotte and me were supposed to start school this year in Illinois."

"Oh?" Emma's voice sounded a bit uncertain.

And no wonder. Mason had been at a loss how Mrs. Hawkins thought his girls could attend school. After all, Charlotte wouldn't be able to hear the teacher.

Again, Birdie's fingers were busy talking to Charlotte.

Charlotte replied in kind and appeared to be scolding her friend.

"Oh, Charlotte still thinks she can't go to school," Birdie added.

Exactly, Mason commented mentally.

"Children need to go to school," Emma said. "All children."

Mason looked away. His little sister would only be the recipient of stares and unkind words. And he wouldn't let that happen.

Only three-quarters of a mile separated the two homesteads, so very soon he glimpsed his place— the sturdy log barn and cabin. After all the years of war and then wandering, he had once again a home to return to and now he had his sister and Birdie, too. His heart twinged at the thought. He was glad, but when he cast a sideways glance at the lady near him, he was sad. He'd hoped to employ finesse over when to meet and get to know Emma. But Birdie had even blurted out the cause of Charlotte's deafness. What might have been would probably never be.

Then he saw something that shocked him. Behind his cabin, a corn field was tall and green and golden, nearing harvest. "What?" He halted right there.

Emma stopped, too. "What is it?"

"I...how do I have a corn crop?"

She followed his gaze. "Oh, yes, Asa planted your fields, one of corn and one of hay."

"He..." Mason couldn't speak from the shock and the feeling of being humbled by a friend's help.

"And ours got wrecked," the silent boy suddenly spoke with plain disgust.

Mason swung to him. "Yours? You mean Asa's crop? Wrecked? How?"

"Yeah, a bad man drove his horses through it, trampled it bad," the boy said.

Mason shifted his attention back to Emma. "What happened?"

"Just what the boy said," she replied, looking unhappy. "The culprit left the county, though the sheriff has a warrant out for his arrest."

Mason couldn't ask any more questions. The thought of Asa planting his crops while losing his own was too much to take in.

"Want me to drive the cows into the barn?" the boy asked.

"Yes, I'll just put the cases inside and be out to help you. Thanks." Mason turned to Emma, ready to let her go. She must be as uncomfortable in this situation as he was. "Thank you for your help."

She paused, studying him. "I will sweep out your cabin before I leave."

She must be offering to do this because of the girls. He couldn't believe she was staying for his sake. "That's not necessary—"

"I know it's not, but you'll have enough to do settling the cattle and getting firewood and water inside. Dusting and sweeping won't take long." She paused to touch first Birdie's, then Charlotte's shoulder. "The girls can help me."

"We can help!" Birdie parroted with glee.

He again realized that Miss Emma was a very kind lady. Gratitude clogged his throat. Overhead the sun was sliding toward the western horizon. He needed to do the things she'd mentioned, get the house fit for occupation so he and the girls could settle in before night. Finally he regained his voice. "Thank you, Miss Jones."

"Thank you, Miss Emma!" Birdie crowed.

Mason hurried ahead, unlocked the chain he'd secured the cabin door with and pushed it open. He set the baggage just inside and shed his traveling jacket on a peg on the wall by the door. Then he turned back to the barn. "I'll go see to the cattle."

"Fine," Emma said, watching Mason go with both relief and a touch of regret. This man, whom she'd already come to respect, carried a heavy load, and she had volunteered to help in the small way she could. But she must not let sympathy lure her from her new, independent life. She brushed away these thoughts of Mason Chandler.

"Girls," she announced briskly, "let's go inside to see how much dust we need to clean away." She strode through the open door and then paused to let her eyes adjust to the dimmer interior. The little girls, one on each side of her, peered in also.

Dust covered every surface of a sparsely furnished one-room cabin—a short counter attached to the wall with a dishpan on it, two benches, one on each side of a table, two handmade straight-back chairs by the central fireplace, and a bed in the corner. Emma surveyed the home that would have been hers if events had followed the course she'd expected.

She much preferred her cozy teacher's quarters where she could do as she pleased. She took off her bonnet and hung it on a peg by the door. The girls shed theirs and she hung them up, too, since the hooks were too high for them to reach.

"It's dusty," Birdie commented.

"It is indeed." Emma glimpsed a broom standing in the corner and several cloths hanging over the side of the dishpan. "I will sweep and the two of you can begin dusting." She glanced down. "Do you know how to dust?"

"Yes, miss," Birdie replied. "We dusted every week in Illinois."

"Good." She handed them each a cloth and claimed the broom.

"We sing while we dust," Birdie informed her.

"What do you sing?" Emma asked, intrigued.

Birdie replied in song, "Ain't gonna let nobody turn me 'roun'; Turn me 'roun'."

Emma couldn't like the *ain't*s, but the song sounded cheerful, and she liked the sentiment. Nobody was going to turn her 'round, either. She had her new course as Pepin schoolteacher set, and she would follow it.

Soon she found herself sweeping up acorn tops and other evidence of squirrels. A thump against the side of the house startled her. Then she heard footsteps overhead. She looked up as if she could see through the ceiling.

The sound of scratching came down through the fireplace.

"What's that, Miss Emma?" Birdie asked, also looking up.

"I think Mr. Chandler may be cleaning out debris from the top of the chimney." She approached the fireplace and craned her neck to look up inside it.

Then she heard it—the sound of boots sliding down

wooden shingles and a yell and finally a thump out-side. Her heart lurched. "Oh, no!"

Birdie cried out in fear and ran to her with Char-lotte close behind.

Emma hurried to the door and outside into the day-light, the girls at her heels.

Mason lay on the ground, flat on his back, not moving.

Emma gasped. How badly was he hurt? She rushed toward him and met Colton, who had run from the barn. Emma dropped to her knees, yet stopped herself from touching him. "Mr. Chandler?" she repeated his name several times.

She looked across at Colton, who stood on the man's other side, looking as worried as she felt. She leaned forward over Mason's mouth and turned her cheek to feel his warm breath. She felt it. Relief ruf-fled through her. "He's breathing."

Then she became aware of the fact that the two little girls were crying. "Don't cry, Birdie. Tell Char-lotte her brother's breathing. He'll be fine." *I hope.*

All Mason Chandler and Birdie had revealed today had captured her interest, her sympathy. But that was all she could give him. Nothing more. She was inde-pendent at last, teaching school, which she'd always wanted to do. She was grateful Mason had released her from their agreement to marry. She would help him now but keep her distance.

Chapter Two

Mason blinked. He couldn't think. But he could see Emma's face just inches above his. "You're so good," he whispered. "And you could have been mine."

Her eyes widened. "Mr. Chandler? Can you hear me?"

Silly question. Of course he could hear her, see her. He realized then that he was lying on the prickly grass, looking up at the blue sky. Crowded around him were his girls and Asa's boy. Why was Emma on her knees beside him? "What happened?" He moved to sit up.

With her small hand on his chest, Emma pressed him back. "Take it easy. You've been unconscious for a couple of minutes. You fell from the roof."

He closed his eyes and the memory returned, his sliding off the roof. That breathless jolt of panic. "I stepped on a loose shingle and lost my balance."

"That could happen to anyone," Emma murmured. She slipped her hand under his head. "You don't have a bump. Does your head hurt?"

"A bit." He appreciated Emma's trying to soothe

his dented pride, but he noticed then that Charlotte was crying and that Birdie, with tears running down her cheeks, was comforting her. He stirred himself. "I'll be all right, girls. Don't worry, Charlotte." He tried to work his fingers to sign but he couldn't. "I'll be all right," he repeated. He watched Birdie sign this to his sister, but she continued to cry. He could see the fear on her face. *I must get up and show I'm all right*, he thought to himself. He tried to sit up again.

Emma pressed him back once more. "First let's make sure you've not hurt anything seriously."

He glanced up at her, very aware of her being so close to him. He hoped she hadn't heard him say, *"You're so good,"* or, worse, *"You could have been mine."* He cringed inwardly, hoping he hadn't said that aloud. The words were true but too personal and embarrassing in the extreme.

"Start by moving each part of you and see if you feel any sharp pain," she counseled.

He didn't want to obey. He just wanted to stand up, thank her for her help and hurry her along home. Her presence was bringing forth feelings he didn't want to explore. But yes, he might have hurt himself, so her instruction made sense. He didn't want to make matters any worse than they were. He obliged her, moving his neck and working down his body, moving each arm individually and rotating each joint— shoulders, elbows, wrists, knees.

All was well till he tested his ankles one at a time. "Uhhh." The pain-filled syllable was forced out when he rotated his right ankle.

Emma glanced down. "I think you can safely sit up.

But perhaps you should first push down your stocking so we can see your ankle."

Once again he obliged.

"Oh, it's swelling," she said as they both stared at the flushed ankle. "But you were able to rotate it, so that should mean it's just a sprain. It will heal in about a week without any further problem. When we were children, my brother suffered a sprain after falling from a tree. I know what to do."

Mason could not believe he was in this situation. And he'd fallen while she was nearby. Humiliation. "I have so much to do. I can't be laid up."

"Well, we can't do anything about that until we take care of your ankle." She rose and rested a gentle hand on Birdie's shoulder. "Explain everything to Charlotte and let her know this isn't serious." Then she turned to Colton. "Please run into the house and bring out a chair. Birdie, please go get the water bucket inside the door."

He tried to make sense of her instructions but the wind had been knocked out of him and he felt depleted somehow. *I guess falling off a roof does take it out of a man.* He grimaced ruefully.

Soon after instructing Colton to stand behind the chair to steady it, Emma helped Mason sit up. "Now the chair is right behind you. When you're ready to stand, I want you to put your hands on my shoulders so I can steady you as you push up onto your good foot. I'm sure you have the strength to stand, but favoring your ankle will put you off balance. So hold on to me." Stooping, she positioned herself in front of him.

He parted his lips to refuse her help.

"Seeing you fall again will only upset Charlotte more," she whispered in his ear.

Her warm breath against his ear stirred him. And her words persuaded him to do as she suggested. "I'm ready." He reached up and gripped her slender shoulders. He pushed up, staggered. She steadied him as he landed in the chair. A touch of vertigo and sharp pain in his ankle vied with his reaction to being so near Emma Jones. She smelled of roses. He closed his eyes momentarily, marshaling all his self-control against the pain and against the temptation to reach for her. He leaned against the back of the chair. "Thank you."

She stifled a chuckle.

His eyes flew open in surprise.

"Sorry." She looked abashed and amused at the same time. "I caught myself just before I said, 'My pleasure.' It's silly how certain words trigger other words, isn't it?"

He didn't feel anything like smiling, but she drew one from him anyway. "I know what you mean." He gazed at this woman who was surprising him in so many ways. She had a sense of humor. He liked that. Then he shifted in his chair slightly, and that tiny movement caused pain to shoot through his ankle and up his calf. He held in a gasp.

Charlotte moved to his side and pressed against him. He put an arm around her and kissed her forehead. He haltingly signed that he would be fine and she shouldn't worry. Or he hoped that was what he said. His grasp of sign language still did not rival Birdie's.

Emma stepped away, primed the pump, filled the bucket and made him rest his foot in cold water up over his ankle. He noted that she tried not to look directly at him and wondered if it was just this situation. After all, she had volunteered only to dust, not to take care of him. Or was it just her not wanting to be here with him?

"I know most people put sprains in hot water," Emma said, standing in front of him, "but my mother always told me that cold water does best to reduce swelling. I hope Judith still has some goose grease. That works amazingly on sprains."

He nodded. The cold water was painful on his throbbing ankle. Goose grease. Good grief.

Emma stood near him, scanning the area and obviously thinking. "Children, we need to do the chores. Mr. Chandler isn't able—"

"I'll be fine. Just give me a few minutes—"

"Mr. Chandler," she interrupted, "of course it's understandable that you don't want us to do what needs to be done, but you are going to have limited mobility for several days."

He wanted to argue but the throbbing in his ankle underlined her words. He nodded, head down.

She turned to the boy. "Colton, Mr. Chandler is going to need a crutch. I want you to go in the woods and find a young tree about this thick." She curved her hands together, leaving about a three-inch-diameter opening. "Take a hatchet and cut it off and bring it here." She turned to Mason. "While you're soaking your ankle, you can fashion it into a crude crutch."

Mason nodded, pulling out his pocket knife. Disagreeing would be pointless and graceless. And he still felt shaken. *I should have been more careful. Why couldn't anything go right this year?* His one hope was that the words he'd said upon regaining consciousness had been inaudible. So far Emma had given him no indication that she'd heard his much too personal words.

"You're so good. And you could have been mine." Mason's words played in her mind much later that unexpectedly stressful day. Now she walked beside him up the forest track on their way to Judith's for supper. He was balancing himself on the crutch he and Colton had contrived out of a young tree, now stripped of its bark with cushioning rags wrapped around the crook under his arm.

"Are you sure—" she began again.

"I can walk the short way to Asa's," Mason said, grimacing as he stumped along on the uneven dirt track.

She sighed inwardly. Men. Sometimes when the bounds that hemmed her in as a "lady" felt onerous, she reminded herself that men also were hemmed in. Men didn't show weakness—period. And then he'd been forced to sit and watch her get his place ready for the night, including the cattle. So she understood how lowering this situation was for him, especially in front of her.

"You're so good. You could have been mine." She couldn't get his words out of her mind. She never appreciated the way people always first commented about her appearance. But this man had mentioned her character and so had proven that he was looking into her as a person, not just at her face. This once again inched her toward caring about him. She resisted it, must resist it. Love was too treacherous a path to go

down again—ever. Just thinking of allowing herself to be vulnerable again caused her to feel slightly nauseated. *I can never do that again. I don't have it in me to love like that again. No.*

"As long as you are patient and don't try to hurry the healing, you should be fine in a week or so." She did not look at him as she murmured this.

"No doubt you're right." He exhaled, releasing his obvious dissatisfaction audibly. "There's just so much to do."

"There always is." And then they were walking around a bend and met Asa, who was already on the road, striding toward them.

"What's happened? I was just setting out to see why Colton hadn't returned," Asa said.

With relief Emma let Mason explain the situation. Now, as they continued toward Asa, she could hurry on to her sister and turn Mason over to Asa. She listened to the men talking, and when Asa reached them, she headed briskly down the road. "I want to go help Judith!" she called over her shoulder. After supper, she would walk home to her own room, her own place behind the school, and relax. And not give this day or this man another thought.

On the Brants' table the wiped-clean plates showed how they had all devoured Asa's wife's good supper. Within Mason the good feeling of being well fed vied with his painfully throbbing ankle. Asa and his wife with their two children sat across from him, his two girls and Emma. Mason noted that the girl Lily did not speak but kept looking at his girls and then away. He hoped she was just shy, like Emma had said earlier.

"Mason, you will just have to stay here," Asa said, "till you get back to normal."

Variations of this had been mentioned all throughout the evening meal. Mason felt exhausted by the day's events and he couldn't take much more. He'd replied politely but finally reached the end of his tether. He stated the truth. "I just want to go home. I've been away from home for months and I want to be in my own bed under my own roof." Without turning his head, he watched Emma out of the corner of his eye as he had throughout the meal. She was gazing at him, her chin downward. What was she thinking? Was it of him?

"But you'll need help," Judith said.

"I can help," Colton spoke up.

Asa, Judith, Emma and Mason all turned to look at the boy.

"I can help." Colton stood up. "I can fetch and carry. Mr. Brant, you helped me and Lily when we needed help. So I can help Mr. Chandler."

Asa gripped the boy's shoulder and smiled at him with approval.

"That makes good sense," Emma agreed. "Mr. Chandler walked here. He has a crutch. He just needs a little help. I completely understand why he wants to be in his own place, don't we all?"

"Thank you," Mason said with emphasis. "Asa, please let Colton go with me and the girls. Thanks to Miss Jones and the children, everything is ready for us to settle down for the night. And that's all I want." He was grateful to Emma for backing him up and to the boy for offering. But he was afraid to look at her and betray more than this. Why did she have to be both lovely and kind? She could do much better than him for a husband.

Asa and Judith exchanged glances. "Very well," Asa agreed. "Colton, gather your things and your bed-roll from up in the loft. Thank you for offering to help our neighbor."

Colton didn't reply but obeyed.

Pressing his hands on the table, Mason pushed himself up. Then he manipulated his crutch and secured it under his right arm. He thought he had just enough energy to get home.

Emma stood also and walked to the door. "I'll bid you all good night. And Judith, thank you for the lovely supper."

Mason watched the woman he had hoped to marry walk away into the gathering twilight. He bound up his mind against thinking of her. She had been help-ful. She has been kind. But she had made it clear with her every glance and every word that she wanted to be only his neighbor and nothing more.

Emma arrived home and soon, in her nightwear, sat in her rocker, sipping a cup of chamomile tea and honey. She still felt stirred up and hoped the tea would soothe her so she could sleep. The day played through her mind. Her shock at meeting Mason Chandler on Main Street, seeing his two little girls—the silent and troubled Charlotte, the bright and sweet Birdie—and hearing the unguarded words he'd said when he woke.

She took another sip of the warm, sweet tea. If only she were young and unmarked by war, she might have reacted differently. But for four bloody years, she had prayed and hoped and kept up her spirits. Trusting that

Jonathan, good-natured and honorable, would return whole and they would spend their lives together. Instead he'd been buried in Virginia. She stopped her thoughts there.

She did not think of Jonathan often anymore. Mason Chandler returning and the words he'd said to her had brought it all back, all the pain, all the waiting. She would keep her distance from him. But then she remembered Mrs. Ashford's remark about judgment and little Lily's unusual reticence. Both of Mason's girls would cause notice in town. They were orphans, Birdie's mother had no doubt been a slave and Charlotte was deaf. Charlotte and Birdie—how could she help them?

Monday afternoon, as the students were finishing the last lesson of the day, Emma tried not to show the roiling pot of emotion in the pit of her stomach. Mason and his girls hadn't attended church yesterday and she could understand that. He'd just sprained his ankle and he didn't have his wagon yet. But she'd hoped that Colton would walk the girls to school today so she could help them get acquainted.

The rumors about Mason's "peculiar" girls had already begun in town. Emma wanted to set the right tone and ease the girls into acceptance. She gazed over the heads of her students and let it rest on Colton's dark head bent over his slate. She didn't want the other children to hear, but she needed to talk to Colton.

"Children, finish the questions and then put away everything. Our day together is ending."

The children obeyed with some murmuring. As

usual, the children lined up in the center aisle and waited for her to position herself at the door. As usual, she spoke to each child, encouraging them and reminding them of what they should be practicing at home that evening. It always included studying their spelling list. The town was insistent that their spellers shine in the spring spelling bee. Her students prepared all year.

When Colton stopped in front, she asked him if he would stay to help with something. He nodded and then moved out of line. "Lily," he called, "I got to help Miss Jones. Wait on the swing."

Soon the school was empty except for her and Colton. "What do you want me to do?" Colton looked up at her.

She didn't try to hide her true concerns. "Why didn't Birdie and Charlotte come to school today?"

Colton frowned. "The little black girl wanted to come real bad. But Mr. Chandler said no, not yet."

Emma was afraid of that.

"What do you want me to do here?" Colton asked, glancing out the open window, obviously wanting to leave.

"You're still helping Mr. Chandler?"

"Yes, they'll come to our place for supper. Mrs. Brant insisted. And then I'll walk home with them and stay there for the night."

"How is Mr. Chandler's ankle?" She refused to let his dazed, whispered words repeat once more in her mind. Or she tried to.

"He doesn't say anything about it. But I see he still needs a crutch." Colton shifted on his feet, reminding her that he wanted to be off and out of school.

"Thank you, Colton."

The boy paused and turned back at the doorway. "When Lily and me started school here, some kids acted strange around us. I think it's 'cause…'cause our parents died. People don't like it when you're different."

The boy's wisdom surprised and impressed her. "I'm afraid that is correct."

"I like Birdie. She's real sweet and always helps."

"That's very true. Thank you, Colton."

The boy left and she walked around the schoolroom, making certain everything was in place. She could understand why Mason wanted to protect his two little girls, but keeping them at home hidden did them no good. They were going to spend their lives here—and they both deserved as good a life as anyone else here in Pepin. If it weren't for the girls and their need for special care, she could ignore this man. But she could see the girls might need her.

Mason Chandler, you are wrong if you keep them home. She knew how stubborn men could be. But it might just be that he needed time. She would give him time, but just so much.

A few days later, in the evening at the Brants', the fragrance of the rabbit stew set before Mason literally caused him to salivate. He bowed his head politely while Asa offered the prayer over the meal. Hearing another man pray heightened the feeling of stone encasing his own heart. Maybe God hadn't deserted him but it sure felt like it. Then he scolded himself. Years ago he'd lost his mother, and months ago his father, but he'd gained a sister and Birdie. He resisted a thought about also losing Emma.

"I caught the rabbits," Colton spoke up. "I used my snares."

For the hundredth time or more Mason found himself glancing at the door. He tried not to but he always looked for Emma to join them. He turned his mind from this. "Well done, Colton," Mason replied, recalling his boyhood days. Then another worry intruded. How could he bring up the unpleasant conversation about Asa's destroyed corn and hay crops? He'd tried twice now but Asa had changed the subject both times.

Birdie and Charlotte sat on the bench beside him. He could tell Birdie wanted to talk to Lily, but the little girl rarely looked at them. Pain twisted in his chest over this. Birdie had wanted to go to school with Colton each day but he had kept the girls home. Why did people judge others on things like skin color and deafness?

"I'm glad you agreed to eat supper with us till your ankle is healed," Asa's wife, sitting on the opposite side of the table, said. "How is it doing? Did the goose grease help?"

At her words, Mason's ankle throbbed as if taunting him with his weakness. "Yes, it helped. My ankle's still swollen some, but it's improving."

"It will be all better soon." Judith forked up a bite of stew.

"I thank you for your hospitality and for Colton's help," he said, grateful, knowing that his girls needed more food than he would be able to rustle up while standing on a crutch by the fire. He decided this was the opening he'd been waiting for. "And Asa, you've not let me discuss your planting my crops—"

"I didn't plant your full crops—"

"You did more than I would ever have expected. And I'm going to share my corn and hay with you. I think—"

Asa tried to interrupt.

Mason forged onward. "I think that if we are careful, we'll have almost enough to make it through the winter and put away some seed for next spring. It will be tight, but we can make it."

"I didn't put it in for that reason." Asa still sounded put out.

"I know, but it's a blessing—for both of us—that you did."

"Asa," Judith said, resting a hand on her husband's sleeve, "Mason is speaking the truth. What you have done for a friend has come back to bless all of us."

The woman's mention of blessing hit Mason squarely in the heart, the heart that had suffered and been stretched this year. "And when November comes," he spoke up, banishing these thoughts, "you'll have to permit me to bring you some fresh meat, Mrs. Brant." He savored the rich gravy, rolling it on his tongue.

"I'm also looking forward to fall hunting," Asa commented. "But now's a good time to start geese, grouse and duck."

Asa and Mason discussed hunting for a while. Birdie was busy signing to Charlotte. Mason often wondered what went on in his little sister's head. He must work harder at learning to talk to her with his hands. "Thank you again, Mrs. Brant," he murmured.

She merely smiled at him. Again, Mason was very aware of the change just a few months of marriage had wrought in his friend. Almost three years ago, when Mason had first arrived in Pepin and found Asa as his neighbor, he'd liked Asa right away. But since they'd last met, Asa had changed, and for the better. Asa now smiled and talked easily, appeared to be more at peace. Mason couldn't stop himself from once again wishing he'd been here in March to meet his mail-order bride. Well, life was what it was.

On Friday afternoon, Mason was in his barn, unhitching the team he'd just reclaimed and fetched from Levi's place outside town to the northeast. He'd left his girls with Asa's wife and rode one of Asa's horses to Levi's. His ankle still pained him. He limped but he'd left off the crutch today.

He turned, startled when he heard his name being called. "Miss Jones." Nearly a week had passed since he'd seen her. He drank in the sight of her like a thirsty man finding water in the desert. He stiffened himself. *Don't embarrass yourself.* "What can I do for you?"

"I'm glad to see you are walking without your crutch," she said, not replying to his question.

Birdie with Charlotte hurried away from the head of one of the horses toward her. "Miss Emma!" Birdie greeted her.

"Hello." Emma bent to talk to them. "Girls, I would like to have a few words in private with Mr. Chandler. Could you go play? I'll talk to you before I leave."

Birdie looked thoughtful but drew Charlotte outside, signing to her.

Mason didn't have to think about why this lady

had come. Colton had repeatedly told him that Miss Jones wanted the girls in school. He gritted his teeth. Evidently Emma was a woman to be reckoned with. His irritation over this vied with his unwelcome pleasure at seeing her here, so fine and determined. "I can guess why you've come. But I wasn't ready to send them to school yet." He focused on working free the horses' harness buckles.

"Your girls are ready. Do you think you are helping them, keeping them out?"

"I'm keeping them from being hurt. Children can be cruel," he said, just short of snapping at her.

"And adults can be. Do you think keeping them out protects them from hurt? Don't you realize that keeping them home is hurting them, too?"

"I can teach them their letters and numbers."

"That's not what I mean." She moved closer and paused, resting a hand on the rump of the nearest chestnut horse. "Isolating them is telling them that you don't think they can handle school. That they are lesser than the other children."

Her words cut through him like a serrated knife, a dull one that rasped painfully. He stepped back, releasing the last buckle, and led one horse toward a stall. Her accusation bounced around in his head.

From the corner of his eye, he glimpsed her standing backlit by the sunshine. She brought to mind a picture he'd seen as a child in a book. It had been the image of an avenging angel protecting the innocent. Miss Emma Jones did not take matters having to do with children lightly.

"Are you ashamed of Birdie and Charlotte?" she snapped.

"No," he snapped back. "They are wonderful little girls."

"Then bring them to school Monday." She turned as if to leave. "Have some trust in me, trust in the children of this town."

She left him without a word to say.

He moved to the open barn door but remained out of sight. He wanted to hear what she said to the girls.

"Birdie! Charlotte!" she called in a friendly voice.

The girls ran to her, Birdie beaming and Charlotte cautious, holding Birdie's hand. "Can you play with us?"

"Just a bit. How about 'Ring around the Rosy'?" Emma joined hands with the girls and they moved in a circle, singing and, at the right moment, all falling or, rather, stooping down.

"I must go now. I'm sure I'll see you Sunday at church." And without a glance toward the barn, she called out, "See you Monday at school. Nine o'clock! Don't be late!"

He watched her go, unable to look away until she disappeared around the thickly forested bend.

The girls ran to him. "Did the lady teacher say we could come to school?" Birdie asked.

He looked down into Birdie's eager face. So many thoughts and emotions swirled in his mind and heart. "Do you want to go to school?"

"Yes!" Birdie signed to Charlotte. "She says yes too. We can see Lily and Colton. And meet other children."

He wondered if Birdie was capable of grasping the concept of prejudice.

"Some children will like us and some won't," Birdie said, answering his unspoken question. "But we want to go to school."

He drew in a deep breath. So be it. He turned to go unharness the other horse. He hoped Miss Emma Jones knew what she was doing. He wanted everything good for his children. But he knew how cruel people could be. This moved him to snap at God, *You'd better keep them safe.*

He then remembered more of Emma's words and realized that he would have to face the whole town the day after next at church. His hurt ankle had given him an excuse to bypass last week's service. But that excuse had lapsed. Miss Emma Jones was right. He must publicly face the community with his girls, starting Sunday.

He was feeling the same dread and anticipation, a heavy weight in his middle, that he'd faced many times in the war. The mornings just before a battle, everyone—except for those who thought they needed to lighten the somber mood—had been silent, barely speaking, girding themselves for the imminent crucible of cannon, gunfire, black smoke and perhaps death.

He tried to shake off the feeling. No one would be firing at him on Sunday. But he worried for Birdie and Charlotte and any negative reactions to them. He didn't want them to be hurt. His only hope was from the friends who'd stood by him. One was Noah Whitmore, the preacher, who'd written the orphan home's director that he was fit to adopt his girls. Would people remember where they were—in God's house? At least no one knew the dark secret he must—above all else—keep hidden.

Chapter Three

Mason thought he'd prepared himself for meeting Emma on Sunday morning, but he hadn't expected them to enter the combined schoolroom-church at almost the same moment from opposite ends of the room, he from the school entrance and she from the teacher's quarters. He halted in midstep.

And so did she. She wore a flattering rose-pink dress with ivory lace at the neck. Her beauty took his breath. But instantly he shook himself inwardly and moved forward. In the past days her kindness to Birdie and Charlotte had drawn his gratitude, making him more vulnerable to her. He steeled himself against regret. *I have to get over missing my chance with her.*

He'd been gone for half the year, but he hoped no one had taken his pew. He forced himself to nod to a few people he knew even though they were gawking. Then he focused on getting the girls settled beside him. Thanks to Asa's wife, the girls' dresses were clean and pressed as well as his own white Sunday shirt.

He tried not to track Emma from the corner of his

eye, but he glimpsed her full skirts swish past them as she joined her sister and family in the pew to his right, forward a row. Bitter thoughts of his father and how once again he had ruined something for Mason rushed into his mind. He bowed his head, willing the thoughts away. What was done was done and could not be changed. He still had his land, his crops and now, his girls.

Hoping that no one would hurt them with unthinking or unkind remarks, he gathered them close to him and kissed their foreheads. "Now, you girls be good," he murmured.

"We always be good in church," Birdie murmured and signed to Charlotte, who looked up at him and smiled timidly.

His poor little sister. She so rarely looked happy. Had what Mrs. Hawkins, the lady who ran the orphans' home in Illinois, said been true? Was hysterical deafness even real? Was there a chance Charlotte might hear again someday? He shook his head. He didn't have that kind of faith.

Tall and middle-aged, Mrs. Lavina Caruthers moved to the front as Noah Whitmore raised his arms. "Let us pray." After Noah's prayer, Lavina led them in singing the opening hymn.

Then Gordy Osbourne, a young deacon, rose and began reading the scripture passage, Numbers 12.

"'And Miriam and Aaron spake against Moses because of the Ethiopian woman whom he had married: for he had married an Ethiopian woman. And they said, Hath the Lord indeed spoken only by Moses? hath he not spoken also by us? And the Lord heard it.'"

Mason never had heard this passage that he could recall. The reading and the story continued, ending with God chastising Miriam and Aaron, the sister and brother of Moses. God had turned Miriam's skin leprous for seven days in punishment of her speaking against Moses because of his choice of a dark-skinned bride. Evidently the word about Mason's girls had spread to the preacher. Noah's boldness in choosing this passage hit Mason as if a rod had been rammed up his spine. Noah's courage in confronting prejudice humbled him.

"Here endeth the scripture for today," Gordy finished and sat down, his face flushed.

Lavina rose again and began the second hymn. The congregation rose to sing, but many cast glances over their shoulders at him, and others stood stiffly facing forward.

Mason hoped that Noah's boldness would not alienate his congregation and cause division here.

At the end of the hymn, Lavina remained standing. "Our preacher has said that I may make an announcement of a sewing and knitting day this coming Saturday morning here. My son Isaiah, who is engaged in mission work north of here with the Chippewa tribe, will be visiting us before winter, and we'd like to have a large donation of quilts, mittens, socks and scarves to send back with him. There is great need among the tribe." Lavina smiled. "Thank you."

Noah approached the lectern and bowed his head in silent prayer. Then he went on to preach about the passage Gordy had read, but without calling attention to the situation of the little black girl sitting beside Mason. Noah preached about God calling Moses a humble man and how prejudice had caused his siblings to react with pride and spite and God's judgment on the proud and unkind. Mason approved. Noah had laid down the precept of God's opinion of prejudice and spite. Mason didn't pray often, but he did now, asking God for kindness to be shown here to his little ones.

Everyone rose and sang the closing hymn, "Jesus, Lover of My Soul." Then Gordy prayed and asked God to bless their week and the coming harvest.

Mason raised his head, feeling refreshed, yet still cautious. Now would come the questions and perhaps the rejection by many of those who had once welcomed him. Against his will his gaze sought Emma to his right. He remembered her kindness to his girls. Again she affected him. He stiffened his resolve to resist the pull to her and led the girls to the aisle.

Indeed, some people brushed past him, but not all. Levi, the blacksmith, and his wife, Posey, stopped. She shook Mason's hand and then glanced downward. "And how are you, pretty little things?"

"We're fine, ma'am," Birdie chirped. "Thank you for askin'."

At that moment, Emma walked by him.

"Good morning, Mr. Chandler," she said in passing. "Good morning, Birdie and Charlotte."

Mason returned the greeting, gripping his tight mask in place. He wished he didn't react to her, wasn't so aware of her.

Then she moved on, greeting others.

Mason turned to Levi's wife again. His heart thumped dully. If Emma had been his wife, he wouldn't feel so alone, so inept caring for his children. What might have been…

Ignoring the pull that wanted her to stay and talk to Mason, Emma moved out into the sunshine. As usual, people milled around in clusters in the school yard after Sunday worship, the social event of each week.

Conscious of her role as teacher, Emma moved from group to group, speaking to the parents of each of her students. Out of the corner of her eye, she glimpsed Mason step out of the schoolhouse. She forced herself not to turn to watch him. But she noted that many others watched, almost gawking at him and his girls. Would someone say or do something rude, hurtful? Her lungs tightened as if she herself were bracing for a blow.

As she moved through the people, she sensed an unusual mood. People nodded to her but they said few words and looked somehow stiff. She experienced an unusual tension herself. She could not stop herself from straining to hear the few words Mr. Chandler spoke to others and his girls.

Still no one spoke of the source of the general tension—Birdie and Charlotte—until Emma approached the Stanley family. Mrs. Stanley, who unfortunately had been born with a wart on the side of her large nose, said loud enough to be overheard, "Seems like you had a near miss." The woman shook her head, and Emma couldn't stop herself from watching the wart wobble. "If you'd married Chandler this spring, you'd be stuck with his baggage."

Emma pressed her lips together to keep from replying sharply. She was aware that Mason was keeping to the edge of the gathering with his children near him. Had he overheard this? Bad enough. Worse yet, the woman had said this with her school-age daughter, Dorcas, standing right beside her. Dorcas would be a classmate of the Chandler girls—if Emma had succeeded in persuading Mason to let them come to school.

Emma chose her words with care. "I admire Mr. Chandler for offering his half sister a home." Her unruly ears strained again to hear his voice.

"Well, he'll be saddled with her for the rest of his life. A deaf girl. No one will ever take her off his hands."

Emma rarely had a violent reaction to anything. But she clenched her free hand down at her side. It itched to slap the woman's face. "My sister and I came here together so that we wouldn't be separated. Having family nearby is a comfort."

The woman scowled at her.

The woman's father-in-law spoke up, "Speaking of family, when will your father be coming back from Illinois?"

"We hope very soon," Emma replied, grateful for his intervention. Her father, who unexpectedly had followed her and Judith to Pepin within a few months of their arrival, had traveled down to Illinois to visit their brother.

"Good. I miss our checker games." The man grinned.

Still tracking Mr. Chandler's progress skirting the gathering, Emma smiled with grim politeness, then excused herself. Her sister Judith welcomed her.

"A strong sermon," Emma whispered into her sister's ear.

Judith nodded, brushing her cheek against her sister's. "Good of Noah," she whispered in return.

Then, as the two sisters chatted about the upcoming sewing day and watched the children playing silent tag around the adults, Emma tried not to continue to track Mason Chandler. When she'd ventured here nearer him, he'd moved away as if fencing with her.

His two girls had not joined in the sedate Sunday game of tag in the churchyard. Charlotte sat on the swing and Birdie was gently pushing her. Birdie's devotion to Charlotte inspired the most tender regard for her. Emma had no idea what prompted little Birdie to befriend Charlotte, but God would reward her selfless love.

Again, Emma tried to keep her gaze from wandering to Mason and again failed. She found ignoring a man who'd assumed responsibility for these two little girls difficult, nearly impossible. His broad shoulders evidently could carry burdens with dignity. She hoped that Noah's support and that of Mason's other friends would smooth the way toward acceptance. She reined in her sympathy so drawn to him. She could not give him false hope.

She could not do more than pray that this situation would resolve itself in a good way. She had come here to marry Mason Chandler, but marrying him would have been a mistake. And God had prevented that. With what remained of her heart, she still loved Jonathan, though he was just a memory.

In the morning, doubts and worry over sending the girls to school lingered. But Mason pressed the girls' dresses and two fresh white pinafores to go over them. He brushed and braided their hair as best he knew how, though somehow the braids ended up slightly crooked. And the bows. He shook his head at the sad bows he'd tied.

However, Birdie was beaming with anticipation. Charlotte kept glancing back and forth between the two of them. Then she did something she rarely did. She patted his arm and signed to him. He caught part of it but turned to Birdie. "What did she say?"

"She says don't worry. Miss Emma likes children."

Moisture flickered in one of his eyes. Emma's good heart drew him almost irresistibly. "She does. Shall we go?"

"Yes!" Birdie answered, and Charlotte sent him one of her rare smiles. Whatever happened at school— evidently his little sister wanted to go.

He set his hat on his head and shooed the girls ahead of him, and then he latched the door. He felt the same way he had reporting for duty in the army years ago. *This must be faced.* He breathed in the fresh air and listened to the crows cawing to each other from tree to tree.

Behind them the sun was slowly ascending from the east and a nip of fall touched the morning air. The three of them walked down the track toward town. He was glad his homestead was within walking distance of school.

When harvest came, he'd be busy in the fields. Just a few more weeks and the corn might be dry enough to pick. The worrying thought of his friend Asa's crop being destroyed unfurled in his mind. Would his fields, and what was left of Asa's, feed the two families with four children for the winter? He hoped so.

Almost to Asa's clearing, Mason glimpsed the children Asa had taken in. He still hadn't heard the story of how that had come about.

The children were coming toward them. Not away toward school.

"Morning!" Colton called out. "We were coming to walk your girls to school!" Lily still seemed hesitant, but she did look at his girls and sort of smiled.

Mason wondered at the children coming for his girls. Had Emma instigated this? He wouldn't put it past her. But he didn't want to question the children. And Birdie, along with Charlotte, was already running to meet the brother and sister.

Colton drifted over to walk beside Mason. "Mr. and Mrs. Brant said it was time we walked your girls to school," Colton said in an undertone, supplying the answer to Mason's unspoken question.

Mason paused and wondered if he should just let the children go on alone.

Then Charlotte broke away from Birdie and claimed his hand, pulling him to come along.

He obeyed.

Birdie and Lily talked on and off as if searching for common ground. Birdie kept her hands busy, including Charlotte in the conversation.

"How did you learn to talk with your fingers?" Lily asked Birdie, appearing fascinated.

"A lady come to the orphanage and taught me and Charlotte. It's easy. See? This is *hello*." Birdie demonstrated the simple motion.

Lily tried to mimic it.

"That's pretty good for your first try," Birdie approved.

Charlotte signed back at Lily, who tried to imitate it again.

In a low voice, Colton told Mason, "Don't worry. I won't let anybody pick on your girls."

The words warmed Mason toward this solemn boy who had helped him when he was laid up. "Thank you."

Colton merely nodded, looking determined.

In a way, this promise was reassuring and in another way, worrying. This young lad expected Mason's girls to be targets of trouble. But the five of them were heading to school this morning, come what may. Miss Emma and the girls were determined about school.

Wondering if Mason Chandler would bring Birdie and Charlotte today, Emma pulled the school bell rope, sounding the signal, and then stepped to the doorway to greet her pupils as usual. And as usual, the children began to run toward her.

Then she glimpsed Mason. Her heart somersaulted. He stood tall and imposing with his jaw set. His hat sat forward, hiding much of his face from her. Whatever his feelings, he'd brought Birdie and Charlotte. Emma began praying silently for the girls and their acceptance here today.

The youngest to the oldest, the children had formed a line in front of the school door. The boys wore flannel shirts, suspenders and dark pants, and the girls wore white pinafores over dresses that ended a few inches above their ankles. "Good morning, students!"

"Good morning, Miss Jones!" the children replied nearly in unison.

Mason with his two girls stood at the rear. The fact that he was trying to hide his concern caused Emma to like him one little bit more. So many parents communicated fear and engendered it in their children, sometimes needlessly. She'd observed that happen this spring when a traveling doctor had come to town and held a clinic. His mission was to vaccinate as many children on the frontier as possible to prevent smallpox. The children whose parents feared the procedure had made the experience more difficult for their children.

Now some of the students were glancing over their shoulders at the trio at the end of the line. Emma ignored this, following her usual routine of greeting each child by name. Finally Mason, his hat in hand, stood before her.

"Mr. Chandler, so glad to see your girls ready to start school." She motioned toward the classroom behind her. "Good morning, Birdie, Charlotte. Since this is your first year in school, please go and sit on the front bench beside Lily."

"Yes, miss!" Birdie crowed and nearly skipped inside, holding Charlotte's hand and drawing her along.

Mason stared into Emma's eyes. She noted he was gripping his hat, nearly bending the brim.

"I'll bid you good day." Emma stepped back.

"I forgot to pack them lunches," he said. "I didn't think."

"That won't be a problem. I'll see to their lunch today."

The man mangled his hat a bit longer. Then he straightened it and put it back on his head. "Thank

you, Miss Jones." He strode away, his long legs
stretching over the wild grass.

Though an unreasonable part of her wanted to
detain him, Emma turned and prepared herself to
face this new challenge. Her students were good children. Some had been orphaned just like Mason's girls.
Some had come from the South like the sheriff's son,
Jacque Merriday, and some from the East. Eight years
after the devastating Civil War, the tensions in the
South continued. It seemed like the war would never
stop hurting them, all of them.

She walked briskly down the center aisle to stand
at the front of the schoolroom. Today Birdie and Charlotte would become welcome members of her school
or she would know the reason why.

At the front of the room, she turned and faced the
class. "Children, please rise for the morning prayer."
Emma read a psalm of David and prayed for a good
day of study at school. Then the children sat back
down on their benches. Many were eyeing the new
girls.

Emma took a deep breath, praying silently for wisdom. "As all of you can see, we have added two new
students today, Birdie and Charlotte, who have been
adopted by Mr. Chandler. I hope you will make them
feel welcome."

Johann Lang held up his hand. "Miss Jones, I spoke
German when I first came here and had to learn En-
glish. How can we make the girl who can't hear welcome if we don't know how to talk to her?"

Birdie bounced up and, following Johann's exam-
ple, raised her hand. "I know how, Miss Jones."

Emma had thought she would be the one leading

this discussion, but perhaps it would be better if the ideas came from the children. "Yes, Birdie, what do you have to suggest?"

"On the way here, Lily—" Birdie gestured toward the little girl sitting farther down the same row "—learned how to say *hello* with her hands. I can teach the other children, too."

"Thank you, Birdie. You may be seated." Emma looked over her students. "I think that might be a very good idea." How to phrase it? She smiled inwardly. A challenge? "How many of you think you are capable of learning to speak with your hands?"

Jacque, the sheriff's son, raised his hand, as did many others, though some students looked hesitant.

"Jacque, you'd like to learn it?"

"Yes, miss, I think it would be fun and I like to know how to do things. Can she, the black girl, show us how to do that sign?"

"Birdie, will you come up and teach us how to say hello to Charlotte? I will sit in your place because I will be the student, too."

This announcement caused a hubbub of murmurs from her students. But Emma passed Birdie, who was nearly skipping to where Emma had been standing.

Birdie beamed one of her contagious smiles. "I was already livin' at the orphans' home when Charlotte come to live there, too. She was very sad and scared because she couldn't talk to anybody. I mean— wouldn't you be if you had to go somewhere you didn't know anybody and you couldn't tell them nothin' and couldn't understand what they were sayin' to you?"

Emma felt the interest of the students. And the aroused sympathy.

"To teach Charlotte 'merican Sign Language, Mrs. Hawkins, who runs the orphans' home, hired a lady who come all the way from Chicago."

A few students *ohhhh*ed when they heard "Chicago."

"I told Mrs. Hawkins I wanta learn to talk with my hands, too. I wanta to be Charlotte's friend 'cause we all need a friend."

Again Emma felt the empathy for Birdie and Charlotte swell all around her. Every child here had come from somewhere else and had gone through the painful process of making a friend. "Excellent, Birdie. Now teach us how to greet Charlotte. We want her to know she is among friends here. Isn't that right, students?"

Different but heartfelt words and sounds of approval flowed around Emma.

"This is how you say *hello* in sign." Birdie demonstrated the hand motion in total and then part by part. Emma along with her students mimicked the sign.

"Y'all did good!" Birdie crowed. "Now, Charlotte, your turn." Birdie signed to the little girl sitting beside Emma.

Hesitantly Charlotte rose and faced the classroom. Shyly she signed, "Hello."

And everyone, including Emma, signed it in return. The children were beaming at this new knowledge.

Emma rose. "Thank you, Birdie. I think tomorrow you will teach us to sign 'How are you?' I think that would be the next thing we would say to Charlotte, don't you, class?"

Affirmative replies sounded around the room and

soon Emma moved the children to their first lesson. Matters had gone much better than she'd expected. Her schoolroom hummed with productive energy. Birdie was not only a sweetheart, but she understood people and how to charm them. Or perhaps Birdie was just being Birdie.

Emma realized something else, too. All through the daily routine of lessons she tried to figure out how to help Charlotte even more. She kept coming up with one answer—no matter how many times she tried to find a different solution. She didn't want the obvious answer to be true because it involved her being with Mason.

And she did not want to give him or anyone else in town the idea that she might be interested in him as a suitor. She could only hope that with time, people's expectations for their becoming a couple would dim. The one thing she was thankful for was that Mason never tried to sway her to look upon him with favor. And then she wondered why that was so.

Emma waited till the end of the school week, and then she walked through town toward her sister's place. She had a standing invitation to supper there and she looked forward to family time with Judith, Asa and the children. But first she passed her sister's clearing and proceeded to Mason's. "Hello, the house!" she called when his neat cabin came into view.

Birdie with Charlotte's hand in hers ran around the house toward Emma. "Teacher! Teacher come to see us!" Birdie called out, her face bursting with joy.

Emma would have had to be solid granite not to

respond. She caught the girls as they cannonaded into her. "Girls, girls. You just saw me at school."

"But you came to our house again," Birdie said.

For the first time, Charlotte took Emma's hand in both of hers.

For this one moment, Charlotte's lost expression vanished. Emma's heart sang.

"Miss Jones."

At Mason's subdued greeting, Emma looked beyond the girls. Mason had come around the side of his cabin. He had rolled up his sleeves and his sinewy, tanned arms drew her unwilling attention. "To what do we owe this kind visit?"

Switching focus, she contemplated his tone—something about it definitely sounded restrained. No doubt he must also feel the awkwardness over the demise of their plans to marry in March. And here once more there were only the girls as chaperones.

He moved a bit forward. "How may we help you, miss?" he prompted.

She tried not to study the way he stood so easy within himself yet with sadness lurking in his direct gaze. "Has Birdie told you that she is teaching the other schoolchildren a new sign every day?"

"Yes, she told me. It's not easy to learn."

"No, it isn't." She gripped her intention tightly and announced, "That's why I've come. I think as the teacher, I should know more sign language than just what Birdie teaches the class daily. I was hoping that Birdie could give me private lessons." *Preferably after school—without you nearby to distract me*, she thought to herself.

Before Mason could reply, Birdie squealed, "Then

you can come to our house to the lessons I give our pa every night!"

Emma's heart sank. Exactly what she didn't want.

"Birdie," Mason said with obvious patience, "maybe Miss Jones can't come every evening. She's a busy lady. Why don't you girls run back and finish your chores while Miss Jones and I talk about this?"

The girls looked up at her and then ran, hand in hand, toward the rear of the cabin. A red cardinal flew overhead. Birdie pointed it out to Charlotte.

Emma walked forward and met Mason, trying to shed her response to the kind way he treated his girls. This seemed to be her Achilles' heel when it came to this man. She could resist his good looks but his character drew her.

"I'm sorry that Birdie put you in an awkward position, miss. She doesn't understand gossip and such. Tongues will wag if people find out you and I are seeing each other regularly—even doing something this innocent."

As he said the words, she felt herself stiffen inside. "I am not one to pay attention to gossips."

"You are in the minority, then." He sent her a rueful smile.

The smile hit her directly around the heart, chipping at the ice there. She resisted this. Learning sign language was the right thing to do. And she was not a weak-willed woman, vulnerable to any handsome man. "Mr. Chandler, when does Birdie usually give you your signing instruction?"

He eyed her. "Usually after supper, but if you're game, why not begin now?"

He had thrown down his gauntlet and she picked

it up. She would not be swayed by fear of gossip. "I have time now. I'm expected at my sister's for supper."

Mason studied her for a moment and then called over his shoulder, "Birdie! Come inside! Miss Jones wants her first lesson now!"

Emma followed him inside, wondering at how she had ended up doing the exact opposite of what she'd planned. She didn't think Mason Chandler was manipulative. He'd merely stated the truth about how people might misinterpret this, and that had goaded her. Well, let the gossips enjoy themselves. She had nothing to explain.

However, the ice around her heart had cracked the tiniest bit and that frightened her. *I can be with him but not let down my guard. Love is a risk I cannot test again.* And then her mind chided, *Mason Chandler has not given you the slightest hint that he wants you to reconsider his original proposal, has he? But the words he'd whispered after his fall might hint otherwise. Or not?*

Chapter Four

Another Saturday morning had come, marking half of September had already passed. Emma dressed in one of her plainer frocks, a faded blue cambric. She wanted to blend in with the ladies coming for their day of sewing and knitting while the men did what was necessary to prepare the school for the coming hard winter. She looked forward to today's community gathering and could not understand why she felt as if she were carrying some heavy weight. Today would be a congenial day of chatting and doing something charitable and useful. Her mind tried to suggest why the weight hovered over her. She refused to listen.

Bustling about, she opened the schoolroom door. The warming wind wafted in the scent of pine. Then she set a coffee kettle sputtering and perking over the fire in her quarters, releasing its enticing fragrance. Yesterday before the children went home, she had directed them in moving the school benches into a large circle. Then they set up the long tables that would hold the food brought for the cold lunch all the workers would share. With a lift of satisfaction, she walked over the room, making sure everything was spit-shined and in place. Not a speck of dust.

She paused by her neatly organized desk that had been pushed back out of the way. There had been some talk of raising funds to purchase real school desks for the children, but that would be in the future. Emma then dragged out the chairs from her quarters for a few of the grandmothers who would have difficulty sitting on backless benches for hours. But all this busyness didn't help her keep her mind off Mason Chandler. Of course he would come today. And what of it?

Foolish question. The man was a constant speck in her eye. The three sign language lessons this week had been times of testing. *I should not feel this way. Going to his home and learning signs should not affect me.* Truer words had never been spoken, but Mason had the power to stir her feelings and cause her to think thoughts she shouldn't think about the breadth of his shoulders or his deep voice. She would just have to be stronger today. She could not care for a man again. Could not. Not would not.

She shoved away memories and marched around, pushing open the windows and letting more warm September breeze in. She caught a hint of cedar this time. Wagons began creaking into the school yard and families arriving on foot. Emma welcomed their cheery voices and distraction. Soon women crowded the schoolroom, all setting down sewing baskets and knitting bags. Outside the children began playing in the school yard, their happy squeals and shouts causing Emma to smile.

She would not be alone with Mason today. She

could keep him at a distance. Though at this resolve a silent sigh eased through her. He hadn't arrived yet, but she was already straining to hear Mason's voice. Irritating but true.

Many mothers of her students paused to look at papers that had merited gold stars and which had been pinned to the back wall of the room. Then Sunny Whitmore, the preacher's wife, entered with her friends, Nan and Ophelia. Everyone noticed but did not comment about the fact that Sunny had loosened her corset stays to their maximum and wore a loose jacket that sought to conceal her condition. The Whitmores were expecting their third child sometime this fall.

Then Charlotte and Birdie burst into the room, the soles of their shoes slapping on the wood floor. "We just wanted to say good morning, Miss Emma!" Birdie announced in her endearing way. Charlotte gifted Emma with one of her rare smiles. Then both girls signed, "Good morning. So glad to see you," to her and she signed a similar greeting in return.

Everyone near her had paused to watch the exchange of sign language. Emma glanced over Birdie's head and there was Mason standing squarely in the doorway, motioning for the girls to come out.

"Now, you girls go and play," Emma said, nodding once toward Mason.

He returned her nod without a hint of a smile.

"Yes, Miss Emma," Birdie said, and the two hurried out to join the children playing.

Emma turned away and caught many, many speculative glances shifting between her and the girls. She raised her chin and smiled as serenely as she could.

"We heard you were going to Mr. Chandler's for special lessons," Mrs. Stanley—the woman with the wobbly wart—said with thick innuendo.

Emma merely glanced at the woman she really tried to like—but couldn't.

"Someone needs to teach those two little ones how to knit and such. Mr. Chandler can't do that," Mrs. Ashford said in a considering tone, and then she sent Emma a pointed glance.

Emma ignored it and was grateful when her sister, who had been unusually silent, said, "I've started teaching Lily. I'll invite Mason's girls over to join us."

Emma smiled and moved next to her sister in the circle of women.

Lavina, the song leader each Sunday, said, "Ladies, let us start our workday with prayer." Lavina prayed for the Lord to bless them as they toiled on the practical gifts and to ensure the items would be a blessing to those who received them.

After the "amen," the ladies found places on the benches and began taking out yarn and needles or cloth and needle and thread. Several ladies had most of a quilt top done and sat close together, discussing the finer points of their quilt design.

Feeling the uprush of joy at being here with her sister, Emma sat beside Judith and began crocheting a scarf of red yarn. Judith was knitting a pair of matching mittens. Both of them were using pairs of their late mother's wooden needles. Judith glanced at her and smiled. But something in Judith's eyes looked worried. Was it just that she and Asa were facing a lean winter? Or something else? Emma regretted she and her sister had not had a moment alone to talk for days. It almost felt as if Judith were distancing herself from Emma. Surely not.

And above the ladies' quiet chatter, still Emma could not stop herself from straining to hear Mason's voice outside with the men. Near the open windows the men were talking about wood supply and about checking the chinking of the log building and the shake roof against the coming winter winds.

"How is Isaiah doing in the Northwoods?" Sunny asked Lavina as she knit a child's navy-blue stocking.

"My son is courting a Chippewa woman there," Lavina said, head down.

Silence greeted this.

"She is a strong believer and is well thought of," Lavina continued, glancing up in a way that repelled dispute. "My husband and I may travel there to meet her as soon as the harvest is in and before snow flies."

Emma drew in a breath. Many women were frowning, but evidently because of Noah's recent sermon, none spoke of the prejudice against a mixed marriage.

"I'm sure she will be a help to Isaiah in his mission," Emma said.

"Yes, but that's not why he's marrying her. He fell in love," Lavina said with a sweet smile.

The way the woman said the words physically hurt Emma's heart. Two young people in love. She bent over her knitting, hiding the tight "stitch" within her.

Then Mason's voice floated through the window. The men were going to hoist someone up on the roof. Her fingers tightened in her yarn. Not Mason. Not Mason.

"No, not you, Mason," Noah said with evident

humor. "You've fallen off one roof this fall. That's your limit."

The men all laughed.

"I must agree," Mason said without evident embarrassment.

"Can I go up on the roof?" The voice sounded young. Emma recognized it as belonging to Jacque Merriday, the sheriff's son. "I know how to check the wooden shingles. My dad taught me."

Rachel, his stepmother, looked up and shook her head. "That boy knows no fear, and he frightens me at times."

"That's the way boys are," Mrs. Ashford said sagely, her knitting needles clicking.

The workday proceeded, and sitting beside her sister, more and more Judith's near silence worried Emma. What was wrong?

At noon the men trooped inside. After the children had been helped through the line of generous sandwiches and cookies, the women waved the men to go first to fill their plates, saying that stacking wood gave a person more appetite than handwork. Emma gauged the distance she would maintain between her and Mason, glad for all the people in between.

However, her sister thwarted her by absently drawing Emma outside with her to sit by Asa, who of course had Mason at his side on a quilt under a blazing red maple. Enjoying the balmy fall day, everyone had settled either on the benches or on quilts outside. A vee of migrating geese honked overhead. What had Judith so preoccupied? Though wondering, Emma did not let her serene smile or her cool demeanor falter.

Mason appeared to be of the same mind as she.

He was polite but did not try to catch Emma's attention, instead giving it to Asa and, of course, his girls. Emma sat quietly, trying to come up with a way to ask Judith surreptitiously what was wrong.

Nearby the sheriff was discussing the newest project nearing completion in town, the new jail, which would be his office and headquarters.

Emma heard a familiar voice calling from up the road, "Hello! I'm here!"

Emma and Judith set down their plates, leaped to their feet and hurried toward the familiar voice. "Father! You're home!"

Emma and Judith threw their arms around the slight, silver-haired man in welcome. Emma had been fearful that he might not return. She knew it was selfish of her to want to keep her father close, but she couldn't help it. She stepped back and studied him. He did not look upset. He looked happy. So his visit with their brother and his wife must have gone well. A relief.

Emma turned and saw Colton rise, set down his plate and come to greet the man. Asa rose and followed the boy. "Hello, Dan! Glad to see you're home." Other people called out greetings to their father, and Mr. Ashford hurried forward and shook his hand. "You've been missed, Dan."

"I've missed everyone and my job. Of course, I know the river season is nearly over, but this winter I plan on setting my own stool near your potbellied stove, Mr. Ashford. I'm looking forward to some checkers and maybe some cribbage." A few of the older men gathered around, clapping him on the back and chatting about the upcoming winter they were planning for.

Emma's heart warmed at the friendship and new life her father had already carved out for himself here. Living in town and having a job selling notions to travelers and new friends had given her father joy and liveliness. For these moments her sister's expression lightened.

Soon Dan settled on the schoolhouse step with a plate and glass. The older man's gaze roved over the men who'd remained outside. Emma and Judith sat beside him now. Emma noted the moment her father's gaze latched onto Mason and then moved to his little girls. "Somebody new come?" he asked.

"Dan, that is Mason Chandler, our neighbor," Asa replied, having shifted closer to his wife.

Dan stared at Mason. "The man who proposed to my Emma and then didn't marry her?"

Mason rose and walked to Dan. He stopped in front of him, composed. "Yes, sir. I'm very sorry about that."

"You gonna still marry her?"

Flushing with embarrassment, Emma felt the intense concentration on them. Everyone had fallen silent.

"Sir," Mason replied, "I was detained by family obligations and Miss Jones has forgiven me that. As for the marrying, I think you need to leave that up to us."

Dan gazed at him steadily. "That so?"

Mason nodded decisively, then walked back to his two children and sat down to finish his lunch as if he didn't notice being the center of attention.

"Leave that up to us."—Mason's words echoed

in Emma's mind. What did they mean? Did Mason think that they might still marry? Emma clamped down on her reactions. She could not show anything here with everyone watching. *"Leave that up to us."* She chewed on those words, barely tasting the delicious food on her plate. But she glanced at Judith once more and worried.

Wednesday, another evening filled with the song of the multitude of crickets, Mason sat feeling once more distinctly uncomfortable in his own cabin at his own table, trying not to look at Emma. His stiff neck hurt from keeping his focus on Birdie, not Emma. Birdie was teaching them how to say the days of the week. He was having trouble with "Wednesday." Birdie was patient with him but his difficulty with the motions embarrassed him in front of Emma. Just as the scene with Dan in the school yard had embarrassed him on Saturday.

He tried the sign again.

"Not 'Saturday,'" Birdie corrected him. "You already got 'Saturday.' We're learnin' 'Wednesday' now. Today is Wednesday."

Thinking of the workday Saturday had tripped him up. He shook his head at himself. "Sorry. Don't know what I was thinking of." At these words his face became heated. He could only hope that Emma didn't guess that he had been thinking of meeting her father on Saturday. The man had not been happy with him.

He hoped these unpleasant incidents over the broken engagement would end soon. Emma was kindness herself. But he had not noted her taking any interest in him—just in his girls. Well, what did he expect?

The lesson finally ended and then Emma surprised him. "Will you walk with me a ways?"

What? She had barely looked at him all evening and now she wanted to talk?

After Emma's bidding Birdie and Charlotte good night, the two of them walked side by side up the trail to the fork that would lead her south to town. The sunset gleamed gold-pink between tree trunks and boughs. Mason champed at the bit, wanting to ask her what she wanted to discuss, but held back. He tried not to notice how her skirt billowed modestly with each step. So feminine.

"I'm wondering if you know of anything that might have upset my sister?" she said finally, still not looking at him.

Sister? His mind scrambled for an answer.

"She's been very quiet every time I've seen her and she just shook her head when I asked on Sunday. Of course, Lily had run up to her just as I asked." She did glance at him then.

Lily, Lily? he thought. An idea came. "Asa said something about a letter from someone in Illinois about the children they've taken in—Colton and Lily."

"That's where the children are from. Was it from a family member? What did it say?"

Mason shrugged, feeling inadequate. Alone on a limb, a squirrel chirped down at them as if telling them to get to the point. "He didn't say much. Asa's not a talker. But he said his wife was upset."

"Well, that helps. Thank you." Emma began walking faster.

He let her go, watching till she disappeared around the thickly forested bend. When he returned to his cabin, Birdie and Charlotte were in their nightgowns, ready for bed.

Birdie looked up at him. "Miss Emma is real pretty."

Mason gazed down at her, catching the underlying message of innocent matchmaking. "Yes, I know. Now you two climb up and say your prayers. Bedtime."

Birdie lingered just a moment longer as if considering saying more. Then she hugged him as she always did, and so did Charlotte and then the two scurried up the ladder to the pallet beds where they slept.

He stood a long time in front of the low fire, seeing again Emma at his table, the movement of her slender fingers that performed signing so much better than his. He rested his head against the rough, bark-edged mantel, watched the flames and thought of the letters he and Emma had started exchanging about this time last year. *I have to stop. I will stop thinking of her.*

Another Friday evening supper at Judith's house. In spite of the fact that Judith had not let her in on her worries, Emma loved being here in this happy home that Judith and Asa had created with their obvious love for one another and for the two orphans they had taken in. And her father sat smiling and chatting with Colton, who had evidently "adopted" him as one of his favorite people. However, the other fly in the ointment was that Judith insisted on inviting Mason and his family every Friday, too. Could her sister be subtly matchmaking? Surely not.

They had just finished a supper of roasted grouse, greens and cornbread when they heard a cheerful, "Hello the house!"

"That sounds like Mr. Ashford," Dan said, turning on the bench toward the voice.

Asa rose and stepped toward the door that had been propped open to let in the cooler evening breeze. "It is. And they have a woman with them."

The Ashfords bustled inside with beaming, expectant faces. "You have a visitor!" Ned announced.

Emma studied the woman who stood between the Ashfords just inside the threshold. She was plump and appeared to be in her fifties, dressed modestly but with an amazing hat, very stylish and flattering to her.

"Asa, this is Mrs. Edith Waggoner," Ned announced.

Judith let out a quiet gasp.

Mrs. Waggoner stepped forward with her ivory kid-gloved hand outstretched. "Mr. Brant."

Emma did not recognize the name and glanced to her sister for a hint of who the woman was.

Judith rose, looking strained. "You're the children's great-aunt."

"Yes, I am—"

Lily popped up from where she sat and ran to the ladder to the loft.

"Don't run, child!" Mrs. Waggoner said. "I've not come to take you away."

Lily paused and turned, worrying her lower lip.

"Why don't we all sit down," Emma suggested, "and discuss Mrs. Waggoner's visit. Come, Lily." She held out her hand.

Lily walked hesitantly over to Emma and climbed onto the bench again.

Soon Mrs. Waggoner was seated at the end of the table on one of the rocking chairs with a cup of coffee, and a subdued Judith was serving slices of juicy, tangy wild plum pie with whipped cream.

"I will speak plainly so that the children understand," the newcomer said after obviously savoring a bite of dessert. "I have not been able to find the children's uncle, their father's brother. Of all the relatives in Illinois, I was the only one who had nothing left to tie me to our hometown. So I've come not to take you children home but to make my home here. Family is important and though I can see that you children have been taken in by a good family, I think you need to have some blood kin nearby. So here I am."

"What will you do?" Judith asked, watchful.

Emma could tell that Judith was worried that this woman might mean she was moving in with them. And with Mason and Asa's much reduced harvest already stretching to provide for two families, another mouth to feed could be a problem.

"The Ashfords have graciously offered to let me board with them," the woman said with a nod toward them. "I am not rich but I have enough to live on. And I hope to think of some business that might thrive in Pepin in the coming spring."

"So you're not going to take us away?" Colton asked, still looking suspicious. Evidently not certain he could trust this stranger.

"No. Unless the Brants want me to?" She gazed at Asa.

"The children are staying with us," Asa stated firmly. Judith nodded in agreement, her shoulders relaxing.

Emma glanced at Mason. He understood how Asa and Judith felt. He'd adopted two little ones this year.

This thought tugged at her heart. She felt the pull toward this man. She looked away. If he hadn't proposed to her, he would be just a neighbor, not a person of special interest to her. But she'd promised to marry him and that promise evidently held power—even when it had lapsed.

Nearing the end of September, an unexpected cold wind had swept down from the north. Another evening and Emma sat beside Mason for yet another language lesson from Birdie, who as usual perched on her knees on the bench across the table from them. The doors and windows were shut against the wind and a modest fire burned, warming the area around the table.

Mason had very obviously been trying not to look at Emma. Maybe if they talked about this tension, it might help.

Or it might make it more intense.

Emma honestly did not know what to do.

This evening they were learning names for foods and now the phrase, "May I have some, please?"

Both she and Mason practiced the signs, sitting rigidly, trying not to look at each other.

Then they both signed the word *please* and what they had been trying to prevent from happening, happened. Their hands brushed. Emma suppressed a gasp. *This is ridiculous.* But she couldn't quell the fact that she reacted to this man. Against common sense. Against her will. *I have to think of some other way to learn this language. But what?*

After they had signed the phrase to Birdie's satisfaction and Charlotte's pleasure, Emma rose. "I need to leave before sundown." Night came sooner each evening. She walked to the peg by the door and lifted down her warm shawl. Mason came and opened the door for her. She tried to read his expression but could not. Did her visits here stress him as much as they did her?

"Good night, Miss Emma!" Birdie called out as Charlotte signed the same.

She lifted her hand and signed the words she voiced to Mason: "Good night and thank you." For a moment, she feared yet hoped he'd ask to walk her to the bend, as he had before.

He didn't.

So she hurried out into the darkening twilight, glad she did not have far to go to reach home. By the time she was walking down Main Street, a large harvest moon had risen.

Her father had evidently been waiting for her in the silent blacksmith's shop where he boarded. He stepped out, pulling on his jacket. "Emma, I was waiting for you. I think it might frost tonight. I'm coming to help you cover your flowers."

The two of them hurried through the crisp fall air in the moonlight. Then they worked together, covering her plants with sheets and dishcloths she brought out. "Thank you, Father. I want to keep my flowers as long as I can."

"Glad to help." He gazed at her in the silvery light. "Are you all right, girl?"

His question took her aback like an unexpected push. "Of course," she replied without thinking or hesitation.

Dan rocked back and forth on his heels, one of

his quirks. It said he was concerned and didn't know how to help. "That Mason seems like a good man."

"Father, he is a good man. But I am happy as I am." She motioned toward the door of the teacher's quarters.

An owl hooted softly somewhere nearby. Her father rocked back and forth two more times and then leaned over and kissed her cheek. Then he turned and headed through the school yard homeward, whistling.

Father, he is a good man. But I am happy as I am. Her own words echoed in her mind and were followed by a hollow feeling. She hurried inside out of the chill and shut the door on the wind and Mason Chandler. She must come up with a way to distance herself. And soon. She could not allow herself to become vulnerable again. Her heart hurt just thinking about caring again, loving again. No.

Chapter Five

Emma had thought that after Mrs. Waggoner arrived but had not wanted to take the children from the Brants, Judith's worry-face would vanish. But she was wrong. Today had dawned a bright and clear, and sunny late September Saturday and after the morning dew had dried, Emma had joined Judith and Lily in the forest to harvest the last of the wild mushrooms. Since the danger of picking something poisonous loomed over them, Lily was merely picking up acorns, which Asa said he knew how to make palatable. What continued to worry her sister?

Judith was stooping over a fallen tree and running her hands over the thick underbrush. Mushrooms could hide and be missed.

Two gray squirrels carried on a loud quarrel while chasing each other through the branches overhead. Emma racked her brain, trying to come up with a way to bring up her concern. "Finding any mushrooms?" was all she could come up with.

Judith didn't reply with words but held up a small

ruffled brown mushroom. She motioned for Emma. "Come."

Emma obeyed. Judith had found a patch of the mushrooms called turkey tails. Emma joined her in plucking the small brown ruffled mushrooms from the downed oak and into their baskets. Unseen chipmunks ran under the fallen leaves around the oak, a constant rustling.

As Emma did this, she wished that Lily had gone to play with Mason's girls. Then she could speak frankly in this rare time when she and her sister would have been quite alone. She recalled the time at home in Illinois when she and Judith had been constant companions in their worry during the war and then in their painful situation with their sister-in-law which had prompted them to seek husbands via advertisement.

Here in Pepin, they had found a new place, a new life. Judith was busy with her own family now. Was Emma just imagining something because she felt left out? Mason's face came to mind. She blinked it away. *I don't need complications.*

"Judith," Emma began to open the agenda.

The sound of voices beyond this part of the forest interrupted her.

"That's Birdie," Lily squealed. The little blonde began to run toward the voices.

Judith called to her, "Lily, bring the girls here!"

Lily's preference for her new neighbors warmed Emma's heart. Was it only a little less than a month ago that upon meeting Birdie and Charlotte, shy Lily had hidden her face in Judith's skirt?

Emma leaned close, taking advantage of this brief opportunity. "Sister, what's worrying you?"

Judith brushed her question away as if it were a mosquito. "I'm fine."

Before Emma could press the issue, Lily came running back with Birdie and Charlotte in tow. And of course, bringing up the rear was Mason.

Emma sighed silently. Her patience with Judith would have to hold a bit longer. Though her eyes immediately wanted to seek Mason's face, she forced herself to stay head down, searching for and plucking the mushrooms. Till finally Mason's shadow fell over her

"Ladies, finding any mushrooms?" Mason's shadow doffed its hat politely.

At his question she had to look up or be impolite. Mason was a tall man, but looking up from where she stooped increased the impression of height. He stood as straight and tall and solid-looking as one of the young maple trees surrounding them. The morning sun flashed between boughs and backlit him, casting his face into shadow, a striking image.

She quelled the flutter of attraction that swirled around her heart and up her throat. "Yes, see?" She held out her oak basket half-filled with mushrooms.

"Good." He turned from her. "Mrs. Brant, you should probably show me which mushrooms are good to eat."

Emma felt his withdrawal from her. Why did it bother her when it was exactly what she wanted?

"I'm sure we'll have enough to share," Judith replied. "Asa told me you're leaving the girls to play with Lily today."

No one had mentioned this to Emma. Another pair

of little ears and less chance of speaking privately with Judith. Emma huffed inwardly.

"Yes, thank you." Mason nodded. "Merriday will pay Asa and me for helping to build the jail. We're meeting to plan it."

"Mason! You coming or not?" Asa's voice carried up the road to them.

"Pardon me, ladies. Duty calls. Coming!" He resettled his hat and walked away with a final encouragement for the girls to mind Mrs. Brant.

Emma could not stop herself from watching Mason's long legs stride toward the road. When she turned back, she caught Judith studying her. "What?" she demanded a bit too sharply.

Judith just shook her head and then turned to the three girls, explaining that they should collect only acorns today. "And stay close enough to see me. I don't want you girls getting lost in the woods."

Emma kept her head down and followed the line of mushrooms growing along the downed tree, vowing not to think of Mason and the girls and the hard winter coming. That's why she and Judith were harvesting all the wild food they could. They would dry most of what they picked today.

Harvesting mushrooms, however, wasn't enough to occupy her. Mason's imposing image had branded itself onto her mind and she could not shake it. Was she a foolish woman? She shook her head. She had a good life now and she didn't need any more complications. The war and its aftermath had brought enough of those. Now she just wanted peace, blessed peace. But when would Judith confide her worry? She bent her head to hide her frown.

* * *

Another weeknight, another signing lesson. Mason tried to concentrate on Birdie's small brown fingers. As usual, Birdie perched on her knees on the bench on the opposite side of the table—across from him and Emma. Usually most of his efforts to hide his emotions had to do with the lady beside him, his attraction to her.

But tonight he was very aware and very worried that this was going to be a bad night for Charlotte. Instead of sitting beside Birdie and helping with the teaching, she was pacing around the room, around and around. Each footfall tightened his nerves another notch.

He didn't want Emma to see one of Charlotte's recurring bouts of distress. He never discussed the little he knew of Charlotte's mother's death. On the day the three of them had arrived in Pepin, Birdie had revealed to Emma the truth. Charlotte's mother had been murdered and everyone was afraid the child might have witnessed it. And that horror might have caused her to become a deaf-mute.

Shutting away these thoughts, Mason tried to concentrate on Birdie, who was making them go through all the signs they'd learned so far. Charlotte's footfalls intruded, disturbing his focus. "Pa, that's not right," Birdie said. "Try again."

Mason tried to focus on his fingers and executing the sign for "More, please."

Thrusting herself between him and Emma, Charlotte climbed up on the bench on her knees and wrapped her arms around the lady's narrow waist.

Then Charlotte began rocking back and forth, butting her head into Emma's midsection.

Worry went through him like buckshot. Mason gripped Charlotte's waist and tried to gently tug her away.

Charlotte wrapped her arms more tightly around Emma.

"I'm sorry," he said, feeling helpless. He could drag the child away, but what would that trigger?

"She havin' one of her bad turns," Birdie observed. The little girl scooted off the opposite bench and came around. She patted Charlotte's back and signed and said, "You feelin' bad, Charlotte?"

Charlotte hazarded just a glance at Birdie and then returned to rocking and butting Emma.

Mason did not know what to do. He looked up and found Emma studying him.

"Is this something that occurs frequently?" Emma asked in a calm voice.

"Just sometimes." He almost began wringing his hands.

"What do you usually do?" Emma asked.

He felt like grabbing Charlotte and then ushering Emma to the door. But he couldn't let his frustration make the situation worse. He'd been counseled by the lady at the orphans' home to be gentle and comforting in the face of Charlotte's troubles. And that made perfect sense. "I usually just hold her until it passes."

Emma nodded and then eased around the end of the bench, sweeping Charlotte with her. Freed from the constraint of the table's edge, Charlotte clambered onto Emma's lap without loosening her hold on the lady's waist. Emma began to stroke Charlotte's back and murmur softly to her. As if suddenly recalling that the little girl couldn't hear her, she fell silent but continued her gentle stroking.

Mason didn't know what to do. He couldn't untangle his reactions into anything clear, anything he could express.

Birdie crawled up onto his lap and rested against him. Sweet Birdie was comforting him. Holding her close, he patted her back as they both watched Emma try to soothe Charlotte.

Long, quiet minutes passed. Birdie fell asleep in Mason's lap. And finally Charlotte did the same in Emma's lap. Outside the windows, the sun had gone down, and crickets clicked their night song.

"Perhaps you could help Birdie to bed first," Emma murmured, still supporting Charlotte on her lap.

He nodded, all his words snared inside him. Soon he had a sleepy Birdie into her nightgown and helped up into the loft. Then he came down. "I usually just leave Charlotte in her dress," he said in almost a whisper, "when she falls asleep like this."

"Probably wise. Here." Emma slid the sleeping child into his arms. He carried the limp little girl one-armed up the ladder into the loft. On his knees, he settled her on the pallet. Birdie cuddled up to her, and he covered them both with the warm, faded and frayed quilt his mother had made him for his child bed. One of the few things he'd taken with him when he left home.

Then he moved back down to face Emma. He didn't want to face her, but he must. He looked into her eyes and found gentle kindness…and sympathy.

"Judith and I lost our mother young, too. I don't

know how a much younger child can…accept that loss, understand it. And I know from Birdie that it wasn't a natural death. The poor child."

Again he had no words. He could only stare at her, stripped of the shield he kept between him and his girls against the world.

Then Emma did something he didn't expect. She stepped forward and claimed his hand. "You know I'll keep this in confidence. And I will do whatever I can to help Charlotte."

Feeling her soft hand grip his stabbed him deeply. He nearly gasped at the gentle pressure. It released all kinds of responses within him. He wanted to pull her close and feel her against him, soft and feminine. He wanted to rest his cheek against her silken hair and breathe in her sweet scent. He wanted not to be alone in this responsibility that was too weighty for him.

All these things he yearned for, but all his words trapped, he could only nod in reply.

A night owl hooted just outside as it flew overhead, shocking him back to reality. The autumn night had closed in around them. A practical concern freed his voice, his body. He dropped her hand. "You'll need a lantern for your walk home. I'd go with you—"

"The girls might need you," she said, forestalling his explanation. She walked to the door to don her thick knitted shawl and wool bonnet.

He turned, fetched his lantern, struck a match and lit it for her. "This will guide you home."

She accepted the lantern but did not walk out immediately. She paused a moment, gazing at him.

Again he couldn't think of anything to say.

"I'll pray for Charlotte," Emma said. "God can heal her heart."

He nodded, still mute.

She walked outside. He stepped out, too, watching her till she turned the bend and the moonlit forest hid her from him. The chill pushed him back inside. He went through his nightly routine of banking the fire and getting ready for bed.

Tonight Emma had seen it all. But thank goodness, she still didn't know it all—that Charlotte's mother had been a woman of easy virtue or that his father had died in a place of shame. As far as the east is from the west was how far God promised to forget sin one repented of, but there was no escape from the past sins of his father. Or the horror that had marked his sweet, innocent little half-sister.

Friday evening had come and Emma, now without planning or wanting to, met Mason and the girls almost at Judith's door. Birdie ran forward, calling out and signing her pleasure at seeing her teacher. Emma's heart lifted within her. The true joy of teaching was the special bond created with the precious children she was privileged to teach each day.

Staying back, Charlotte clung to Mason's hand.

Emma let Birdie draw her toward Mason.

"Good evening, Miss Jones," he said formally, removing his hat.

Ignoring the sharp and invisible pull toward him, she parroted the same sentiment back to him and then stooped and cupped Charlotte's cheek. She signed carefully, "Let's go. See Lily."

Charlotte had been quiet the past two days at school, and now she barely glanced up into Emma's face.

On impulse, Emma leaned over and kissed Charlotte's forehead.

The little girl flung herself into Emma's arms.

Lily popped outside the door.

Birdie stepped in front of Emma and Charlotte, automatically shielding them. "Lily, hi! We're here."

Taking Charlotte's hand, Emma rose smoothly and also greeted Lily. Mason walked behind them into Judith and Asa's home.

Soon they all sat at Judith and Asa's table. Mrs. Waggoner had joined the large group around the table of both Mason and Judith's families. Emma tried to sit quietly and not call attention to herself, trying to ignore but not appear to ignore Mason.

After the troubled evening signing lesson in which Charlotte's wounded heart had been revealed, at school Emma had behaved as if nothing had happened. She didn't know if that was right or wrong. But she could not get the event of that evening out of her mind. What could she do to help Mason? Was she the person to help Mason? Maybe he should talk to Noah Whitmore, the pastor?

In his wry tone, her father, Dan, was recounting some of the interesting people he'd met at the pier where he sold notions from Ashford's store to travelers. "So the fella paid me a dime for the tobacco and tried to give me a penny tip. I mean, a penny? I gave it back to the penny-pincher. Said 'Mister, save it for a beggar.' Most people are generous. But some…" He shrugged.

Dan's happy face and eager voice soothed some of

Emma's restless, troubled spirit, but just some. Two people at the table—Mason and Charlotte—pulled her in two different ways. Sometimes she still wished Mason hadn't returned, his presence disrupting her assurance that she was living the life she was meant to.

On the other hand, Charlotte drew her. How could she help this little child who'd witnessed something so horrible? How could she help Charlotte and avoid Mason?

Why didn't life just go along smoothly? And then there was her sister.

Surreptitiously she watched Judith. No doubt to everyone else, Judith appeared normal. She wasn't pale or drawn-looking, but something was not right. They weren't identical twins, but after all they'd been through together, they were closer than most sisters. She could do nothing about her attraction to Mason and she couldn't heal Charlotte's deep hurt, but she could tackle her sister. But when? Where?

"We'll be seeing you in town tomorrow, Dan," Asa said, his arm around Judith's waist on the bench across from Emma.

The sign of their affection crimped around Emma's heart.

"Oh?" Dan said.

"Yes, we're going to keep working on the new jail. The sheriff hired me and Mason, remember?"

"Well, why don't you let Colton come to town too?" Dan asked. "He can meet boats with me. Our river-boat season will end in just a few a months. Hard to believe when the weather's been so mild."

Colton beamed at the invitation.

Asa agreed to this and began to talk about the stone foundation that Noah Whitmore would oversee them set for the jail.

Emma was glad to hear about this new work for two reasons. This would bring needed income to both families and it would leave Judith alone tomorrow. Perfect. Tomorrow she would beard the lioness in her own den—or cabin—and not leave till she knew what was troubling her sister. That she could do. She smiled at Judith. *Tomorrow you'll tell me and that's that.*

Emma rose earlier than usual on a Saturday morning, one of the final days of September. She ate her breakfast and dressed simply for a confrontation with Judith. She would find out what was wrong or troubling her sister today or know the reason why. She set off with the golden sun, shining through the tree trunks to the east. But the sunshine did little to warm a northern breeze. Her shawl held tightly around her, she walked out into the clearing that opened onto Main Street and saw Judith letting Asa, Colton and Mason off the wagon farther up the street where the new jail would rise. Noah Whitmore stood there, obviously also working today. Birdie, Lily and Charlotte remained sitting in a row in the back of the wagon. They waved goodbye as Judith unexpectedly drove toward the road that would take her a bit south and then east of town.

Though this altered her plan to go to Judith, Emma stood by the side of the road, waiting.

Appearing a bit disgruntled, but hiding it, Judith slowed when she reached Emma.

As they exchanged *good mornings*, Emma climbed up the step into the wagon. "Where are we going, sis?"

"I am going to visit Sunny Whitmore. She's getting closer to her time," Judith said, lowering her voice so as not to elicit questions from the children about "what time."

"Perfect. I'll keep you both company." Emma set herself on the wagon bench beside Judith and folded her hands in an *I will not be moved* attitude.

For a moment Judith said nothing. Then she slapped the reins in a disgruntled way and started the wagon forward.

Emma let a few moments pass and then patted her sister's leg and whispered, "Little ears."

"Exactly," Judith replied, acknowledging the presence of the girls.

They entered the forest, where golden leaves fluttered overhead in the sunshine and scarlet ones drifted down. The wagon moved slowly, rocking up the rutted trail. In spite of this, Charlotte climbed over the back of the bench and planted herself on Emma's lap. The little one didn't look up at her, merely laid her head against Emma's bodice. Emma accepted this, setting a protective arm around the child. Maybe Judith, who had taken in two orphans, would have some advice on children, but she couldn't reveal the secret, the reason for Charlotte's distress.

Through the whisper of the cool fall air, they traveled the trip of a few miles to the Whitmores', and then they were drawing up to the pastor's cabin. Sunny appeared at the window and motioned them inside. Little blonde Dawn Whitmore and her toddler brother scampered out to greet the girls. All the children, save Charlotte, who chose to stay with Emma, gathered outside to play in the brisk autumn sunshine.

When Charlotte wouldn't be parted from Emma, Judith sent her a questioning glance over the top of Charlotte's head.

Emma mouthed, "Later." She let Charlotte cling to her hand as they entered the cozy cabin.

In the privacy of her home, Sunny wore a large, comfortable dress without any hint of a waistline. Some called these dresses Mother Hubbards. However, the loose dress could not hide Sunny's advanced maternity. She looked uncomfortable and she had gray smudges under her eyes.

For a moment Emma tried to imagine what it would feel like to carry a child within. Well, that wasn't going to happen. She brushed the thought away.

"I'm so glad to see you. It was going to be a lonely day with Noah gone to supervise the laying of the jail foundation." Sunny pressed a hand to her lower back as if it ached. "May I offer you a fresh pot of coffee?"

"No coffee, thank you," Judith said.

Sunny lowered herself into a rocker by the hearth and motioned them to sit nearby. Judith settled into the companion to the first rocker with Emma drawing up the straight-back chair to join them. The fire warmed her fingers chilled from the drive here.

Judith sent her sister a glance filled with irritation, saying something like *I wanted to come alone.*

Emma replied with one that said, *Too bad.*

Sunny paused, evidently observing the exchange of glances. Silence settled over them.

Judith drew in a loud breath of frustration. "Emma, would you please go out and take care of the children? I need to discuss a topic not for little ears or maiden ladies."

Maiden ladies. Emma gawked at her openmouthed.

Another moment of strained silence passed. Emma cleared her throat. "Charlotte can't hear a thing we say."

"Oh, that's right," Judith said, looking shamed.

"If you don't mind—" Sunny shifted on her chair as if not quite comfortable "—I know that you two don't have a mother living, and I think sometimes too much is kept from maiden ladies. Your sister will most likely marry someday and I, for one, don't think she should be kept in complete ignorance."

Judith looked surprised. "I hadn't thought of that."

"Well, when another young wife moved into this area, she didn't even realize she was in the family way. Her mother was living but never discussed such matters with her." Sunny pursed her lips. "That's wrong in my opinion. Now is this just a general question or something that you don't think your sister, not just a maiden lady, should hear?"

Emma liked Sunny's frank ways.

"Emma can stay." Judith accepted the challenge and sat up straighter. "I am wondering if I am... I might be...in the family way."

The question shivered through Emma, but she realized it had already hovered at the back of her thoughts. She wanted to be happy if this were true, but childbirth brought its own dangers.

"What makes you think that?" Sunny asked, once again pressing low on her back.

"I... I've felt strange, tired even when I've slept. And queasy sometimes in the morning. Especially at the smell of the first morning coffee. Mrs. Ashford mentioned these signs to me privately after Asa and I wed." Judith blushed.

Sunny nodded gravely, still pressing her low back. "Those are all symptoms that could mean you're expecting. I must ask one more personal question."

"Very well." Judith's voice sounded strained.

"Have you missed your…your monthly flow?" Sunny asked, glancing away as if offering Judith a bit of privacy.

Emma was shocked. Not since she and Judith were around thirteen and their neighbor Anne had explained to the two motherless sisters about this female phenomenon had anyone ever mentioned it within Emma's hearing.

"Yes," Judith whispered. "I've missed two…"

"Well," Sunny said, sending a smile to Judith, "I'm not a doctor, but those are all the signs of pregnancy."

Emma started slightly at Sunny's final word, another one never spoken in polite circumstances.

Sunny pressed her index finger to her chin. "Two months. So that would mean August?" Sunny counted off nine on her fingers. "You may be a mother around April—next spring."

Judith gasped sharply, a hand flying to her mouth. "Do you think so?"

"I think so." Sunny drew in a long, pained-sounding breath.

With sudden realization, Emma tingled from head to toe and back again. "You're going to be a mother. I'm going to be an aunt!"

Then they were all chuckling and smiling. Judith

leaped to her feet and hugged Emma. "Oh, I'm so happy. Asa will be so glad."

Emma dabbed away joyful tears. "I'm so happy, so happy."

Charlotte looked up and signed, "What's happening?"

Emma tried to come up with a reply she knew in sign. She settled for, "We're happy." She had so much more sign language to learn, and why did she have to learn it primarily sitting beside Mason Chandler?

"Oh!" The word sounded forced from Sunny who had remained seated.

Emma glanced at her and was shocked to see a puddle forming beneath Sunny's chair. "Oh," Emma parroted.

Sunny shut her eyes.

Emma was embarrassed for her. But why had this happened?

Sunny opened her eyes. "It's good you two came today. What has just happened means that I am going to have the baby—today."

Judith froze and Emma gasped.

"What do you need us to do?" Emma asked quickly.

"I'm going to ask you, Miss Jones," Sunny said, rising, "to drive back to town and get Mrs. Ashford. She's the local midwife, and also, Noah needs to know. Mrs. Ashford will send her husband to tell him. And then I'll need you to come back and take care of the children." Sunny reached for Judith's hand. "You'll stay with me, Mrs. Brant?"

"Of course," Judith said stoutly, though her voice warbled slightly.

Emma hopped to her feet, signing to Charlotte that

she had to drive to town. "I'll be back as soon as I can!" She hurried out the door, sweeping her shawl around her. Charlotte ran at her heels.

They reached the wagon. Swinging the child up before her, Emma clambered up the step, untied the reins and turned the wagon around. She could hear Judith telling the children that Miss Jones would be back soon.

The day had not gone the way Emma had planned at all. Charlotte sat close beside her as Emma steered the team back down the rutted trail to town. All she learned today about…pregnancy would have to wait for later reflection. Goodness, how fast did babies come?

She slapped the reins, hurrying the team, but she had to be careful. The trail was curvy and uneven. She must not injure a horse. Sunny wasn't alone. Judith was there. Oh, my, Judith was about to be steeply educated about motherhood. Emma began praying for Sunny's safe delivery of a healthy baby.

Chapter Six

Guiding the team a second time today along the track to the Whitmores', Emma tried to hide her breathless feeling. Wrapped in a warm shawl, Mrs. Ashford sat beside her with a carpetbag at her feet and as calm as if delivering a baby were an everyday occurrence to her. Very soon after they'd left town, Noah on his horse had passed them. Emma sent up another prayer for Sunny's safe delivery and for a healthy baby. Next spring Judith, her dear Judith, the best sister ever, would be the one giving birth. This thought pressed down on her lungs even more.

A gust of wind unleashed a veil of golden leaves as she drove up and halted the team with a "Whoa!"

Noah with another man was pacing in the yard, watching the children. Mrs. Ashford slipped down from the bench and, carrying the carpetbag, headed for the door. Setting the brake, dismounting and then walking toward the house, Emma recognized the other man with him, the deacon from church, Gordy Osbourne, a close neighbor to the Whitmores.

The men touched the brims of their hats politely

and then, without a word, the two of them left her alone in the front yard to oversee the children. Birdie was happily playing with Dawn and letting Dawn's little brother tag along. Right now they were trying to catch locusts that hopped in the high grass and fallen leaves. However, Charlotte stayed close to Emma. Soon, from the direction where the men had disappeared, she heard the sound of chopping wood—not a bad way to keep busy while waiting. How long did it take to deliver a baby?

As a maiden lady, she knew she would be expected to stay strictly away from what was going on in the cabin. Maybe that was for the best. Still she strained to hear anything. But the chill in the late September air meant the windows and door stayed shut. After an hour in the chill, she drew the children into the barn. Upon returning, Noah had left his horse in the stall. Dawn invited Birdie to curry the horse. Emma let them.

Sunny's toddler son appeared sleepy, so she held him till he was quite asleep. Then she laid him in the fresh straw in a manger by the cattle stalls nearby. Charlotte clung to her skirt and wouldn't leave her side even though Birdie invited her repeatedly to help comb the pretty horse. Emma was pleased that she was beginning to understand more of the hand language.

Out of the wind, they were warmer, and the quiet of the well-kept barn settled over them. Emma sat on an overturned barrel and watched the girls. Charlotte rested her head in Emma's lap. Occasionally Emma would pat or stroke Charlotte's back, trying to keep her calm. Mason would be humiliated if the child showed her secret distress here.

Mason. Thinking his name released within her a stream of remembered images of him—as a father. His surreptitious attempt just before entering church to straighten one of the sad bows he'd tied in the girls' hair ribbons. His walking the girls to school, holding a hand of each. His stooping to look his girls in the eye as he tried to speak to Charlotte with his hands, and patiently receiving correction from Birdie. He was a wonderful father. The thought wrapped around her heart.

She rose abruptly. She saw a broom near the door and reached for it. Charlotte looked upset. Emma swung her onto a three-legged stool near the door and signed, "Please wait here." Then Emma began sweeping the barn floor, which did not really need sweeping. She also began singing the song "Frog Went A-Courting" for the girls. And to keep her mind too busy to think, to feel.

Finally she heard her name being called by Mrs. Ashford. Opening the bar door, she leaned out. Mrs. Ashford was waving her to come to the house. Emma gathered the waking boy in her arms and herded the girls out into the crisp afternoon sunshine. She glanced overhead, estimating the time at nearly midafternoon.

"I'm hungry," Birdie said, running toward the house.

"I've made sandwiches for the children!" Mrs. Ashford called. "And Dawn and little Adam can see their new…brother!"

The children hurried inside and were hanging their jackets on low pegs by the door.

Hesitating, Emma felt a bit awkward stepping inside, and then she saw Judith. Her sister was holding a swathe of baby blankets that must contain a baby. Emma had read about faces beaming, but she had rarely witnessed Judith absolutely radiating joy.

"Emma, will you sit the children around the table and get them eating their late lunch?" Mrs. Ashford asked. "I'm going to call the men." The woman flung a shawl around her and shut the door behind herself.

Emma couldn't move for a moment, gazing at her sister, thinking that next year Judith would be the new mother. *But I won't be the one helping her through labor. I'm a maiden lady.* The feeling of being cut off, separated from Judith, sliced through her. The children gathered around Emma.

Judith, still aglow, walked over and showed Emma the tiny babe she held. "It was amazing," she whispered to Emma. "A little stressful but amazing."

Emma nodded dumbly.

"I want to see," Dawn said on tiptoe.

Judith lowered herself onto the bench by the table. Dawn and Birdie hovered over the baby.

"Is he supposed to be all red like that?" Birdie asked.

"Yeah," Dawn replied. "Adam looked just like that."

Then Charlotte took one step forward and Emma heard it. Charlotte let out a sound—of wonder. The first sound she'd ever heard from the child.

From outside the men's voices reached them. Judith rose, swiftly moved to the bedroom and ducked behind the curtain. She returned to the main room in time to greet Noah. He received their congratulations on his way to see his wife and new son. After looking in at the bedroom curtain, Gordy left to take the good news to his wife.

A longing rose within Emma as she imagined the tender scene of herself as a mother introducing the father to his newborn son. *I'll never do that.* Again Mason's face flickered in her mind. She shut it out as she and Judith busied themselves feeding the children and eating with Mrs. Ashford.

"Well, all's well that ends well," Mrs. Ashford said, eating one of the sandwiches.

"It's been quite a day," Judith said, glancing at Emma with meaning.

"Yes, it has been." Emma had discovered her sister would be a mother in the spring, and in a very important way, that would distance them. When Judith had married, that had removed her one degree from Emma. When she became a mother, that would move her another step away. Emma would be busy with her students and Judith would be busy with her growing family. Why did that upset Emma, leave her feeling somehow lost, left out?

Mason's image standing over her in the forest on the day they'd harvested mushrooms tried to overwhelm her. Emma turned to Mrs. Ashford and asked about the spring wedding plans for her daughter, Amanda. Anything to keep from thinking these thoughts.

A few days later, October had begun, and Emma released a breath, filled with tentative relief. Another evening signing lesson was coming to an end. Outside the last of the daylight waned. As usual, Birdie perched on her knees on the bench on the opposite side of the table. The "little teacher" always sat Emma and Mason side by side so they could see her better. Occasionally Emma thought even this sweet little girl was matchmaking. Tonight a calm Charlotte sat beside Mason and often helped him form the signs. His large hands had trouble with the intricate motions.

Emma tried to ignore Mason's strong profile. His hair needed trimming. Fortunately her hands were too busy to give in to the temptation to smooth back the stray strands that had drifted over his ear and onto his cheek. The longer hair on his collar also tempted her.

Irritation with the situation roiled up in her midsection. Why couldn't Mason be sixty years old with a stooped back and hair growing out of his ears and maybe a few warts? The word *warts* jogged her mind to "dear" Mrs. Stanley, who'd managed outside church to slip in a not-so-subtle hint that everyone knew why Emma was "really" going to Mason's house in the evenings. At this thought Emma found herself grinding her teeth. She loosened her jaw and practiced again with her fingers, "How may I help you?"

Mason tried and Charlotte helped him several times.

Emma could feel frustration radiating from him.

"How am I ever going to learn all this?" Mason said under his breath so softly she barely heard him.

Her mind transformed it to, How am I ever going to learn this without sitting here beside this man?'

Some other way to learn sign must exist. But what? Then a thought came. Was that possible? She chewed her lower lip as she imitated Birdie's fingers teaching her, "Yes, I will." Well, she certainly would try. The idea might be a good one but would take some time. Yet in the end it would free her from enduring these side-by-side sessions with Mason. And anyway, winter was coming. Not a time she wanted to be out walking at night, and sitting here with this man who was becoming a temptation.

Another Saturday in town, first week of October. Mason preferred working on weekdays when Emma Jones was busy at school. The fall season was advancing this far north. So the new jail needed to be finished before snow flew and the ground froze. He and Asa hoped a hard freeze would wait till November. Besides, he needed the money. And while he worked, Birdie and Charlotte were safely playing with Lily at Asa's, and Asa worked beside him here. Colton had walked into town with them and was spending the day with Dan.

Mason and Asa were making another batch of cement, mixing sand, clay and lime in a large, low tub. The cement would be the mortar between the stones of the new jail, and later, when the iron bars arrived, they would make more to cement those into place. Mason stirred a long hole in the thickening slurry. His muscles heated, warming him against the sharp wind. Trees were losing their leaves steadily now. Dry leaves blew around his ankles and sometimes into the cement. He regretted missing summer here.

Then the jolt Mason had dreaded came. From the direction of the school south of town, Emma walked onto Main Street. She was dressed neatly in a flattering blue cape and bonnet. And of course, he couldn't be looking the other way or turned away. He was facing her so, of course, he nodded politely in her direction. She nodded in return and headed toward Ashford's store—not toward him.

He felt relief and irritation all rolled into one.

"What's up?" Asa asked, prompting Mason to start stirring again.

Mason muttered, "Sorry." And began swirling his pole in the thick slurry of cement, staring down into the gray mess. Maybe the strain on his muscles working on the future jail would distract him from thoughts of the pretty teacher.

Of course Mason snagged Emma's attention, standing there, his sleeves rolled up in spite of the chill, his muscles clenching and relaxing as he worked on the jail. Emma had hoped to avoid Mason's notice, but of course that hope had been dashed. Pepin was a small town but really…did they have to bump into each other every day? She'd hoped that her mission this morning would release her from the evening signing lessons at his table. That would help the situation of her growing response to him and stop the gossip that evidently had started—or really never stopped— about her and Mason.

Inwardly shaking her head at people, she walked up the two steps to Ashford's. Mrs. Waggoner, Lily and Colton's great-aunt, was sweeping the porch and greeted her with a cheery, "Good morning!"

Emma replied in kind and stepped inside, instantly breathing in the scent of drying apples, which hung in rows on long strings from above. The store hummed with voices, a welcome sound to her. She wanted Mrs. Ashford to be too busy to ask what she was shopping for. A few people glanced her way and smiled, then went back to examining merchandise. Mr. Ashford was busy at the shelves behind the counter, gathering an order for a customer, the warted Mrs. Stanley. The woman turned and gazed at her with a knowing look. "I see Mr. Chandler is working on our new jail."

"It appears so." Emma set her paper-thin polite smile in place and moved to the corner where the catalogs were kept. She sat on the stool at the counter and began to look through the various books for the one she needed.

Mason hadn't expected the sheriff to work alongside them. But Brennan Merriday had rolled up his sleeves and began hefting the stones that had been gathered by the town over the past year into a wheelbarrow. He moved some to different sides of the stone foundation that had already been set deep into the ground under Noah Whitmore's direction. Noah not only was the local pastor but also a fine stonemason. He would arrive soon to teach them how to set the stones so that the jail walls would be as strong as the foundation.

With a glance toward the store, Merriday leaned close to Asa and Mason. "I don't want you two to breathe a word of this. But I've contacted the sheriff in Illinois where the Farriers, Colton and Lily's parents, were from."

"Why?" Asa asked, his head down toward the cement.

"Well, I want to make sure that this Mrs. Edith

Waggoner is who she says she is and is here for the reason she gave."

"What could she want from two orphans?" Asa asked.

"A place to stay?" The sheriff grunted as he continued loading rock into the wheelbarrow.

"Well, why didn't she just move in with us, then?" Asa asked.

"That's what an honest person would-a done," Merriday replied. "Just asked and could you refuse? An older woman alone? No Christian man could send her away, not if she was kin."

Asa frowned, obviously chewing on this idea.

"But if she runs out of funds to pay the Ashfords in the middle of winter, what can you do?" Merriday stated the obvious.

Asa grunted at this. He obviously couldn't argue with fact.

Mason didn't really follow the sheriff's logic. However, a sheriff heard more about how people twisted things to their own advantage. And after spending days with his father as he died, he didn't doubt that as the Bible said, "The heart is wicked above all things." Still he couldn't think of any other less than honest motive for this woman to come here.

"Maybe it's better to be safe than sorry, Asa," Mason suggested.

"That's my motto, all right," the sheriff agreed. "It doesn't hurt to investigate and make sure she is who and what she says she is and wants what she says. If she comes up and asks something that sounds unusual, let me know."

Both Mason and Asa, becoming winded with working the thickening cement, merely nodded.

Sitting on the stool at the lowered end of the counter, Emma sorted through the catalogs Mr. Ashford kept so people could order special items. He had one just for books she'd used to order a few reference books for school already. She ran her finger down the table of contents, trying to find what she was looking for.

"And how is our pretty schoolteacher today?"

Emma glanced up, trying not to look irritated at the interruption. Since she didn't want anyone to know what she was looking for, she rested a hand over the catalog. "Mrs. Waggoner, how are you getting used to living here in Pepin?"

Two women near the windows were watching and discussing Asa and Mason and their work. Fortunately Mrs. Waggoner's voice overwhelmed their quiet conversation. Emma ushered out of her mind her earlier sight of Mason's muscular arms stirring what must have been cement.

"It is difficult to leave behind a hometown," Mrs. Waggoner said. "But you know that. I heard that you and your sister are from northern Illinois, too?" The woman gazed at her inquisitively.

"Yes, we lived near Rockford." Emma rested her other hand over the first. Was the woman lonely or fishing for…what?

Mrs. Waggoner nodded. "Yes, I know Rockford well." The woman looked as if she wanted to say more but instead she smiled and walked away.

Emma went back to the catalog. But though she

searched it diligently, the catalog failed her. It listed no book about American Sign Language. She closed it with a frustrated slap. There was no one here she could ask.

She turned and gazed out the front windows, trying to come up with another way to find the book she needed. She almost hated to walk outside. She knew the whole town was watching her and Mason, and much of the town was outside, keeping track of the work farther down Main Street.

She suppressed a sigh. And tried to come up with another way to find what she needed to free her from sitting beside Mason Chandler at his table three evenings a week. Without warning, like a gust of wind, the contrasting feelings of sitting so close to the man she'd planned only months ago to marry and now holding herself stiffly apart from him rushed through her. *I can't do that much longer. I can't. Who would know where I can get the book I need?*

Another Saturday in mid-October, Mason did not want Emma to be here at Asa's. But Judith had asked her sister to come and watch the children while Ellen Lang, the first woman who'd taught school in Pepin, taught Judith and Mason how to make cheese. The cabin was shut up tight against the sharp wind and a cheerful fire crackled on the hearth. The Mississippi River would freeze soon enough and that would end the food shipments to town. Ashford was stocking up on staples for the long winter ahead.

The harvest had finally started and Mason wanted to be out with Asa and Colton, haying. But he needed to see how to do this, too. He had a snug barn and two cows, with a steady supply of milk that he could learn to turn into cheese for his girls. If only Emma weren't here and if only during the last signing lesson, he hadn't felt her withdrawing further from him in some way.

"This is the easiest recipe," Kurt Lang's wife was saying.

Mason tried to concentrate on her, not on Emma, who was playing with the Langs' two toddler boys at the far end of the room. The boys were building with wooden blocks. Outside. Lily, Birdie and Charlotte were playing hide-and-seek. He could hear Birdie counting loudly as the others were hiding. Mason's mind insisted on going over the last signing lesson. Emma's sweet, light fragrance, the way the lamplight had caught the gold in her hair. He clamped down, trying to stop remembering. And worse, Emma had barely looked at him. But that's what he wanted, right?

"We start with two gallons of milk." Ellen poured it into a large pot. "We heat it, but don't simmer or boil it."

Staying a few inches back, Mason joined Asa's wife peering into the pot over the fire.

"How do you know when it's warm enough?" Judith asked.

"I test it on my wrist. It should be warm but not hot. Think of the way water feels when you're making yeast bread and don't want to kill your yeast."

Judith was writing the recipe down and he would copy it this evening.

The lesson continued and Mason tried to concentrate, but there was a lot of waiting between steps, and Emma's voice kept intruding. She murmured to the boys, often entertaining them with a nursery rhyme. The desire to move nearer her and to draw her up and into his arms taunted him. He'd never even held her hand and he thought he was going to hold her? Where did these ridiculous ideas come from?

In spite of all the waiting, the cheese-making was moving more quickly than he'd thought it would. He studied the pot of solid white new cheese.

"Now you see the curd has formed and we need to pour the whey off." Ellen demonstrated, pouring the cloudy liquid off the curd into jars. The women discussed the uses for the whey. But his mind focused on Emma. She was singing "London Bridge Is Falling Down" to the boys.

Letting in a gust of cold, Charlotte burst into the cabin and made a beeline for Emma. She thrust herself into Emma's lap and buried her face against Emma's dress.

Mason tried not to show his tension at this sign. He didn't want others to see Charlotte in distress. Usually playing with Lily and Birdie kept Charlotte content, happy.

Emma was soothing her and still entertaining the boys. Her compassion with Charlotte drew him even as he fought it. If only their evening sessions could end. No.

Though Mason's mind preferred thinking of Emma, he must follow and finish this lesson. And then he would flee to the field and join the men harvesting.

Emma looked over her shoulder and their gazes connected, hers filled with sympathy. The pull to her almost overwhelmed him. *I must begin putting dis-*

tance between us. If she didn't have to come for signing lessons, I'd rarely see her and not so close. But when he thought of Emma not coming to his cabin, a shaft of loss chilled him. *I must not feel this way.*

"She won't be coming tonight?" Mason repeated, staring down at Birdie.

"That's what teacher say. 'Please tell your father that I won't be coming tonight.'" Birdie did not look happy.

Charlotte had begun to circle the room, a bad sign.

Birdie's gaze followed Charlotte and she glanced up, her worry plain. "I think it upset Charlotte."

Anything new or unexpected could set her off. And Charlotte had connected with Emma, which was good in one way and bad in another. If timing had worked out differently and Mason, newly married, had brought these two home to his new wife, Emma, the situation would have been more settled. He and Emma would have been forced to work it out together. But because of his father's letter, that hadn't happened. His resentment over this grated inside him still. What if Emma decided to move to a different school? He dismissed this. Emma's sister and father were in town. He doubted she'd be leaving.

That meant that at least he could count on Emma remaining a good presence in his girls' lives. He felt so completely inadequate to the challenge of raising his damaged sister. Why did God think he had what it took to do this? Anger at his father boiled higher inside him. He tried to pour cooling thoughts onto it. But it bubbled up anyway. He shut his eyes, praying for calm.

"Miss Emma, she ask me about Mrs. Hawkins at the orphan home."

His eyes snapped open. "She what?"

"She ask me about what the orphan home name be and what town it in." Birdie looked up at him, her expression saying that she thought these questions unexpected, too.

His mind reeled. Had he said something that caused Emma to want to find out more about Charlotte? About him? The secret of his father and where he'd died remained a tight ball of cold dread in his stomach that Mason couldn't shift. If this family shame became known, he'd have to leave Pepin. And the girls had just gotten accepted here. What would another move do to his little Charlotte? He just wanted the past to stay in the past. Why was Emma digging into it?

Chapter Seven

Near the end of the school day just a few days since Emma hadn't come to sign, Mason walked into town, holding on to his hat. An unexpectedly blustery wind had practically blown him there. In the face of the advancing cold weather, after supper last night he'd had the girls try on the winter coats they'd worn last winter. His girls had outgrown them. The buttons wouldn't button and their arms had stuck out like scarecrows'.

So today, late in the afternoon, he walked into Ashford's store to order them warm coats. The bright autumn sunshine would soon be giving way to bleak winter. He blew on his gloveless hands to warm them as he drew nearer the potbellied stove in the middle, warming the store. Thank goodness for the money he'd earned building the new jail. They were still waiting on the iron bars. When those arrived, he and Asa would finish it up. And they hoped they'd have enough money put away to make it through the winter without asking for help.

When the chill had left him, he approached Mrs.

Ashford. She'd have to help him with this. What did he know about sizes and such? Fortunately the store was relatively quiet. He hated having to ask for help and didn't want an audience.

"How can I help you?" Mrs. Ashford asked.

He explained the situation.

"Why are you ordering coats?" she asked.

The unexpected question silenced him at first. "Well, because they'll need them."

She pursed her lips. "Store-bought coats are expensive and not as good as homemade."

This opinion struck Mason as odd. Wasn't she the storekeeper's wife?

"But the girls need coats and I can't sew them." He managed sewing on buttons and sort of mending, but that was the extent of his sewing.

Mrs. Ashford frowned. "We'll have another sewing day and we'll sew those coats."

Mason held up both hands. "I can pay—"

"You will pay for the fabric, thread and buttons." Mrs. Ashford waved him to follow her. "Come here and see if we have what you want. What colors were you thinking?"

Ushering in a blast of chill wind, two schoolchildren ran inside and headed straight for the candy counter, trying to keep their excited voices low.

Mrs. Ashford stepped away from him, toward the rear of the store, and called out the back door, "Mrs. Waggoner! I could use your help please!"

The children were eyeing the candy displayed and discussing what to buy, their breath clouding the glass case.

Then Mrs. Ashford returned to him, showing him fabrics that were warmest and would last the best.

He didn't know how to do this. Why wouldn't the woman just let him order two ready-made coats?

Mrs. Waggoner entered from the rear and went to wait on the children.

"Mrs. Waggoner," Mrs. Ashford murmured to him, "is so agreeable. She likes to help out wherever needed."

He nodded, thinking about the sheriff's inquiries about the woman. He hoped the lady would prove to be what she appeared. "Mrs. Ashford, I don't know which fabric is best," he admitted finally.

She sent him one of those superior female smiles. "Are you picking up your girls from school?"

"I told them to come here—"

And then the door flapped open. "Pa!" Birdie called out.

He turned to greet them. And with a jolt saw that Emma had come to the store with them. The low afternoon sun cast her into shadow so he couldn't see her expression. *I've missed you.* The words nearly burst from his lips. He pressed them together. She hadn't come for a signing lesson for over a week, a very long week.

"Good afternoon, Mr. Chandler, Mrs. Ashford," Emma said politely and nodded toward Mrs. Waggoner. She went to the wooden tray on the counter where people dropped off their outgoing mail.

Birdie's voice played in his mind: *"Miss Emma, she ask me about Mrs. Hawkins at the orphan home."* Suspicion sprouted within him. Was Emma writing to Mrs. Hawkins? Why? To find out more about him and the girls? He found himself having trouble swallowing.

He managed to acknowledge her greeting with a nod and then looked down at Birdie, who was trying to tell him about her day at school. "And Charlotte spelled the word right. And everybody read her fingers. Miss Emma say maybe Charlotte can be in the spellin' bee."

"Well…good," he stammered.

"I don't know if the judges will allow that," Mrs. Ashford pronounced.

"I told the children the same," Emma said, coming closer. "And I'm leaving it up to Charlotte as to whether she wants to compete." Emma paused to smile down at Charlotte. "But I think it's good for her to practice with the other children."

"I think that's wise," Mrs. Waggoner said, joining the conversation.

Mason barely followed the exchange, his mind on that letter. Who was it to? He tried to battle his curiosity and failed. Too much was at stake.

"Miss Jones, maybe you can help Mr. Chandler," Mrs. Ashford said, gesturing Emma closer. "He is having trouble choosing fabric for winter coats for the girls."

Emma drew near the fabric counter. "I always think a quilted lining is warmest."

Mason stepped back and let the children wander the store while the women debated the merits of different fabrics. When he noticed Birdie going near the wooden tray, he drifted over to her. If he could just get a glance at the letter, see who it was addressed to…

"Birdie!" Emma called.

He startled as if caught in wrongdoing. He covered

it by leaning against the counter. He kept his gaze trained on Emma and the women gathered around the fabric counter. The women were asking Birdie what color the girls preferred for their winter coats. Evidently the task of getting the girls ready for winter had been taken out of his hands.

He casually glanced over at the tray. Drat. The letter had landed facedown. He glanced over at the winter coat discussion group and, pulling up his audacity, with one finger he flicked the letter over. It was addressed to Mrs. Felicity Hawkins at Barney's Home for Orphans. Ice shot through his veins.

With effort he kept his posture casual while his heart thudded. What was Emma writing to Mrs. Hawkins for? His knees had turned to jelly and he was glad he was leaning against the counter. Mrs. Hawkins knew Charlotte's story, the story of a murdered mother, and Mrs. Hawkins knew where their father had died and what he had done to merit shame. *If this becomes known here, I could lose everything I've worked for.*

He glanced up and found Emma had come forward, and her gaze focused on him. Was his distress visible?

She studied him, and then her gaze dipped to the wooden tray beside his elbow. A little line appeared between her brows. She looked up into his eyes as if asking a question.

Had she noted that the facedown letter had been flipped over? He braced himself.

"Mr. Chandler," Emma said, "Birdie would like a red winter coat. And Charlotte has chosen blue. Is that all right?"

"I'm fine with that," he muttered, pushing away from the counter. He just wanted to leave now, run.

For a moment Emma studied him and then turned away.

All he'd done was flip over a letter. Guilt flooded him, though. Yet he forced himself to appear unmoved. But he didn't join Birdie and Charlotte, who remained near the fabric section.

He tried once more. "I still just want to order them ready-made."

"Nonsense," Mrs. Waggoner said. "I have time on my hands. I can start them right away. It will give me something to do." She glanced at Mrs. Ashford. "I do what I can to help out upstairs, but with Amanda, there are three women to share the chores and help Mr. Ashford in the store. There's not enough work to go around."

Mrs. Ashford chuckled at this. "So it's decided, then. Red wool for Birdie. Blue for Charlotte, and warm quilted linings. And we'll have fold-up cuffs and deep hems so they can last another year."

"Will the coats have pretty buttons?" Birdie asked, standing on tiptoe, looking at the button display under glass.

The women smiled indulgently, and soon the girls were examining and discussing buttons.

Mason's tension did not ease. He felt as if he were in a room where the walls were inching closer, closer, and he could see no door. An oppressive feeling, one he'd felt before all those days when he'd kept his dying father company. His heart cried out, *Please God, don't let people find out the truth. I can't put the girls through another move, another new beginning.*

Then he admitted more powerful than that was the fact that he couldn't bear Emma knowing the truth. Even thinking of her finding out the truth about his father caused him to cringe as if ducking a blow.

On Saturday morning, Emma sat at the table in Mrs. Ashford's upstairs quarters, where she had lived the first few months in Pepin. A robust fire burned in the hearth. The surroundings were so familiar, and Judith was here, and Mrs. Waggoner and their hostess. In spite of these things, Emma felt uncomfortable or stirred up.

She knew that outside, Asa, Mason and the sheriff were setting the iron bars into the jailhouse windows and hefting up and hanging the barred door of the one cell. Her mind kept bringing up Mason leaning against the counter downstairs just days ago. She was certain he had read or had been trying to read the address of the letter she had set in the outgoing mail tray. Why had it appeared to affect him?

The ladies were busy doing the hand-sewing on four winter coats for Lily, Colton, Birdie and Charlotte. Mrs. Waggoner, who had insisted on paying for the fabric for Lily's and Colton's winter coats, had cut out the fabric and, using Mrs. Ashford's sewing machine, had put the four coats together and done an excellent job. At the moment Judith was mending her father's winter coat. A brisk wind buffeted the windows, rattling them slightly at times.

"This will be our first winter in Pepin." Emma hadn't expected her thoughts to come out in words. *I'm in an odd mood.*

"Yes, you came right at the end of winter this March," Mrs. Ashford said, not looking up from the buttonhole she was sewing. "That's not so long ago, but it seems like you and your sister—" she nodded toward Judith "—have been here forever."

"I take that as a compliment," Judith said, pausing with her needle in the air. "I do feel very at home here. And now that father has moved here, too..." She sighed. "It was a good move for all three of us."

A good move. Emma nodded in agreement, but her mind took her back to Mason standing by the outgoing mail tray. She finally decided that it had to be the expression on his face that day that kept drawing her back to him. What had been in his expression? She couldn't put her finger on it, but Mason's face had looked stricken. That was the word, *stricken*. Why? Why would her writing to the orphans' home cause him such a strong reaction?

Tonight, a school night, Mason and Asa were going to assess where they were in regards to the harvest progress. He wished Emma hadn't come to supper tonight at the Brants' cozy cabin. But he couldn't voice this and tried not to show it. Remembering the letter she'd written to the orphans' home and all the possible disastrous revelations it could unleash sat in the pit of his stomach, a cold brick of dread.

And that wasn't the only reason he wasn't happy to see her here. More and more he realized that he was in danger of letting his growing attachment to her show. Merely trying not to sit so near and gaze at her was a challenge.

As usual, Emma sat on the same bench as Mason, and he let himself drink in the way little curls evaded her bun and graced her neck. He forced himself to look away. "A delicious meal, Mrs. Brant," he murmured as he finished the last bite of vanilla cream pie.

Judith smiled at him and rose to clear the table.

Asa put out a hand. "You sit, Judith." He looked to the children. "Lily, why don't you let Birdie and Charlotte help you clear the table tonight?"

"Can I do the dishes, too?" Lily asked, looking eager. "Mrs. Brant says I'm old enough to be careful."

Asa nodded.

Birdie popped up from the bench, too. "I'll help. We help Pa every night." Charlotte joined the two of them. Lily stood on the stool by the counter and began the chore.

Colton rose and donned his jacket. "I'll check on the stock." And he went out the door, shutting it against the cold.

That left Mason, the Brants and Emma at the table. Mason kept his gaze lowered, but that meant that he focused on Emma's lovely hands and not her face. Why, oh, why had she written to the orphan's home?

Asa got up and brought a notebook and pencil to the table. "I'm glad we're having this talk tonight. I think that everything is going to work out this winter."

Mason did not want to discuss finances with Emma here, but he couldn't object. She rested her wrists on the edge of the table, and he had trouble not staring at her slender wrists.

"Now, Mason, I'm grateful to you for combining

our harvest," Asa began. The girls were talking softly as they worked together, a homey sound.

Mason shook his head at his friend. "I'm grateful you planted so we have a harvest."

Asa ignored this. "We need to go over what we know we have and what we will need for winter. And we will pool our resources for the best of all."

Mason nodded grudgingly. He liked to take care of himself. Though grateful, he did not like the fact that the ladies had sewn the girls' winter coats. Sure, he'd paid for the fabric and buttons, but he didn't want to accept charity. But to say so would be graceless. Emma shifted beside him, releasing a breath of her fragrance, something that reminded him of spring flowers.

"The corn and hay harvest is going along better than I thought," Asa said.

"And the potatoes did well," Judith put in. She had brought out her knitting and didn't glance up.

Asa sent his wife one of those small smiles just for her.

Envy squeezed Mason. After all, he was the one who'd nudged Asa last year about this time to go along and advertise for brides, and now Asa had a wife and Mason didn't.

"And you will also be making cheese," Emma commented, glancing his way.

Not meeting her gaze, Mason nodded reluctantly. "And we have the money from building the jail. That will help."

"So the Lord has provided," Asa said, pushing the notebook toward Mason, pointing to the page of numbers. He rose and added another couple of logs to the fire, warming the room.

Mason studied the figures and realized that Asa was right. But again the irritation over having to depend on someone else's labor—even from a friend like Asa—tugged at him. He had always made his own way, and though he needed to be humble enough to accept help and work a job off his own land, he didn't like it. Asa's figures on the page in front of him did indeed show that they would make it but just barely. It would be a tight winter.

For now he should just be grateful. He'd come home and had the girls and friends and enough to make it through the winter. Why wasn't that enough anymore?

"I'm still wondering if the forge is the best place for father this winter," Judith said, her needles clicking together.

"What's your concern, sister?" Emma asked. She turned to Judith, wanting to focus on her, not Mason, who kept silently demanding her unwilling notice.

"I worry about whether it is going to be warm enough in the loft. And should he be climbing that ladder every night and morning?" Judith's forehead furrowed with worry.

Emma shared these concerns.

"Judith, Dan's happy there," Asa replied. "He likes being in town near the store and the other checkers players. And the forge is the warmest place in town." Asa patted her arm.

Watching this gruff man show such tender regard for her sister caused Emma to ache. After all, she was the one who'd found the ad in the Dubuque paper and cajoled her sister into responding. If Emma hadn't, Judith wouldn't have a good husband, Lily and Colton and a baby on the way. It didn't feel fair. Then Emma felt a little ashamed for thinking that.

Judith sighed. "You're right, Asa, but Father won't be peddling to the riverboats much longer. The river will freeze and even before that, the passenger trade will slow. And I don't like him having to take his meals at the Ashfords'. He's not their kin, but it's so much closer for him, especially in winter."

"I know how you feel," Emma said, swallowing down that last of her envy. "They fed me for months, and I tried to help out upstairs and downstairs in the store, but I still feel beholden to them."

"Why don't we just accept the fact that they like Dan and like to have people at their table?" Asa suggested. "I've already told Ashford that I will do some repairs to his roof before winter, and I noticed a few other things that need attending to."

"Oh, Asa, that makes a difference," Judith said, touching his hand on the tabletop.

"One thing I've learned is that people here like to help, and that's good," Emma said, sensing Mason's discomfort at this sentiment. All his fuss over their making coats for his girls.

Colton entered, bringing in the harsh breath of an October night. "It's starting to snow a little."

Emma rose. "I need to get home before it's too late." She quickly bundled up in her warmest cape, scarf, mittens and wool bonnet and then headed out into the deepening early dusk, facing the cold. Unable to stop herself, she glanced over her shoulder at

Mason, feeling a sudden sharp loneliness. She swallowed it down. Why was she feeling lonely? She had family here and a host of friends and all her students.

Through the side window of the schoolhouse, Emma watched Mason arrive to walk his girls home. He didn't do that every day, but she'd been hoping he would come today. Something had arrived in the mail yesterday that she wanted to show him. October was advancing relentlessly, carrying them toward colder November. It had been a few weeks since she had written to the orphans' home and a while since she'd gone for an evening signing lesson.

"Now, remember to take home your new spelling list," she said to her students, who had put away their chalk and slates for the day. And then school ended and she was standing by the door in the cloakroom as the last of her students escaped into the brittle sunlight. Mason had stepped inside out of the wind. His girls had run outside to spend a few moments on the swing, in spite of the wind.

"Mr. Chandler, do you have a moment? I'd like to show you something." She turned and led him farther inside. She thought she would feel liberated now that she had what she wanted, but confusion swirled within.

He looked puzzled but followed her to her desk.

She lifted the book out of the drawer. "We are approaching winter," she said the rehearsed words, "and I don't think I'll be able to keep up with our evening lessons." Something gave way inside her—what? Some feeling she couldn't identify.

She kept a tight grip on her words. "So I wrote to the lady who runs the orphanage where Birdie and Charlotte lived and asked if she knew where I could get a book on American Sign Language." Unaccountably she felt then as if all her strength had drained out. She rested a hand on her desktop. What was causing this distress? *Isn't that what I wanted, to be free of sitting beside this man?*

Mason held on to his calm expression, though he did not feel calm. So that's why she wrote that letter. He fought to control the relief he was experiencing, a kind of rumbling through his midsection. "I see," he managed to say.

"Mrs. Hawkins did not just send me a reply. She sent me the book she had. I didn't expect that."

"She is a very gracious lady," Mason agreed, making sure his voice didn't reveal his upset.

"I was very glad to hear the other night that you and Asa have had a good harvest."

Mason nodded, not wanting to pursue this topic. "Yes, well, I should be going now."

"I'll bid you good day, then."

He bid her the same and hurried outside to gather Birdie and Charlotte. So Emma hadn't been curious about him. From her expression and words, he had detected no hint that she had been told anything more than what he had revealed to everyone here.

Birdie and Charlotte left the swing and ran to him. He took their hands and led them toward home. He was safe, then. His secret shame had not been revealed. And probably would never be revealed. So why didn't he feel better? The answer was simple. He'd liked having Emma in his cabin, but of course, she'd just come for lessons, nothing more. And that was how it should be.

Mason had come to town to help Asa check and fix the Ashfords' roof and chimney. October chill folded around him as he carried replacement wooden shingles or shakes up the ladder to Asa. The sky overhead was a flat gray. Layers of clouds hid the blue sky. Once again he'd have preferred to work when he knew Emma would be busy at the schoolhouse, but rain had once again delayed them.

From his perch on the ladder he glimpsed Emma in the doorway of the blacksmith's shop, where she was probably visiting her father. Then he forced his attention away from her. A riverboat was edging to the pier. In town, speculation about when the river would freeze was rife. Listening to Asa nail shakes into place, Mason watched the lone passenger, a black man wearing a battered blue Union forage cap, step onto the dock.

Dan came out of the blacksmith's shop and called out to the stranger, "You need anything?" Emma appeared in the slight opening of the doorway.

"No, sir, I thank you. But I am looking for someone."

"Who?" Dan asked.

"Mr. Mason Chandler, I hear he be livin' in Pepin."

"He is!" Dan replied and then pointed in Mason's direction. "Up there!"

The newcomer halted, setting down his carpetbag.

He looked up at Mason. "Mr. Mason!" he called out. "It's me, Eb!"

Stunned, Mason nearly lost his footing. "Eb?"

"Yes, sir! Eb!" The man started hurrying forward.

Hand over hand on the side rail, Mason lunged down the ladder rungs, urgency prodding him. Eb? Here? He couldn't believe it. He met Eb in the middle of Main Street. "How? Where?" Mason couldn't stop stammering questions. Then he threw his arms around the man he thought he'd never see again. "Eb... Eb." He fought tears.

Eb slapped him on the back and wiped away his own tears with the back of his hand. "I been lookin' for you for a long time, sir."

"Eb," was all Mason could reply. He scrubbed his face with his hands as if this were a dream and he was trying to wake. When he opened his eyes, Eb was still there. "I never thought I'd see you again."

"Well, the war ended and I been travelin'. Seeing the country and looking it over. Wanted to see where to settle. Then I read... I learned how to read, sir. I read about your daddy in the paper. He died—"

Panicked, Mason suppressed the urge to clap a hand over Eb's mouth.

"And they mentioned you—" Eb sent him an understanding look " —and I figured you been to see him before he died. I found out you had and where you gone so I decided to come."

Mason sorted through this information, realizing that Eb had given nothing incriminating away. Obituaries were common. Of course his father hadn't had a normal one. His passing had been viewed as God's justice, and Mason hadn't been surprised to read about it in papers in Missouri. He shoved his hands in his back pockets. "I'm glad, Eb. I'm glad to see you."

"Hey! Where'd my assistant go?" Asa bellowed from atop Ashford's roof.

Mason turned. "Eb, I'm in the middle of a job."

"He can come into the blacksmith's shop," Dan invited. "It's warm in there."

Mason did not want Eb to go into Levi's shop. He might unknowingly tell more than Mason wanted known. Emma was there, too. But what could he say? "I won't be long, Eb. And then I'll take you home with me."

"That be fine." Eb grabbed up his bag and followed Dan.

Mason hurried back to the ladder and hefted another shoulder load of shingles, his mind racing. He was grateful to see Eb, more than grateful, but how would he be received in Pepin? Birdie had wormed her way into almost everyone's heart, but Eb might not be able to do that. And was he here to stay or just for a visit? Or some specific reason? What would Emma think?

Emma stepped back to let her father and the newcomer inside the warm forge. She'd witnessed the reunion and heard most of what had been said between Levi's hammer strokes.

"This is Eb, a friend of Mason Chandler's," Dan said to Emma and Levi, who'd paused in his hammering.

Eb removed his hat. "Good day to y'all."

Emma offered her hand.

Levi remained where he was and merely nodded toward Eb.

That struck her as unusual. Levi was always jovial and friendly.

Disconcerted, she waved to where she had been sitting with her father. "We just have a bench."

Levi went back to work, hammering, ignoring them.

"Turn over that bucket," Dan said, pointing toward a galvanized tin bucket.

"Thank ya," Eb said, sitting down on the overturned bucket.

"How do you know Mason Chandler?" Dan asked over the sound of the hammer.

"Well, that's a long story," Eb replied.

"I got time," Dan said, settling with his back leaning against the wall behind.

"Well, Mr. Mason and me were raised on his daddy's farm in Missouri." Eb paused, studying them. "I was his daddy's only slave."

Emma drew in a sharp breath. Living in Illinois, Emma had met a few former slaves, and a neighbor had harbored runaways before the war, but Eb's announcement brought up a dozen questions. The foremost was why a former slave would come looking for his former master's son and embrace him—like an old friend. What was she missing?

"I heard a bit of South in Mason's way of speaking," Dan commented.

"I don't want you to think wrong of Mr. Mason. He didn't like that I was property." Eb paused. "In fact, he's the one who helped me get free."

Emma felt her eyebrows rise, taken by surprise, but then wondered why. Of course Mason Chandler would help a slave escape. She knew his character. And that was a danger to her—her independence and her peace.

She glanced up to catch Levi frowning and staring at Eb. Birdie had been accepted by the town, but would this man accept Eb? But perhaps Eb was just visiting. Had he simply come to see Mason, thank him? Would a sermon silence the reaction to a black man coming to town?

Chapter Eight

Twice that day, high on the ladder, Mason nearly dropped shingles. Eb's arrival caused images, some good, some awful, to stream through his memory.

Asa stopped a few times to peer down at him and once asked, "Is everything all right?"

Mason was tempted to shout back, "Nothing ever goes right!"

But that wasn't really true. *I'm glad to see Eb.* And he was. Eb was the closest person he had to a brother in this world. How many times had he thought about him, wondered where he was, if he'd survived the war?

A few times when people entered the blacksmith's shop, Mason heard the familiar sound of Eb's harmonica. That too caused a wave of memories, some just feelings, sensations. His mother clapping her hands in time to a tune. Bittersweet.

Finally the Ashford's roof was ready to weather another winter. Chilled to his core from hours in the chill wind, Mason and Asa warmed themselves by the store stove, Mason preparing himself to be with Eb again, facing the past.

Ashford bustled over. "I can't thank you two enough for taking care of that for me. There was a day when I could have been up there myself." The man smiled ruefully.

"We were glad to help out," Asa said. He leaned forward and lowered his voice. "We're grateful for the way you and your wife make Dan welcome at your table."

Ashford tilted his head to one side as if considering. "We like Dan. He always livens up the dinner conversation and is good for an after-dinner game of chess or checkers. With him and Mrs. Waggoner at our table, the winter won't be so lonely in the evenings."

Asa nodded. "He's a good man."

"And my girls love their new coats," Mason added, though he still couldn't understand why the women hadn't just let him order ready-made. Yet three men understood the implicit deal they had settled over an exchange of labor, meals and goodwill.

"We'll come back another day and see to those loose floorboards in your storeroom," Asa said.

"I'd be grateful." Ashford paused and then looked to Mason. "Who was that stranger you met on the street?"

Mason groaned inwardly. Eb was impossible to overlook. Now the reaction to his presence would begin. He tightened his jaw. "That's Eb. We grew up together. Haven't seen him in years."

The bell on the door rang. Ashford turned to greet the new customer, saving Mason further questioning.

"Well, are you warm enough to walk home?" Asa asked Mason.

"Yes, I need to get Eb." Mason didn't worry about Asa's reaction to Eb's arrival. He didn't let his mind go further than that.

The two of them bid Ashford farewell and headed across Main Street to Levi's. They let themselves in and the heat from the forge melted the last of the chill from the day. Only the scant light from the small windows and the red light from the forge illumined the shop. After a day outside and in the full view of the whole town, Mason nearly sighed, aloud in the thawing warmth and comforting shadows.

Then he tensed when he recalled that Emma had been here with Eb nearly the whole afternoon. What might Eb have said that would bring unwanted attention or questions from her? He sucked in the warm, moist air of the forge and hoped for the best.

"Eb, I want you to meet my friend Asa Brant," Mason said as Eb rose. "Asa, this is Eb. We grew up together."

Asa offered his hand and Eb shook it with a smile. "Any friend of Mason's is a friend of mine. He's the one who advertised for wives for us. If it weren't for him, I'd still be a lonely bachelor."

Asa's cheerful words stabbed Mason. *I'm still a lonely bachelor.* And he couldn't stop his gaze from seeking Emma.

She rose and began preparing herself to go out into the sharp wind. "Eb had proved an interesting observer of life."

"Yes, indeed. I've never been a well-traveled man," Dan said from his place on the bench against the wall, his silver hair shining in the dim light. "He has taken us on quite a tour of places I'll never see. Thank you, Eb."

"My pleasure, sir. Traveling is fine but often lonely."

"Father, are you sure you don't want to walk with us to Judith's for supper?" Emma asked, buttoning her gloves at her wrists.

Mason could not stop himself from watching her elegant hands do this intricate chore. And then her words penetrated his fascination. She was going to supper at Asa's? Walking with them? He thought they'd be leaving her in town. Now that Eb had come, he wanted to be alone so they could talk. He tried to look away from Emma, the forge flames casting shadows over her pale, arresting face.

"No," Dan replied, rising, "I think I'll finish the game of chess Ashford and I started last night. You young folk go on. Give Judith my tender regards."

When Mason finally tore his gaze from Emma, Eb sent him a knowing glance. Mason could have kicked himself for being so obvious.

Levi remained by his forge, watching but not taking part in the brief conversation. Recalling Levi's welcome when he'd returned to Pepin, Mason suffered a sharp pang over his friend's hesitance and tried to ignore it. Then, with Emma, he and Eb and Asa were heading out of town.

"I hear from Mr. Dan you have a little sister?" Eb was asking Mason.

"Yes, half sister." Mason dreaded this kind of question. Eb knew too much that Mason didn't want known. Emma's skirts swished as she kept pace with them. The toes of her kid boots peeped out in a steady rhythm, catching Mason's attention.

"I didn't think your daddy would marry again," Eb said, shifting his carpetbag from one hand to another.

Well, he didn't. But Mason could never say that—that would brand sweet little Charlotte as illegitimate—so he merely shrugged. "After I left for the war, I didn't have much contact with him." Or before that, either. Once again the old ache plagued him. What had gone so terribly wrong inside his father in the years after his mother had died?

Asa's and, more important, Emma's presence kept their conversation to surface matters. Mason was almost grateful. But this would only be a delay. Tonight he and Eb would be talking the truth. At cross-purposes, he dreaded, yet wanted, someone he could talk truth with. He swallowed a ragged sigh.

He couldn't wait to pick up Birdie and Charlotte, say farewell to Asa and Emma and head home where he and Eb could be alone.

The three men let Emma enter the cabin first, then shut the door behind themselves. As usual, Judith had something fragrantly meaty simmering in a large pot over the fire. Mason braced himself for her reaction to Eb. Asa and Judith had welcomed Birdie at their table, but he doubted they would do the same for Eb.

"Well," Judith said, looking up at Eb's face, "who's this?"

"Judith," Emma said, not doubting for a minute that her sweet sister would welcome the newcomer, "this is Eb, Mason's friend who's come to visit." Emma held her rampant emotions in check. Eb's arrival and story about escaping slavery with Mason's help had opened something inside her, something like a river of feeling. She tried to resist being swept away in it.

Judith gazed up at the big man. "Hello. My, you're tall."

Bowing politely, Eb chuckled, deep and low. "Ma'am."

Emma drifted toward the fire, seeking something she could do to help, to distract herself. And needing to distance herself from Mason. Her inner river was sweeping her toward him. She could not analyze it. So, turning, she looked to see how Charlotte would react to this stranger. However, Birdie was true to form.

Birdie hurried from where she'd been playing jacks with the other children. "Mister, you look like me!"

Eb stooped down to be at eye level to the child. "And you look like me. Mr. Dan told me your name. You must be Birdie, right?"

"I am Birdie. Mr. Chandler 'dopted me." Birdie turned and gestured behind her. "And that be Charlotte. She's my 'dopted sister."

Emma moved toward Charlotte, who'd also risen.

Warily Charlotte skirted far around Eb. Hurrying toward her brother, she wrapped her arms around Mason's thigh.

Though resisting a similar pull toward Mason, for the child's sake Emma moved closer and stroked Charlotte's back and then signed, "Don't be afraid. He is nice."

Mason glanced at her and she saw her own worry reflected in his dark eyes. The river flowing toward him pulled at her, relentless. She stood her ground.

Eb claimed Birdie's hand. "I hear from your teacher you talk with your hands and she say you as bright as can be."

Emma murmured her agreement, so aware of Mason that she felt as if she were breathing with him.

Birdie glowed at this praise. "Thank you, Mr. Eb." She waved. "Miss Emma."

"Well, girls, we need to be getting along," Mason announced.

His tone and announcement startled Emma. She nearly reached for him.

"No," Judith also objected, "I prepared enough stew for all. One more mouth won't make any difference. The girls helped me peel and dice the turnips and wild onions. Colton caught two rabbits today. And I baked three loaves of soda bread. We've plenty."

The way her sister phrased it, refusing would seem to imply that she didn't have enough to share. A slight. Would Mason see it that way? Charlotte claimed Emma's hand and tugged her closer to Mason. Emma stiffened herself against the flow trying to carry her away from good sense.

"I don't know about Mr. Mason, but you got my mouth watering, ma'am," Eb said. "Much obliged by the invite."

Mason and Eb exchanged a significant glance that Emma could not read. As she busied herself helping her sister set out the meal, Emma concealed her inner confusion over Mason. She'd already realized that Mason Chandler was not commonplace, yet now Eb had come with his story and it had opened her to this response. She sensed that even more might lie hidden within Mason and his life. She imagined herself reaching for him and shivered as she hid it.

They all sat at the table. Birdie and Charlotte had claimed the places on each side of her. Mason flanked Charlotte and Eb drew up a chair to sit at the end of the table. They all bowed their heads and listened to Asa saying a quiet, heartfelt grace. Then Emma helped dish up food onto Birdie's and Charlotte's plates, keeping her gaze forward, away from the man she could not ignore.

But her eyes betrayed her. She glanced over Charlotte's head and found him looking at her. The expression in his eyes puzzled her. What was he thinking? Did he feel the pull toward her that she felt toward him? He never said anything about it. But…

She again recalled what Eb had revealed to them in the blacksmith's shop. That Mason Chandler had gone against his father and helped free their only slave. This was not out of character. And then she thought what the consequences of Mason helping this man had been. Had his father known what Mason had done? Why couldn't Mason Chandler just be an average man, a homesteader with no heroic actions? And no way to snare her?

The meal finally ended. Emma wished she had been able to taste Judith's delicious stew and flaky soda bread, but the flow, the river within her, overwhelmed her senses. The girls were helping Judith clean up, so she rose and went toward the door, wanting to escape before she betrayed herself.

"Mason, why don't you walk Emma a ways?" Asa said. "There's not much moonlight tonight and the path is still uneven from the summer storms. I don't want her to twist an ankle."

Emma wanted to object and she sensed Mason's reluctance. But what could either of them say?

As she left, over her shoulder she could see her sister sending her glances that said, *We'll talk tomorrow.* Emma nodded slightly in acknowledgment. But did she really want to let anyone, even her sister, know how stirred and mixed up her mind was?

Opening the door, she stepped outside into the chill night.

Mason offered her his arm.

Since everything within her wanted to accept, she knew accepting his arm could be dangerous. But she couldn't refuse, not with Judith, waiting at the door, watching after her.

The two of them started over the worn path to the track to town. She tried to concentrate on anything else but the man beside her. The October twilight, so chill and gray, sent cold shivers around her face. Summer twilight wrapped its soft arms around one. And soon winter twilight would arrive and it warned one to stay inside.

However, the presence of the extraordinary man walking beside her, supporting her over the rough ground, bombarded her with feelings she did not want to feel, sensations she had long forgotten. "Mason," she said his name. It had bubbled up from deep within.

He slowed. "Yes?"

They had walked around the bend in the road and were totally alone, shielded by the thick forest. She halted and turned to face him. "Eb told us what you did for him."

Mason looked down. "That was a long time ago."

She didn't like him looking down. She lifted his chin with her gloved palm. "Don't look away." She gazed into his eyes; in the moonlight they glistened.

He said nothing in return, but merely met her gaze.

All the turmoil, all the feelings that had been cascading within her over the past hour or more surged to flood stage. She recalled the spring flood here, and what she was feeling mimicked what she'd witnessed then. She drew in a ragged breath, trembling. As if he were the North Star and she a compass hand, she felt herself leaning forward, forward.

And then she rested her cheek against his chin and neck. She felt him swallow. His arms came around her and he was holding her. She let go and let herself lean into him. Oh, the comfort, the blessed peace of being near him. She was a ship that had come to its harbor, home at last. She felt his lips graze her hairline and rejoiced.

"Emma," he whispered.

She felt his lips move against her forehead. "Mason," she breathed.

Then a night bird swooped overhead and let out a screech.

The sound shocked her back to her senses. She jerked and stepped back from him. "I'm so sorry. I guess I felt faint for a moment," she babbled.

"Are you…are you all right now?"

"Yes, yes." She righted her bonnet, which had fallen back. "I'm fine now. Good night!" She began striding away as quickly as her skirts would permit. Her heart pounded, and her breath came quickly. *What was I thinking?* But she hadn't been thinking.

She had been feeling, moving toward this man, this extraordinary man.

She was at last hurrying down Main Street when Mrs. Ashford hailed her from an upstairs window. "Come up, Miss Jones!"

Emma stifled her frustration. She did not want to be interrogated by Mrs. Ashford. She still tingled from being held in Mason's arms and was trying to minimize that. Impossible. But she might as well face the woman, get it over with.

And Eb must be considered. She had no doubt that Mrs. Ashford wanted to know more about him. Perhaps Emma could make things easier on Eb while he spent time here. She walked around the back and up the familiar stairs. Mrs. Ashford waited for her just inside the door. "Oooh, I can feel the coming winter in the air."

Emma shed her outerwear in the back hall and then entered the cozy parlor–dining room and immediately went to the fire to warm her hands. Mrs. Waggoner sat by the fire, knitting. Dan and Mr. Ashford sat at the table, playing chess.

"Is it true that Mason Chandler helped that man escape from his father?" Mrs. Ashford asked, coming to stand by Emma. Evidently Dan had revealed everything Eb had said at Levi's this afternoon. Emma still trembled slightly from her moments of resting against Mason, but perhaps Mrs. Ashford would take it that the cold caused her shivering.

Here and now, after what had just happened, Emma did not want to talk about Mason. But what choice did she have? "That's what Eb told us today."

"I don't know what to think," the older woman said.

"It's natural, Katherine, with their history, that the man would want to visit Mason," Mr. Ashford said.

Mrs. Ashford chewed her lower lip.

"Mrs. Ashford," Emma began, trying to find the right words, "we are a welcoming community. And from Eb's cap, I think he might be a Union veteran. He seems an honest man."

"After all, he will be leaving before the river freezes," Mrs. Waggoner put in.

Emma didn't contradict the woman, but would Eb be leaving or staying? She'd obtained a book to free her from the signing lessons that had brought her too close to Mason. Yet again she was being drawn even deeper into Mason's orbit. And she'd allowed herself to be drawn into his arms tonight. She pressed a hand to her forehead. Why had she let that happen? How?

Mason walked back to Asa's in a daze. Had he really held Emma in his arms? How had that happened? He recalled pressing his lips to her forehead. It seemed like a dream, a dream too wonderful to be true. What had she been thinking? What had prompted her to lean against him?

Too much had happened today. Too much. Eb appearing and now this moment with Emma. What did it mean?

Inside the cabin again, he surveyed the gathering. The children except for Charlotte seemed to be drawn to Eb and sat around him, asking questions and telling him about the other children at school. Charlotte rushed to Mason and clung to him. He led her to the bench and she climbed onto his lap. As he comforted her, Mason tried not to show his impatience.

He just wanted to get Eb home where they could send the girls to bed and then talk. The longing to be totally honest with someone for once swept through him, forceful, insistent.

With Eb he could discuss his father, try to work out what had caused him to run off the rails like he had. Only with Eb could he have this conversation.

And somehow he would put aside the tender interlude with Emma. It wouldn't be repeated, but he could treasure it safe in his memory—her softness against him, the scent of spring flowers.

Finally Eb rose and said, "I'm plum tuckered out."

Mason stood also and motioned for the girls to follow them to the door, where they dressed to face the chill night. Charlotte still kept Mason between her and Eb. But outside, Birdie claimed Eb's hand and skipped along beside him. Fatigue, however, finally caught up with her, and when their cabin came into sight by the light of the veiled moon, Birdie sighed loudly.

Before long, the girls were in their warm flannel nighties and up the ladder to their pallets. Mason tried to reassure Charlotte with an extra hug but she still appeared worried by Eb joining them.

Mason waved Eb to sit by the fire. He wished he had comfortable rocking chairs like the Brants but straight-back would have to do.

"You got a snug place here," Eb said.

Mason nodded, staring into the flames. He wondered if the girls were asleep yet. His mind brought up Emma's soft skin resting against his chin. He rubbed it and regretted that this late in the day it had been rough against her.

"What's between you and that pretty teacher-lady?"

Mason started on his chair. "What?"

"You heard me." Eb grinned.

Mason let his chin drop and rubbed the back of his head. What was going on between him and Emma? "Asa mentioned that we advertised for wives last year about this time, and in March we were supposed to each marry a sister."

"And?"

"And I got my dad's letter the week before Emma arrived. Said he was dying. Wanted me to come and make peace." This memory along with the dark walk home left Mason chilled. He shivered, stirred the fire with a poker and added more wood chips from the bucket.

"Ah. Your daddy always did have a way of upsettin' matters."

Mason grunted unhappily.

"So he died in prison," Eb said in a voice just above a whisper.

"Yes, and nobody here knows that." The wind shushed against the windows, a lonely sound. Secrets isolated him.

"They won't hear it from me." Eb stretched his long legs toward the fire and stared down. "What went wrong after I left home all those years ago?"

"I think things went wrong before you left...after Ma died."

"Your ma was good to me, an orphan." Eb's voice

softened. "She never treated me like I was less than you."

"I know." Mason rose and set another log on the fire and then propped the poker against the fireplace.

"But you're right. She died and your daddy started drinking and not tending to the farm." Eb sucked in a breath, shook his head and stared into the orange flames.

What could Mason say? Eb spoke the simple truth.

"What happened after I run off?" Eb asked again.

"He got worse. I got a whipping for helping you. He drank more and began hanging out at the saloon every night. I started doing most of the farm work but I was just a stripling. I needed his help." The lost feelings rushed back to Mason, nearly overwhelming him for a few moments. Those sad days—no ma, no Eb, just an angry father who couldn't work in the mornings, hungover.

"I shoulda stayed." Eb turned toward him.

"No," Mason said adamantly. "He got meaner and he would have ended up hurting you bad." The firelight flickered over Eb's dark, earnest face, a face Mason had never expected to see again. This face released such memories. Mason rubbed his face with both hands.

Neither had to voice how all those years ago his father had taken his anger out on Eb with increasing violence. That had scared them both, and in the end, Eb had run away.

"I've thought about all that a lot." Eb paused. He leaned forward, resting his elbows on his knees. "I think that your ma was your daddy's North Star. She kept him going in the right direction. When he lost her, he lost that."

Mason considered this. "He said...toward the end that my ma was the best thing that ever happened to him, that he never had deserved her."

Eb nodded solemnly. "She was special, your ma, a true Christian."

Melancholy but determined, Mason drew up his courage, hating what he must face. "You read that he rode with Quantrill in the war? And the James gang afterward?"

Eb shook his head sadly. "I read it in the newspaper when they wrote it up after he died. It's hard for me to believe that he went that far wrong."

Quantrill's Raiders had been a byword in Missouri and beyond. They had been "bushwhackers," Confederate guerrilla fighters, who did unspeakable things to stray Union soldiers on leave and to civilians who supported the Union. The James brothers had ridden with Quantrill, too, and after the war had continued their lawless ways. "I thought when he wrote me from prison, he wanted to make peace."

"He didn't?"

Banked sadness and loss unfurled within Mason. "The anger still burned inside him. It was everybody's fault but his. I nearly left a few times, but I knew I had to stay with him. Maybe at the last moments of life, he would repent and we could have a few moments of...peace together. I wanted that so bad." Voicing this admission cost Mason, but who else could he share this with? Emma's face flickered in his mind and he shook it away. The moment they'd shared tonight presented a mystery he couldn't solve.

"Did it happen? Did he repent?" Eb glanced at him, his eyes catching the firelight.

Mason let out a long breath. "Not really. I did try to talk to him about Ma and seeing her again. But his heart was hard. The only thing he finally revealed was little Charlotte." Mason inhaled. "He wasn't married to her mother."

"Not surprising, but did he want you to take care of Charlotte?"

"Yes, he didn't want her to end up like her mother." Mason didn't have to explain. Eb would understand.

"I'm glad you brought her home with you and that little sweetheart, Birdie."

"She's a godsend, all right." Mason felt some better. Sharing the burden of his father's sins and lack of repentance with a trusted friend had helped—a little.

"Well, I'm going to head out to your barn and settle in the loft." Eb rose.

Mason held up a hand. "You don't have to do that. Just bed down by the fire."

"No, I think I'd better bunk in the barn. It looks snug and I got two good wool blankets. People 'round here will take it better if I'm not living in the cabin with you and the girls."

Mason stood. He wanted to argue with Eb but knew he was probably right. "I'll come out with a lantern and help you get settled. It is a snug barn and I've got my team and two cows in there. It's usually warm."

Soon Mason was hurrying back to the cabin. He banked the fire for the night and got himself ready for bed. He ached with fatigue from a long day of working on a ladder, climbing up and down and carrying shingles and nails. He lay down on his rope bed and listened to the wind grazing the windows. Eb had found him and slept just a stone's throw away. He knew the town would be stirred up by Eb coming but he didn't care.

He thought over the conversation with Eb, the only one who'd known his father before he changed, the only one who knew the truth of where he'd died, the Missouri State Prison in Jefferson City, and now knew all the truth. Mason wished he could be free of the secrets, the shame. He wished for the thousandth time that his father had voiced some words of regret over the life he'd led. He rolled onto his side.

"Emma." Mason whispered her name and couldn't figure out why she'd let her guard down tonight. His muscles ached and his heart ached. He wanted to tell her everything. And if they'd married, he would have. But his father's timing had been perfect—perfectly dreadful, interrupting their plans to marry. And somehow he knew that holding in all the secret shame was changing him in some way.

He hated keeping this in, but what could he do? This didn't concern only him. It touched Birdie and Charlotte, especially his little sister, who could be hurt by the truth being known. An outlaw father and an unmarried, murdered mother of questionable virtue— who in town would not look at her with prejudice?

And secretly, deep down, he wondered since his father had changed from an honest man to an outlaw, could he be changing that way? Did bad blood come out in the end? Did the sins of the father come through the son? Dear God, no.

Then he realized that tomorrow was Sunday, so tomorrow he'd face Emma after those secret moments. And the whole town with Eb at his side. He didn't feel up to the challenge, but life didn't ask if a man was ready. It just happened.

Chapter Nine

Sunday dawned, chill and bright. Outside Emma's window, sunlight glinted on frosted fallen leaves. She had suffered a restless night, not the usual for her. She moved away from her cold window to stand in front of her fireplace, buttoning the tiny buttons on her rose-pink and ivory lace Sunday dress. Her lapse in self-control with Mason last night chased her thoughts around like a dog after its own tail. *Why did I let him hold me?* Worse yet, why had she enjoyed it or craved it?

Another thought intruded. What about Eb?

The black man immediately struck her as an honest and good-hearted man. He had revealed more of Mason's past, one that showed great conflict and family trouble. Emma knew something about that. Her Kentucky sister-in-law had motivated both Judith and her to accept proposals from strangers to get away from a troubled home. And her brother was still fighting a private war against drunkenness.

She rubbed her tight, worried forehead and then went to the mirror hanging on the wall to smooth her hair. She'd braided it today and coiled it on top of her head. She gazed into the mirror and saw a mental image of Eb and Mason together. And little Charlotte and Birdie. No doubt today they would all come to church and then "the talk," gossip or controversy, would begin again. Emma exhaled in frustration.

Birdie had been accepted by most in town and ignored by the rest. But big and black Eb would be hard to ignore. Impossible to ignore. She didn't want to face anything today. After a sleepless night, she felt drained and flat, but that was no excuse. Eb was Mason's friend, actually more than a friend, almost family. She recalled how she and Judith had come here together and their joy at seeing their father settle here, too. Family was so important in this worrisome world.

She could not predict how Eb would be received. But for Mason's sake, she wanted Eb to be welcomed here in their church for as long as he stayed. For some reason, white Christians did not worship with black Christians. She'd expected this to change after the war and the end of slavery, but it hadn't.

If Eb wasn't welcomed, she must do something to help the situation, but what? Then into her chaotic thoughts, a memory glimmered. Studying history and great battles had its uses. She recalled a phrase uttered by some general long ago. *"The best defense is a good offense."*

With this in mind, Emma was waiting in the schoolhouse-church as Mason, the girls and Eb walked into church. Merely smiling at those who greeted her, she moved down the center aisle toward Mason.

Just inside the schoolhouse door, Eb paused in the

cloakroom. "Maybe I better linger here," Eb muttered to Mason. "Keep some separation."

Reaching the doorway in time to hear this, Emma hid her irritation over Eb's words and greeted them, "Good morning." She leaned close to Eb. "You didn't give me your surname last night."

Eb bent down a few inches. "Mason. I call myself Eb Mason."

Emma noted that Mason stilled and then his gaze swung to Eb's face. Hadn't he known that Eb had taken Mason as his surname?

"Eb—short for Ebenezer?" she asked, sensing that those nearby were watching.

Eb nodded. "Mason's ma gave me a new name when I come to them, named me Ebenezer. It means 'Hither by thy help I'm come.' She said it because I was an orphan and God had brought me to her."

Though noting the suddenly somber expression on Mason's face, Emma beckoned Eb. "Come to the front so I can introduce you to a few people."

Eb hesitated.

But she waved him on. She would not let Eb hide in the back, waiting to be rejected. Better to make him prominent and hard to send away. She strode forward, smiling at everyone, making the most of her position.

Birdie trotted after them. Emma hazarded a glance over her shoulder. Charlotte had hung back with Mason. Looking back was a mistake. The secret glance unleashed all the sensations from last night's lapse, all she was trying to forget.

In the instant of hearing Eb's words about coming to live with them, Mason had recalled his mother, just a glimpse of her. She was standing outside their door and had one hand on his shoulder and one on Eb's. His breath hitched for a moment as he remembered her. She had been a good woman to two skinny boys, one black and one white.

Mason decided to keep Charlotte with him. He did not know what Emma was about to do, but he wasn't about to counter her here in public. Besides, he'd learned trying to stop Miss Emma Jones from doing what she thought right did not work. Avoiding making eye contact, he led Charlotte to their usual bench and sat down. From this vantage point, he watched Noah welcome Eb with a handshake. No surprise there. Noah had proved to be an exceptional man. Then, after meeting a few others at the front, Eb walked back.

Mason motioned him to come sit with him, but Eb merely shook his head. Over his shoulder, Mason watched Eb situate himself on one of the short benches at the rear, just within the cloakroom, using caution in this new place and waiting to see what his reception here would be. It griped Mason. As boys, they'd slept together in the same loft like Birdie and Charlotte. Now Eb must sit in the rear. When would this type of injustice end?

Birdie joined Mason, sat down next to Charlotte and patted his sister's back. Evidently Birdie was able to sit with him and not cause trouble because she was a child. She and Charlotte were inseparable—just as Eb and Mason had been as children. Mason tried not to show his frustration and uncertainty.

Noah raised his hands, and the congregation quieted as he prayed and began morning worship. The preacher's new son began crying in his mother's arms on the bench near the front. Sunny carried the child into Emma's quarters, as women did. Many watched her leave.

Mason also noted the backward glances that people were casting toward Eb. When tall, sweet-faced Lavina, who led the singing, began to rise, Noah held up a hand. "Just a moment, Mrs. Caruthers. I need to introduce our guest." He motioned toward Eb, who rose but stayed at the rear.

"I'm sure you've all noticed that another Union veteran has come to town. His name is Eb Mason. He's an old friend of Mason Chandler's and is staying in Mason's barn while he's here. I'm sure you'll extend a warm Pepin welcome to him." Then Noah motioned toward Lavina, who came forward and began the singing.

When Mason was standing, facing forward and singing, he heard Eb's harmonica begin to accompany the song. Heads turned but no one frowned—at least for long. The mellow tones added to the singing and brought memories back to Mason. The harmonica had been a Christmas present to Eb one very prosperous Christmas. Mason had almost forgotten that. The Sunday service followed its usual routine but with this new musical dimension. Mason noted that the singing was more enthusiastic with the accompaniment. Leave it to Eb to know how to charm people.

When Noah said the final "amen," Mason felt somewhat restored. He was glad his mother had taught him not to forsake the assembly. If only his father had continued to go to church instead of frequenting the saloon. He pushed his father from his mind. He had Eb to think of now.

Mr. Ashford was already shaking hands with Eb in the cloakroom. "Thanks for the music. We haven't had any musicians come to town in a long time."

"Glad you enjoyed it, sir. I love to play." Eb folded his arms with his harmonica prominently on display.

"Come to my store any time and bring your harmonica. I heard that Abraham Lincoln always carried one with him."

"That so?" Eb said. "I hadn't heard that." Eb held up his harmonica. "I didn't know I had anything in common with that great man."

Mason noticed that several people had gathered around Eb and were listening. Then a few hurried past, making it clear they would not be welcoming Eb. Well, Mason had expected that, more than those who welcomed Eb. He drew in a cautious breath. He wondered how everything had gone so smoothly. Then he realized that Emma's forthright welcome had set the stage for Eb in a favorable way. She was one smart lady. But he'd known that already. And he tried not to think of holding her so close. Emma...

As he and Eb walked out into the bleak November sunshine to the sound of crows cawing overhead, he overheard one woman, the one with the wart on her nose, say, "Well, he's just visiting. We don't have to worry he's staying."

Eb leaned close to Mason's ear. "She's got that wrong. I found you and I'm going to homestead here. Unless you have an objection."

Mason glanced sharply up the few inches that Eb stood taller than he did. His heart pounded. "No objection." No matter what the backlash might be, he wanted Eb here. After all the lonely wandering years, he wanted family close. If only Emma could be his family...

On the sunny and chilly Saturday afternoon, Emma glanced at the rear window at her sister's house. Golden sunshine poured in through the small window, though she'd seen her breath as she'd walked here. Out in the nearby fields, the men were finishing the harvest today, cutting and stacking the last of the hay and checking for any potatoes that had been missed. Here inside, Birdie and Charlotte flanked Emma on a bench at the table. Opposite them, Lily sat beside Judith.

Mrs. Ashford and Mrs. Waggoner sat on the rocking chairs at the end of the table, near the fireplace. The older women had been given the more comfortable chairs and the warmest place to sit. They had come with Emma to Judith's to knit for their families and for the northern tribe mission for the coming winter. No doubt the two older women also had come to coach as Emma and Judith taught Lily, Birdie and Charlotte how to knit. They had been impossible to dissuade. Emma tried not to show her amusement at this.

Emma wished they hadn't come for yet another reason—to question them about Eb or Mason. She did not want to talk about Mason, stirring feelings she didn't want to have.

Finally she wished she and her sister could enjoy some time together, just the two of them. It seemed as if there were always people around whenever Emma wanted to be alone with her sister. How was Judith feeling now? Was everything all right with her pregnancy? Then Mason's face popped into her mind, unbidden. And worse, the way his stubbled chin had felt against her face the other night.

"So, Birdie, let me see you knit another stitch," Emma said, interrupting her own rampant thoughts and looking to the little girl sitting on her right on the bench.

Birdie slowly inserted the short wooden needle and drew the bright red yarn around the needle and then off. Birdie had chosen yarn that matched her new winter coat.

As Emma watched, she was concerned about Charlotte, who was not trying very hard to knit and seemed upset. Emma signed, "Are you all right, Charlotte?"

Charlotte just shook her head and then looked down at her idle needles and royal-blue yarn that matched her coat.

Emma turned her attention back to Birdie, watching her knit another stitch. "Well done. But you need to hold your yarn tighter."

"But not too tight," Mrs. Ashford put in.

Pausing with her knitting in hand, Mrs. Waggoner looked past the knitters at the table to the front window. "The harvest will be finished today. Winter will be here before we know it. When does Pepin hold its Harvest Dance? It will have to be soon."

The first observations had been commonplace, but the ending question brought Mrs. Ashford up short.

"Harvest Dance?" Mrs. Ashford parroted.

"Yes, at home we always hold it at someone's barn before it gets too cold. Though with everyone dancing, we hardly feel the cold. I still dance at least once. Brings back such memories like the first time I danced the Virginia Reel with Mr. Waggoner. The way he looked at me." The woman sighed as she smiled over the memory.

The vision of dancing with Mason flickered in Emma's mind. Definitely not. That would cause the tongues to wag. A regretful thought.

"Some people here don't hold with Christians dancing," Mrs. Ashford said, obviously trying to be diplomatic.

"Well, there is dancing and there is dancing," Mrs. Waggoner said, also sounding diplomatic. "I'm not talking about a grand ball where people dance the waltz and such and where men put their arms around their partners. Just a good old-fashioned country dance where everyone dances, young and old."

"I like dancing," Birdie agreed, bouncing on the bench. "We learned how to dance in Illinois. There was a dance on our street and Mrs. Hawkins let us go. We danced that Ginny Reel, like you said."

"Yes." Mrs. Waggoner beamed at Birdie. "It's fun, isn't it?"

"I loved dancing," Birdie agreed with a more enthusiastic bounce that upset her yarn.

Emma helped the child recapture the stitch she'd managed to lose.

Mrs. Ashford looked thoughtful. "What would we do for music?"

Emma tingled as another way to help Eb become a part of the town came to mind. "I enjoyed Mason's friend's harmonica on Sunday. It really made our music a more joyful song to the Lord."

"Indeed," Judith agreed.

"I like it, too," Lily said shyly from Judith's side. "I never heard a 'monica before, but it was nice."

Mrs. Ashford nodded regally. "I agree."

"And if people don't want to come, no one's forcing them to," Mrs. Waggoner added reasonably.

Mrs. Ashford nodded regally once more. "I must admit that I've enjoyed dancing in a barn once or twice. But I don't know of any barn around here that's big enough."

"Perhaps the idea of a street dance might be best," Judith said, venturing into the conversation. "That way no one person is hosting it but it will be open to whomever wishes to come. And we could have fires burning for people to warm themselves at and benches around them for people to sit and watch."

"If we could persuade Eb to play his mouth harp for us, it would be very merry," Emma said, guiding Birdie through another stitch. Once more she banished the vision of her dancing with Mason from her mind.

Charlotte dropped her knitting, jumped up and began pacing around the end of the room.

"What?" Mrs. Ashford asked, sounding surprised.

"Oh, ma'am, Charlotte's just havin' one of her spells," Birdie said, moving to put down her knitting and rise.

"I'll take care of her," Emma said, standing up. "You continue to practice your knitting."

Emma went to Charlotte and began walking beside her. She didn't want to do anything that might spark more pronounced distress.

"What's happening?" Mrs. Ashford asked urgently.

"Miz Ashford," Birdie explained, "my sister gets real sad sometimes and she has a spell where she just not happy and she paces. Pa says we just got to love her and she'll get better."

Emma was aware of all the women watching. Charlotte paced and paced in a circle at the end of the room where the ladder went up to the loft. Emma wished she could think of a way to help, but nothing came to mind.

"Should we do something?" Mrs. Waggoner asked, sounding sincerely concerned.

"You a sweet woman, ma'am," Birdie replied. "But Miz Hawkins at the orphans' home say—only God can heal a heart."

"It would be best," Emma said, "if you ladies just went on knitting—"

Charlotte suddenly veered into Emma, grabbing her around the waist and bumping her head into Emma's stomach.

"I need one of those rocking chairs," Emma said, lifting Charlotte into her arms. "Please."

Mrs. Waggoner leaped from her seat and stood aside.

Emma murmured her thanks and then sat down, settling Charlotte onto her lap and beginning to rock. She stroked the little girl's back as Charlotte continued butting her.

"I was sad when I lost my mama and pa," Lily said. She laid her head into Judith's lap.

Setting her knitting on the table, Judith began to stroke her back and murmur to her.

Birdie looked around, went straight to Mrs. Ashford and climbed into her lap. The woman looked startled, but within a few moments, she set her knitting into her basket on the floor and began to rock Birdie.

Emma chewed her lower lip. Mason would not be happy that others had witnessed one of Charlotte's spells, but she could do nothing about that. Emma began praying for this sweet little girl, that God would heal her heart. The thought almost caused Emma to touch her own heart. How many times had she felt her own heart breaking over Jonathan? But today she hurt for this little child.

Something occurred to Emma. Until this moment she hadn't realized that she had been feeling different. But how? Then she realized that the longtime ache from losing Jonathan deep within her had been healing. The realization startled her, upset her equilibrium. Was God healing her heart? She hadn't thought that possible.

A few days after harvest, though night was nearing, Mason with Eb at his side entered the store after hours. Mr. Ashford, Sheriff Merriday, Martin Steward—a school board member—and Kurt and Ellen Lang sat on benches around in the warmth from the store stove. Overhead the strings of drying apples hung like fragrant decorations. Unbuttoning their jackets and removing their hats, he and Eb greeted and were greeted. Kurt Lang even rose and offered his hand to Eb. And his wife smiled at them both.

Mason looked over the gathering and reckoned that they weren't meeting upstairs because he'd been asked to bring Eb. He also surmised that Ashford had handpicked these highly respected people in order to present the best foot forward on this "controversial" topic, a harvest street dance.

Then Mrs. Ashford and Emma entered the store

from the rear. "It's so nice of you to help me dust this evening," Mrs. Ashford said.

Mason became instantly alert in that special way that came over him whenever Emma was within sight.

"I'm happy to do it," Emma said. And the two women proceeded to claim wool dusters with short handles and to begin to dust shelves.

Mason was as certain as he could be that Mrs. Ashford had not been invited to the meeting but did not want to miss it. He hid a smile, and tried not to watch Emma's back. Her hair caught the low light and shone golden like a beacon.

"Well, let's get started," Ashford said, looking at his pocket watch. "You all want to get home by the fire sooner rather than later. So we're here to decide whether to have a Harvest Dance or not." He looked around the circle expectantly.

Mason tried to stop himself from glancing toward Emma, who was moving slowly around the perimeter of the store. How did she manage to look elegant even doing such a common chore?

Martin Steward cleared his throat. "Noah did not come. He is not opposed to a dance but he doesn't want it to create a controversy in the church."

"I do not understand why dancing is not gut here," Kurt said with his German accent. "It is just dancing."

Ellen patted her husband's hand. "I agree, dear, but some people here think dancing is too…too free."

Kurt still looked confused.

"You dance in Germany, Mr. Lang?" Eb asked.

"Ja, we dance. It is fun."

"I agree," Ashford said. "Katherine and I met at a barn dance. It's good for the young people."

"And I think," Mrs. Lang said, "that we should have a street dance. Then no one person is hosting it. If people want to come, they can. If they want to stay away, that's their choice. And now that we have music—" she nodded toward Eb "—that makes a dance possible."

"I don't want to cause trouble," Eb said.

Mason trained his gaze to the group around the stove, but he still tracked Emma's progress around the store with that heightened awareness he could not rid himself of.

"You're not causing trouble, Eb," Martin said with force. "I think Noah will be able to present this in a way that will quell dissension."

"Well, then we are agreed. A dance next Saturday night?" Ashford said.

Everyone around the stove assented with nods.

Ashford clapped his hands together. "Excellent! Katherine and I will keep the store open for the older folks to sit inside or come in to warm themselves. And if every family will bring a bench for outside and some food to put out on the tables up on the porch, it will be fun! I'll make sure the word gets around."

Mason rose with some misgivings and could not keep himself from glancing toward Emma. Mrs. Ashford and she were putting away their wool dusters.

"Eb," the sheriff said, "did I see ya'll go into the land agent's office yesterday?"

"Yes, sir, I filled out papers to homestead." Eb paused and looked at the man.

Ashford seemed surprised and then frowned. "That's odd. He usually brings the paperwork right over to be mailed off. I didn't get any new papers to send in to Washington."

Looking grim, Sheriff Merriday rose. "I'll visit the land agent and see what the holdup is. Sometimes that man is a bit slow in doing his job. I'll check on that for you."

"What land did you claim, Eb?" Martin asked, sure the sheriff would make sure Eb's claim was processed.

"A place that belonged to a family named Brawley. Guess they left."

"Then you'll be close to the Brants and your friend," Ellen said, joining them.

Mason forced himself to keep his gaze on Eb, not Emma.

"Yes, after wandering so many years," Eb replied, "I wanted to be close to…friends."

Eb bid everyone a cordial "Good evenin'."

Emma donned her coat and hat and moved toward the front door.

And though Mason tried to hurry Eb as they dressed for the night chill, they stepped outside in the company of Emma. The Langs and Martin followed them out, got into a two-wheeled cart and drove away eastward over the ruts on the southward road out of town.

Emma started down the steps.

"Mr. Mason, I think you should walk the lady home," Eb announced, gazing upward.

Mason halted on the last step, stunned by the suggestion. First Mrs. Ashford brought Emma down to dust while the meeting was going on, and now Eb wanted him to walk her home?

"That's not necessary," Emma began to beg off.

"It's dark already and bear might be out," Eb interrupted her, glancing downward. "You two go on. You can catch up to me, Mr. Mason." Eb started down the two steps, his back to them.

Mason knew this was a bad idea, but he went down the last step and offered Emma his arm. They walked toward the school yard south of town. The clear night sky was studded with stars and moonlight. The air was still but felt brittle.

"Bear? Really?" Emma murmured to him.

He shrugged slightly. He would have spoken but his tongue had become a wooden slat.

"What do you think about this idea of a street dance?"

He shrugged again. With her so close, he was unable to draw up words. But the image of taking her hand and sashaying up a line of dancers was more than appealing.

"I love to country dance," she said. "We always danced in Illinois on the Fourth of July and at the harvest. But I'm the teacher here."

He nodded this time and managed a sound acknowledging her concern.

She let out a frustrated gust of breath. "It's hard to know what to do."

He swallowed and brought out, "I see that."

Those were the last words spoken on the moonlit walk down the path into the school yard. Mason was aware of every night sound, mostly the swish of bird wings overhead, but primarily every breath Miss Emma Jones drew in and let out. He tried to break his concentration on her, to no avail. Finally they arrived at the teacher quarters' door.

"Well, thank you for guarding me all the way home, Mr. Chandler," she said with wry amusement.

He knew he should say something polite and leave, but as frozen as his tongue was, his feet now appeared to suffer from the same malady.

She paused on the step and gazed at him. Moonlight gilded the front of her hair, but hid her face within the shadow of her hat brim. He wanted to see her face, must see her face.

He moved onto the step and found himself a whisper away from her.

She tilted her head to one side and the moonlight illumined the lower half of her face, her lips, so perfect and full.

He couldn't look away and then he felt himself leaning forward. Nearer. Nearer.

"Good night, Mr. Chandler." She'd reached behind her and now opened the door. And stepped inside.

Then he was left standing and facing the shut door. If he could have, he would have kicked himself. What had he been thinking? Well, he hadn't been thinking. He'd just been reacting, doing what he wanted to do. Almost. He hadn't succeeded in kissing her. He tried to convince himself it was for the best. But most of him wasn't buying it. *I must keep my distance.* But this wisdom failed in light of the fact that in this small town, avoiding her was almost impossible.

In a party dress under warm outerwear, Emma stood on the Ashfords' porch and watched as the party gathered. On the Sunday before, Noah had given a sermon on brotherly love and unity among believers and peace in the church. And now, on the following Saturday, those who wanted to celebrate the harvest—dancing or not—began appearing on Main Street. Emma had pondered whether she should dance or abstain. Part of her longed to, and mostly she saw herself dancing with Mason. Not a good idea. Finally she had decided that she should take the middle road. She would attend the dance but not dance. That way she might not offend either the pro- or anti-dancing factions.

To distract herself from watching for Mason's arrival, Emma watched as the men built a huge bonfire at the south end of the street. Red-gold sparks flew skyward, and behind her, the Ashfords' store glowed with lamplight. On the long, wide porch, people greeted her as they approached the refreshment table and set down bowls of popcorn, plates of cookies, pans of cakes and doughnuts. She mentioned to them that a barrel of apple cider warmed over the forge across the street. And they showed her they were prepared with cups or mugs in their pockets. Every face shone with anticipation.

Eb's arrival set off a cheer and applause.

Emma couldn't have asked for a better response as she scanned the early November twilight for Mason but didn't see him. Wasn't he coming?

And within minutes, on the street in front of their store, the Ashfords organized everyone into two lines facing each other for the Virginia Reel. From his pocket, Eb pulled out his harmonica and began playing a lively and familiar tune. Emma remained on the porch, humming to the music. The older folk gathered in the doorway of the store, clapping in time or tapping their toes.

Then Mason with his girls along with her sister's family arrived. Charlotte clung to his hand with both of hers.

Emma hoped this new event wouldn't spark one of her spells.

Birdie ran ahead, straight for Emma. "We're gonna dance!"

Emma nodded and smiled, still humming.

Birdie ran to the end of the line dancing and began clapping, calling out, "Dance! Dance!"

Other children gathered around her, and then they formed their own lines and began trying to mimic the steps of the adults' dance.

Emma tried not to keep track of Mason and Charlotte, but in vain. He walked over to the porch and greeted everyone, touching the brim of his hat politely. Charlotte turned to watch the children. Birdie waved to Charlotte and, wonder of wonders, Charlotte hurried down the steps and was welcomed by her classmates.

At the joyful sight, Emma couldn't help herself. She spontaneously reached for Mason's hand, watching to see Charlotte join in the dancing.

But still the child hung back.

"That's right," her father said. "Mason, you're not going to let my daughter be a wallflower, are you?"

Emma froze, holding Mason's hand. She tried to form words of objection and failed.

Mason appeared surprised.

"Father," Emma began.

"No, sir, can't let that happen." Commanding her, Mason drew Emma toward the end of the line of dancers.

Emma tried to tug away.

Mason leaned forward and said for her ears only, "It will be good for Charlotte to see you dance."

Emma didn't know if this was true. She glanced and found Charlotte watching her. But it was worth a try. "Let's dance, Charlotte!" she signed and then held up the hand Mason's clung to.

Charlotte clapped once, took the hand another child was offering and began to dance with the children.

A thrill at the sight shot up through Emma. Then she and Mason joined the adults, he with the line of men and she facing him with the women. They bowed to each other. Mason moved forward and gripped her gloved hand, then led her around by the right and then by the left, moving in time to the lively beat, aided by the dancers and bystanders clapping. She gazed up at him. Moonlight and the light from the bonfire lit his face, so ruggedly handsome and yet so kind.

She couldn't believe she was dancing, yet she recalled the steps easily. She'd danced it at gatherings since she was Birdie and Charlotte's age. She couldn't stop the smile that blossomed from within. She almost didn't feel like herself. She had stepped into one of those storybooks she'd read as a child. She was Cinderella at the ball but she had no fear of midnight. This was real.

Then they were sashaying up the center, everyone around clapping. Mason claimed her gloved hand as they ducked under the bough of clasped hands, and then suddenly he was laughing out loud.

And she felt her face stretching into another smile that equaled his. The merry dance continued, bow to each other—right-hand turn—left-hand turn—both hands around—sashay down the aisle, and they took their turn holding their clasped hands high for the others to duck under. Then she was laughing, too. The chill of the evening receded as the dance steps pumped her blood. When the dance finally ended, Emma was warmed and breathless and beaming.

Birdie and Charlotte ran to them. "That was fun! We danced! We all danced!"

Everyone applauded Eb, who beamed at them. "Before the next tune, I need to wet my whistle," Eb announced and walked toward the forge.

Birdie with Charlotte in hand ran after him. The other children followed him as if he were the Pied Piper of Hamelin.

Mason and Emma were left standing in the middle of Main Street, facing each other. Doubt rushed in. Should she have danced? What would people say? Taken by unexpected shyness, Emma looked away and moved toward the steps of the Ashfords' store. Mason followed her.

"It did my heart good to see both my girls dancing with fine young men," Dan announced.

Emma was caught off guard and couldn't find a word to say.

"I was just fortunate to be at hand," Mason said modestly. Then he moved down the porch and selected an oatmeal cookie from a plate. His withdrawal left her feeling let down, and the lush sensation of floating on air vanished. Shaken, she looked down to hide her disappointment.

Emma didn't know what to think. She'd loved dancing with Mason, but here in front of everyone—had it been wise? As town schoolteacher, she had to be so careful not to show preference for any man. But this would be her only dance. She could justify it for Charlotte's sake if anyone made an issue of it. She calmed herself.

Then she looked up and found all the older folk smiling at her in the most knowing way. She tried to come up with some way to deflect their interest and speculation. And failed.

Honesty prompted her. *I wanted Charlotte to enjoy this. Also I wanted to dance. And I wanted to dance with Mason. I loved dancing with him. I'm not fooling anybody. Why am I trying to fool myself?*

Chapter Ten

After school on Monday in the crisp early November sunshine, Emma, Mrs. Waggoner, and Mason's and Judith's children walked up the path toward Judith's house. At Lily's cheery shout, Judith came out, dressed against the chill, and joined them as they turned to head toward Eb's just-claimed cabin.

Welcoming the distraction, Emma had brought along rags, old newspapers and a bottle of vinegar to clean with. Mrs. Waggoner sported a broom at a jaunty angle over her shoulder and Judith brandished a mop and pail with a bar of soap. They were going to clean the cabin for Eb, something else that would keep her mind off the Saturday night dance.

Asa, Mason and Eb had gone hunting today. A dusting of snow last night had presented a perfect day for tracking. Venison would be welcome on everyone's table. And if they thinned the population, the local deer herd would survive the coming winter in better shape. Emma had seen deer starve in bad winters in Illinois. It wrenched her to think of the beautiful creatures reduced to that. Would the coming winter be a hard one?

"Children, how was school today?" Judith asked as they walked northward away from her homestead. Overhead, squirrels jumped from bough to bough, gathering acorns.

"Fun!" Birdie chirped.

Colton shook his head at the girl. "You think everything is fun."

Judith patted Colton's shoulder. "Did you learn something new today?"

"We're learning how to multiply. I have to learn my times tables." Colton tried to look glum and failed. He lifted the pail from Judith, lightening her load. The bar of soap slid and clanked within the pail.

"I remember learning them." Judith glanced at Emma. "Do you remember us sitting with Ma and her testing us?"

With Charlotte holding her hand, Emma instantly recalled the scene. "Yes." She blinked away the moisture that quickened in her eyes. She wasn't sad and it wasn't a sad memory, but her emotions had been like a pot boiling over since Saturday night's dance. She had gone to the dance because she didn't believe it was wrong and didn't want to appear disapproving of those who'd come to dance. But choosing the middle road, she'd had no intention of dancing, least of all with Mason Chandler.

The dance with him had been a misstep in so many ways. The knowing glances she'd received that evening and then the next day after church had made that clear, very clear. She could ask herself why she'd done it but she knew why. She danced with Mason Chandler because she wanted to dance with Mason Chandler, to feel young and free again. And she'd enjoyed every breathless, exhilarating moment, but the experience had fostered gossip and left her unsettled, to say the least. Wading in the deep confusion, she could not make sense of what she was feeling.

A gust of wind and golden, crimson and bronze leaves cascaded down around them. Charlotte lifted her face and one hand toward the leaves and then Emma heard it. The little girl voiced a tiny sound of happiness. At this, Emma's step faltered for a moment but she concealed it.

This precious little girl had suffered something so dreadful it might have robbed her of hearing and speech for the rest of her life. Would she ever come back to normal? Emma was convicted of her sin of self-centeredness. Her lapse of judgment in dancing with Mason was nothing compared to Charlotte's woes. She beamed at the little girl. "I love pretty leaves," she signed.

Charlotte bobbed her head and then skipped a few steps.

And Emma's spirits rose.

"That's it, isn't it?" Mrs. Waggoner asked, motioning toward the cabin ahead. High weeds covered the yard and the windows didn't gleam in the clear autumn sunshine as Judith's did.

"Yes, I was here yesterday afternoon with the men," Judith replied. Then, in the distance, they heard a gunshot. The women paused.

Emma noted that Judith looked worried. Hunting for meat was a necessity but dangerous, too. Emma knew that Judith would worry about Asa till he came home safe tonight. Emma's mind tried to carry her toward worrying about Mason but she merely started walking faster. *He's not for me to worry over.*

Soon the women had propped open the door and surveyed the dusty interior of the one-room cabin.

"If nobody was livin' here, how come everything gets dirty anyway?" Birdie asked, her pert nose wrinkled.

The women all broke into laughter.

"That is the age-old question, Birdie Chandler," Mrs. Waggoner said. "Women have been asking that question for thousands of years."

"Dust and dirt just come of their own accord," Judith said with a sigh.

Soon Colton was outside pumping water for scrubbing, the rusty pump creaking. The girls took turns standing on the step stool, cleaning as much of the two windows as they could reach.

As Mrs. Waggoner dusted every surface she could, Judith swept away the ceiling cobwebs with a broom while Emma swept the half-log floor. Another shot rang out a little nearer. The women paused again almost as one, glancing toward it. Would the hunters come home safe and with the much-needed meat?

For a moment Emma let herself think of a family and a cabin of her own. She pictured herself in Judith's life—a wife and mother with a husband out hunting for the family. But she had chosen a career, a different path. She wanted independence, but now she realized that independence could be lonely, very lonely.

Once again today's inappropriate reaction, the recurring moisture rushing into her eyes, had to be blinked away. *I have chosen my path. Mason has cho-*

sen his. I must be more careful in the future. No more dancing or anything like it. This weakness, these rampant reactions, will ebb and I'll go back to normal.

Mason lowered his rifle. Another miss. Frustration burned in his chest. One of them needed to bring down a young buck, thin the herd. To his right through the forest, he glimpsed Asa and then to his left, Eb. For safety's sake, they were careful to keep in line as much as possible, not get ahead where they might become unintentional targets.

After long hours of tracking the herd, Mason was chilled to the bone. It was uncanny how the deer seemed to sense hunting time had come and they had hunkered down. The hours of walking and not talking had given Mason way too much time to go over Saturday night—every detail of dancing with Emma. The brief dance had heightened her attraction. What a wonderful woman, and she could have been his. Anger simmered inside him once more—over missing his chance to marry her. Why was it that anything connected to his father never went right? If his father's letter had come just two weeks later...

Eb moved stealthily near him. Mason's anger eased. Eb had found him and was settling only a couple of miles away, as near as Asa. And then Mason recalled now he'd gained Charlotte and sweet little Birdie. But were they enough? The memory of Emma holding his hands and sashaying face-to-face with him down the dance line triggered a longing he could not deny.

A shot rang out.

"I got him!" Eb shouted, and then the three of them

were running. Their first deer! At last, the long first day of hunting would come to an end and Eb, Asa and Mason could feed their families. Regret and anger over the past and the shame his father had brought to him must be put away. Life had to be lived and he was a father now. Emma's face fluttered in his mind, and he ignored it or tried to. He'd probably never be a husband, but he was a father.

Today after church the finally finished new town jail had been opened to the public. After service that day, they'd held the first fall potluck. The summer picnics had been put away with summer bonnets and parasols. The potluck meal had been enjoyed, and now the coated and hatted and scarfed townspeople headed to Main Street to take turns touring the jail—the sheriff's office with the one cell in the rear. High wispy clouds rushed over the blue sky but the sun still shone.

On the way, Mason held back from the hurry toward the jail. Eb walked beside him, and though the town appeared to be adjusting to Eb's presence, the word had gotten around that he'd moved into the old Brawley cabin and was staying. Mason worried that someone might take this chance to be rude and he didn't want that. Wouldn't let Eb face it alone.

But also, he was keeping his distance from Emma. After last Saturday night's dance on Main Street, there'd been renewed and increased interest in him and Emma. So today on the way to the jail, he let the girls inspect every fallen leaf and interesting pebble and was glad when Emma and her sister passed him on the trail between the school yard and town.

Despite his slow pace, the four of them finally

reached the jail and joined the line waiting to see the finished project. Standing there looking at the stout stone walls, Mason couldn't help the tug of pride he felt over the workmanship he and Asa had performed.

His silver hair peeping out from his hat, Dan greeted him with a handshake and nodded to Eb. "You and Asa should be proud of your work. A fine job."

"Thank you, sir," Mason said. "We learned a lot from Noah Whitmore. He's the one who taught us how to do stone like masons."

"A handy man, our preacher," Dan agreed, gazing up as geese flew overhead, honking.

"Is this where the sheriff will put bad men, Pa?" Birdie asked, gazing up at him, hanging on to his hand.

The innocent question brought a rush of scenes from the prison where he'd gone daily to visit his father in the infirmary. He recalled the sorrow, followed by irritation and humiliation. "Yes," he said belatedly.

"Why do men do bad things?" Birdie asked.

"That's a question, all right," Dan answered, saving Mason from trying to come up with a reply. "It all goes back to people wanting their own way, not thinking of others. You girls listen when the preacher talks and to your pa and when my daughter teaches you the right path. Then you'll never end up in a place like this."

"Women go to jail, too?" Birdie looked shocked.

"Unfortunately that does happen," Dan continued. "But I know you girls are never going to do bad things."

"I'm not," Birdie said fiercely. "And neither is Charlotte. We're good girls. Miss Emma says so."

Dan nodded. "That's right. I see how you always help and think of others."

Mason was glad that Dan had handled this conversation.

Then Johann, a schoolmate of the girls, ran over. "Come! We will play hide-and-seek. It is fun!"

Birdie in her bright red coat and knit hat looked up, silently asking for permission.

"Go ahead," Mason urged. "Have fun. But stay in town."

"We will!" Johann said, pulling Birdie toward the children gathered in the midst of the street. Charlotte in her royal-blue winter wear went along but reluctantly. Soon Mason saw Johann standing with his face to the outside wall of the blacksmith's shop with hands over his eyes, counting very loudly.

Two couples came out of the jail. Two more entered. Then, finally, Mason and Eb's turn arrived. They stepped inside onto the log floor and gazed around. The stone walls would keep out the wind. And the barred windows had wooden shutters outside for more protection. A Franklin stove sat in the center, warming the large room. Mason, Eb and Dan first moved there to warm themselves.

The sheriff's imposing desk sat to the right of the door with a chair and another. At the back of the room stood a wall with a door that would lead to the one cell that spanned the back of the jail. As Mason scanned the room, he sincerely hoped that the jail would never hold an outlaw. Bad memories of those he'd seen in Jefferson City rushed through his mind. He hoped Pepin would remain free of such men. And this jail empty.

Eb and he took their time inspecting the map of the county framed on the wall. Merriday came to stand beside them. "Quite an area to patrol. Once a month I make the circuit t'all the towns. So far all I've dealt with is minor thievin' and a suspicious fire. Hope it stays that way. I don't like that I have to ride a day to reach a telegraph office."

Mason nodded but couldn't think of any reply. It was a lot to expect a man to be the law over such a large territory.

As if reading Mason's thoughts, Merriday said, "I can always deputize men when I need assistance. And I have already deputized a few men in the farther towns so the townspeople have someone to send for me. But we need better communication if I'm to do a good job."

True, but Merriday was highly respected, and if anybody could do it, he could. Finally Mason and Eb returned to the street. The children had nearly finished their game of hide-and-seek. Birdie was among the "found" and was looking here and there, probably for Charlotte.

Mason scanned the street looking for Charlotte's bright blue coat. He didn't see her. Worry niggled into his mind. He shoved it away. Charlotte never strayed far from Birdie's side. She's just enjoying the hide-and-seek game. And that was good, right?

"Are you all settled in, Eb?" Dan asked, looking upward.

"Yes, sir. The cabin was a bit dusty—" he paused to nod toward Judith nearby "—till my good neighbors came and cleaned. But the cabin's in good repair. I want to buy some chickens soon, and I'm looking for a heifer to raise up over the winter. Need a milk cow."

"I'll keep my ears open. If I hear of anybody with extra stock, I'll let you know."

"Thank you. 'Preciate it, sir."

Mason kept an eye out for Johann bringing Charlotte to the "found" group.

The other two men went on to discuss various farmers Eb might approach directly. Chickens appeared to be available.

As Mason listened, he watched as more and more children arrived back in the center of Main Street. Evidently Johann was doing a good job of finding children. Still, Charlotte in her bright blue coat remained absent.

Finally Johann appeared, looking distracted. The boy paused and visibly counted the children he'd found who'd gathered in front of the forge. "Where is Charlotte, Birdie?" the boy asked. "She is the last one. I have looked everywhere and I cannot find her."

Birdie stepped out of the crowd of "found" children. "I don't know. We were together and then I turned my back and she was gone. I thought she found a good hiding place, is all."

"I have looked everywhere." Johann scanned the street. "Did anyone see her?"

The children shook their heads no and looked around.

Mason moved forward, worry lapping over him like cold water. He couldn't hold back. "What's wrong? Where's Charlotte?"

Johann turned to him. "I do not know. I have found everyone else."

Birdie ran to Mason. "I just thought she was hidin' good."

Stooping, Mason folded Birdie in his arms. "Don't worry. We'll find her. Don't worry." He tried to make himself believe his own soothing words, but he couldn't.

"Charlotte gone missing?" Eb said from behind Mason.

Dan called out, "Charlotte! Charlotte! Come out!"

"Beggin' your pardon, sir. She can't hear you," Eb said.

"Oh, that's right," Dan said, looking abashed. "I forgot."

Mason rose. "Eb, why don't you take the high side of the street and I'll take the river side?"

Eb touched the brim of his Union pea cap and headed toward the high side of the street.

"Will you watch Birdie?" Mason asked Dan. "I don't want her to get lost looking for Charlotte."

Dan mimicked Eb's salute. "Will do. Birdie!" He waved. "Come here, child."

Mason tried to control his concern, but Charlotte had never left Birdie's side before. Worries swirled around Mason like a swarm of spring mosquitoes. He tried to ignore them as he began searching the river side of the street.

The news that Mason Chandler's deaf sister might be missing hit Emma like a slap in the face. Charlotte, where could she have gone? Soon the street came alive with mothers keeping their children close while the men combed both sides of the street, looking in every cranny and crevice, behind every boulder and up every tree. Emma stood by her father, Birdie between them. Emma patted Birdie's shoulder. "They'll find her. Don't worry." Her own words mocked her. She couldn't stop herself from fretting.

The search continued and broadened. Other mothers drew nearer their children, speaking quietly, reassuring them that Charlotte would be found, not to worry. The afternoon shadows lengthened. And Charlotte remained missing. Soon night would fall. Women and children started moving to wait in the warmer store or the forge or the jail, waiting for husbands to find the girl so they could all go home.

Mason appeared in front of Emma. His distraught expression wrung her heart. He stooped. "How are you, Birdie?"

"I'm scared. Where did she go? Why?" Birdie moved up and down as if in pain. "Charlotte, my Charlotte."

Emma stooped also and wrapped her arms around the child. "Birdie, God is watching over Charlotte."

"But bad things happen," Birdie wailed. "I want my Charlotte."

Emma had never seen Birdie in a panic. She felt her own panic building inside her. What if Charlotte had somehow gotten too close to the river and been swept away in the current? She capped this line of thought mercilessly. Her gaze met Mason's.

"I'm going to take Birdie with me to the forge," Dan spoke up. "We'll sit by the fire and have some cookies. And we'll pray."

"We're gonna need lanterns!" Sheriff Merriday called out. "If you live near town, go get a lantern! We don't want that child out all night!"

Emma stood. "Birdie, go with my father and stay with him. I'm going to get my lantern."

With one last glance at Mason's crestfallen face, Emma hurried away toward the school to fetch her lantern. With every quick step, she offered a prayer for little Charlotte's safety. No strangers had been in town. This must be a simple case of the child getting lost. Emma tried not to think of the dark forest that surrounded the town and how frightened Charlotte must be. *And we can't even call her name!*

Through the last of the day's light, Emma hurried to her door and let herself in. She picked up the lantern she kept by the door and reached for a match from the metal match holder mounted on the wall when something plowed into her waist from behind. She cried out and nearly dropped the lantern.

Then she realized it was a small body that was clinging to her and butting her from behind. "Charlotte!" She set down the lantern and turned to embrace the child. Something had set the girl off and she was suffering one of her spells again. The head-butting became frantic. Emma reached for a match and lit the lantern so she could see better.

She lifted Charlotte into her arms, carried her to her rocking chair and sat down. She wrapped Charlotte close to her in the afghan that lay over the arm and began rocking. Charlotte's distress was palpable and the worst Emma had seen. Emma began praying aloud, "Help, God. Help me please. What can I do for this sweet, troubled child?"

The rocking didn't seem to comfort Charlotte, so Emma began kissing her forehead and smoothing away the tears on her small cheeks. How she wanted to murmur comforting words. Then she realized she could sign them. She began signing, "Don't worry. You are safe." She wished she was more accomplished in sign but she did her best.

Then she began to worry about those in town searching for Charlotte, who was here and safe. How could she let them know? She rocked and signed and soothed the child. Then she recalled—the school bell.

She got up, carrying Charlotte, and managed to hurry through the nearly dark schoolroom to the rear. She set Charlotte down and grabbed the rope and pulled. Charlotte actually wailed, the sound tearing at Emma's nerves. But she rang the bell three times, then picked Charlotte up and returned to her room, pushing the outside door open with her foot.

Not much time lapsed and she heard voices, lots of voices, coming nearer. "Emma!" Judith called. "Are you all right?"

"Charlotte's here!" Emma shouted in return.

Soon her sister and Mason and many others crowded into her small quarters. She stayed in the rocker while her sister lit more candles and Mason stirred up the fire. She heard the Ashfords outside explaining that the search could end. The child was safe and people began leaving for home. November dusk had about drawn to night and the moon was only a quarter moon. They needed to get home while there was still enough light.

Finally only Mason, Judith's family, Birdie, Dan, Eb and the Ashfords remained. Charlotte finally sat up and looked around.

Birdie signed, "Why did you come here?"

Emma translated the question for the others.

Charlotte's reply came with emphatic fingers. "Want my mama!"

What she wanted she could not get. Emma felt like weeping for the child.

Birdie translated Charlotte's words and signed back, "But your mama is dead."

Charlotte's fingers slashed through air again. "Want Miss Emma for my mama!"

Emma's mouth dropped open. She couldn't think what to say or do.

But Birdie dutifully announced to all what Charlotte had signed.

Silence dropped over them all like a window slamming shut.

Mason could not think of anything to say to this. He stood dumbfounded, facing Emma with Charlotte on her lap in the rocker. No one moved. No one said a word. The silence overwhelmed the room.

"Well, I think Ned and I will head home," Mrs. Ashford said.

Mason's head snapped around. The woman was leaving?

"That's probably a good idea," Judith agreed. "Birdie, you come along home with us. We need to let your pa handle this." Their family turned toward the door.

Dan followed them out and Eb was the last to leave. "See you tomorrow, Mr. Mason." And he shut the door behind himself, leaving Mason alone with Emma and his sister.

The sudden departure of all the others created a vacuum, an emptiness, in the lantern- and fire-lit room. Shadows from the flames in the hearth danced and flickered on the walls, on Emma's lovely face. Now that Charlotte had delivered her demand, she relaxed against Emma and yawned.

"Mr. Chandler, won't you pull up a chair?" Emma invited.

Mason suddenly felt exhausted, as if he'd laid stone all day and then harvested a field of hay. He drew one of her straight-back chairs from the table nearer her. Her golden hair glimmered in the low light. For many minutes they sat just looking at each other.

"How are we going to handle this?" she asked finally.

He opened his hands. He had no clue. "Do you think the Ashfords will spread this?"

"No, I don't. Mrs. Ashford likes to talk but she doesn't gossip. She will probably corner me and want to discuss why we haven't…"

"Our plans to marry were disrupted and I released you from our agreement," he said, his voice catching on "released."

She nodded. "And I have begun teaching. I love it." She'd said something similar before but this time her voice came out softer.

He settled back into his chair. After inhaling deeply and slowly, he said, "So the real problem is that Charlotte has become attached to you and wants you as her ma."

"Yes."

"So what do we do?" he asked, letting himself watch the play of the light on her pale face.

"If she had not gone through the shock of losing her mother, I would know the answer to that. But this is not about facts. This is about emotions, isn't it? About sorrow?"

"I know I'm not the best at trying to care for Charlotte," he admitted. A log broke on the fire, a subtle sound.

"But it's obvious that you love her very much. And you provide all you can for her—not just in food and warmth but in caring."

Emma's words were balm. "She's mine, my blood." His voice came out rough, low.

"And she loves you. I know she does."

He shrugged, embarrassed.

"Children want a mother and a father. That's just natural."

He repeated, "So what do we do?"

"Well, you and I aren't marrying just to care for your sister. I know that's why some couples get together. But we aren't forced to by circumstances."

Yes, some couples did marry for the sake of children. But how could he marry Emma unless he was completely honest with her? And why would any woman marry him after she knew the truth?

"For a man, I think you're doing well caring for two little girls. I find that very admirable," she said with a lift of her chin.

"Thanks," he said wryly. "Your sister helps a lot."

"Judith is the kindest person."

Silence dropped over them again, this time like a warm shawl. Finally he rose. "I need to take Charlotte home."

"Yes, I don't think giving in to her would be best. But let's tell her that I will visit soon. Do you think that would help?"

He shrugged again. "It can't hurt."

In the end, Charlotte made it easy for him. She had fallen into that deep sleep of exhausted childhood. Not even a trumpet blast would have roused her, so he hoisted her limp body over one shoulder and headed for home.

He was aware that Emma stood outside her door and watched him till he walked out of sight. He thought over what Emma had said and how she had said it. In some way he had detected a change in her. She had sounded less adamant about her single state. Was there a chance they might get together? Or was that just his wishful thinking? And did it change anything about him and his secrets, secrets he could never reveal?

Chapter Eleven

Wednesday after school, Emma walked toward the Ashfords' in the crisp November air. Dried leaves swirled around her ankles. She'd promised to help Mrs. Ashford prepare supper and would stay as she did most nights to eat it in the cozy upstairs rooms over the store. It was a blessing to have somewhere to go, not sit alone with her churning thoughts.

Not even by today had Emma completely calmed down over Charlotte's demand on Sunday night. *"I want Miss Emma for my mama"* played over and over in her mind, chilling her like the puffs of cold wind that ruffled her hem. And then followed Mason's devastated expression at those words.

And on top of that, a new troubling idea gnawed at her. She sighed and saw her breath white in front of her.

What had happened to Mason while he'd been away those six months earlier this year? She'd sensed for a time that he carried more than just the grief over losing his father and finding a wounded sister. When

Eb had arrived, he had provided more hints about a troubled family.

Emma sighed again. *It's none of my business.* Easy to think, hard to dismiss. She decided to enter the Ashfords' through the front store entrance, hoping to see her father there. That would cheer her up. She walked up the two steps and into the warm store, fragrant with spices. Mr. Ashford was not in sight.

Mrs. Stanley and another woman, relatively new in town, were at the rear, looking over fabric, their heads together, their back to Emma. When the bell over the door rang, they didn't look around.

"Did you hear what they're saying that little deaf girl said?" Mrs. Stanley asked.

"I didn't know she could talk." The other woman lifted the edge of a bolt of navy-blue fabric as if trying to decide.

"That little black girl told it out loud—anyway, she said she wanted the schoolteacher for her ma—"

Emma halted in midstep.

Mr. Ashford came in from the rear entrance. "Miss Jones! Hello!" he called out.

Emma smiled, her lips stiff, and greeted him, avoiding the gossiping women. She had hoped no one outside had overheard Birdie, but someone must have stayed behind, perhaps out of curiosity.

Trying to behave as if she hadn't overheard the women, she went directly to the stove in the center, leaned over and kissed her father's cheek. He and two other men near his age lounged around the stove on the short benches there. A coffeepot sat on top of the stove and the cracker barrel within reach.

"Emma girl," Dan greeted her, rising, his glance

straying toward the women. The other two men rose slightly in deference to her.

"Hello, gentlemen. Please be seated. Have you solved the world's problems yet?" She gestured toward the open newspaper on Dan's lap. The men merely chuckled in reply. She sat down beside her father and let the warmth of the stove soothe her. She couldn't control what people chose to gossip about or the fact that they chose to gossip. But she wondered how Mrs. Stanley would like it if others discussed her business here.

"We're starting a friendly competition," Dan said as if trying to fill up the strained silence that had overtaken the room. He pointed to a chalkboard set on the counter at the far end of the room.

"Competition?" She unbuttoned her coat now that the stove was warming her.

"Yes, we're letting people post their guesses of what day the river will freeze over this year," Dan said.

"And what do they win if they're right?" she asked with a forced grin.

"Bragging rights, a-course," one of the other men said and chortled, slapping his knee.

"So, Emma, what do you think of our handiwork?" Dan motioned toward the chalkboard. "Ashford pulled this out of the back for us and we've marked off a grid of the days from today through December to mid-January."

Emma rose and walked over to the chalkboard propped at the end of the counter. The men had obviously used a yardstick and taken great care in designing the grid. "Well done. You all get an A."

The men chuckled merrily at this.

Wearing his white store apron, Mr. Ashford came over. "I think it's the kind of thing that people will get a kick out of. We might as well be cheerful about winter. It's coming whether we like it or not."

This friendly man's banter soothed her sorely ruffled feathers. "Indeed. I might do the same for the children at school and use it for a few science lessons about water in its various states."

Mrs. Stanley and the other woman motioned for Mr. Ashford.

He walked to them and rang up their purchases on his new brass register.

As the two women reached the door, unable to resist, Emma called out, "Mrs. Stanley?"

The woman halted and turned, her cheeks a bit pink. "Yes?"

"Dorcas is doing really well with her spelling again this year."

"Oh, oh, thank you!" Then both woman hurried outside.

Emma walked back to her father. "As much as I'd like to stay and chat, I've promised Mrs. Ashford that I would come up and help with supper. I'll see you upstairs, Dad?"

"Yes, we're going to play another game of cribbage and then I'll come up with Ned when he closes for the day."

Emma waved to the men and headed for the back door to go upstairs. She probably shouldn't have given in to temptation and stopped Mrs. Stanley on her way out, but she couldn't resist giving the woman a moment of guilty panic. Still, none of this helped. Emma's stomach and mind could not settle down. She'd given Mason the logical response to Charlotte's demand. They couldn't marry just to please the child, could they? And except for asking her to dance, Mason never made the slightest effort to attract her. No. He held her arm's length.

Emma had no answers. She walked up the stairs and went inside. "I'm here!"

In her ruffled blue-and-white-plaid apron, Mrs. Ashford greeted her. "Tell me about school."

As she donned an apron to help, Emma thought over the past year. She was the one who'd replied to Mason's ad and she was the one who'd persuaded Judith to accept the letters of proposal. But at that time at home, they'd been at their wit's end and in such misery.

Now her sister Judith was happily married to Asa and in the coming year would give birth to the new little Brant. *And I'm happy teaching. I love the children and all the activity and the way I get to use my brain.*

But what about your heart? whispered through her mind. She forced herself to begin chatting to Mrs. Ashford. *But what about your heart?*

On the cold Saturday afternoon, under a slate sky, Mason and Eb worked side by side to fell an oak on Eb's claim. The former homesteaders had left some firewood, but Eb would need much more before the end of the winter. Aged wood burned cleaner and easier, so they were really months behind time already. Mason had left the girls with Judith. *I'll have to think of some way to thank Asa's wife.*

"That Mrs. Brant is sure a true Christian," Eb said, as if he'd read Mason's mind.

"Yes. Asa's a fortunate man." Mason swung his ax and felt the sharp blade sink into the hard wood and the resistance shiver up his arms.

Eb swung again. "What you gon' to do about Charlotte wanting Miss Emma for a mama?"

Mason glared at Eb. "Miss Emma does not want or need me."

"I don't know 'bout that. Mostly womenfolk would be better off without us but they put up with us anyway." Eb grinned in that old mischievous way he had.

"No doubt," Mason agreed drily.

The two of them continued taking turns till they backed away and watched the mature oak crack, fall, bounce and settle. They both attacked the smaller branches with hatchets, preparing for the next step, turning the tree into logs.

In the midst of this chore, Eb looked over at Mason.

At Eb's teasing expression, Mason paused. "What?"

Eb chuckled. "I think I make you wait. I know how you like surprises."

"I hate surprises."

Eb laughed louder and deeper. "I know. And I got a big one comin'."

Mason didn't even try to think what Eb's surprise might be. He just hoped that it wouldn't be anything that would call any more attention to them.

The weekend came and Emma sat at Judith's table along with Mrs. Waggoner, Mrs. Ashford and Judith.

All had knitting in hand. They were finishing up their gifts of knitted scarves, hats and mittens for the northern tribe. Song leader Lavina's son was due to arrive at any time from Lac du Flambeau, and he would carry their handiwork back with him to the mission. A large pot of soup simmered on a hook over the fire, the lid shuddering once in a while, letting off steam. And the kittens lay in front of the fire like rugs.

Today after another brief knitting lesson, the three little girls had been released and were outside playing tag. A relief because Emma had almost cried off from coming. Perhaps it would be better if she tried to limit her interaction with Charlotte to school. At least Mason wasn't here. Mrs. Ashford had been hinting around, wanting to know more about Mason and Emma. But there was no "Mason and Emma."

Now Colton and Asa had paused by the door to dress warmly. "We'll be home before dark, Judith," Asa said, wrapping a scarf around his neck. Today Asa was taking the boy out to learn about tracking animals. A light dusting of snow had coated the ground overnight, making it a perfect day for the lesson.

"Very well." Judith walked over and rested a hand on Colton's shoulder. "I know you'll do well."

"Yes, ma'am." Colton was nearly dancing with anticipation.

Judith brushed the hair back from his forehead. "You both need haircuts again."

"Hair grows." Asa grinned. "Come on, boy." And the two left, cold air rushing in behind them.

Again a whisper of envy over her sister's full, settled life plagued Emma.

Judith had just sat down and picked up her knitting when Mrs. Waggoner asked, "Have you and Mr. Brant thought of legally adopting Lily and Colton?"

Emma paused in the middle of a stitch. The woman's question returned her mind to Charlotte's demand. *"I want Miss Emma for my mama."*

Judith glanced up. "Asa and I have thought about it, but is it necessary? I mean, everyone knows that they are ours now."

"You're probably right. I was just thinking that making it official might help the children feel more secure," Mrs. Waggoner said. "I'm glad they found such a good home. It's a comfort to me."

"I'll discuss it with Asa," Judith promised.

"Everyone has been asking me about what little Charlotte said Sunday night," Mrs. Ashford said, suddenly bringing up the topic Emma dreaded. "Of course, I have done my best to…minimize the talk. But do you think the poor thing will have another spell?"

"The poor thing." Hearing Charlotte called this caused Emma to tense. She understood, however, that Mrs. Ashford meant it in the kindest way. And Emma shared her concern. She consciously released her tense neck muscles. Would these spells continue, worsen, fade away? A solid brick of worry settled into Emma's stomach. She drew in a deep breath. "Mason is doing the best that he can. And I'm doing my best at school—"

"But why don't you two make any move to court?" the storekeeper's wife asked, checking the stitch count on her needle. "Mason Chandler is a fine man. You are a sweet, loving woman. And those girls need a mother—"

Interrupting, Judith came to Emma's rescue. "Sometimes matters aren't as easy as they appear."

An understatement. Emma forced her fingers to begin moving again. How could she stop people from thinking she and Mason would marry? Of course, that was a silly question. She had no control over what people thought. She realized her own rampant thoughts had defied her control.

"Well, sometimes people make things harder than they should," Mrs. Ashford commented, not looking up from her handwork.

This forced Emma to speak. "Mason has made no overtures toward me," she murmured.

At this, Mrs. Ashford looked up and her mouth formed a perfect O.

Blessedly the little girls burst inside, a welcome distraction. "Mrs. Brant!" Lily said. "We got cold."

Judith chuckled. "Hang up your things and stand near the fire. Maybe you girls would like some tea and cookies?"

"Yes! Please!" Birdie replied with a bounce.

Judith paused to serve tea, and the ladies and little ones sat in the glow of the warm fire, listening to the wind outside. Now that December loomed so near, the afternoon shadows began early. Soon Mrs. Waggoner and Mrs. Ashford bundled up and left for home. Emma stayed behind, hoping for a few minutes alone with her sister. The girls settled on the floor by the fire, playing jacks again.

"I wonder why Asa isn't back yet?" Judith whispered to Emma as they stood by the window, their arms around each other's waists. The early November twilight draped over the sky. Knowing it would be dark when she left after supper, Emma had brought along her lantern for her walk home.

"Well, they weren't hunting, so there couldn't have been an accident," Emma replied softly, hoping that was true. "They probably just went farther afield than they expected to. Maybe following tracks."

"The bear haven't gone into hibernation yet and are foraging in daylight," Judith whispered back.

Emma tried to come up with a way to comfort Judith. She leaned her head against Judith's. "Father God," she murmured into her sister's ear, "you know where Asa and Colton are. Please bring them home safely. Our trust is in you and you alone."

"Amen," Judith whispered.

Charlotte appeared beside Emma and tugged at her skirt.

"She always senses moods," Emma whispered to Judith. She turned around, lifted Charlotte high and smiled at the girl. Then she swung the girl to her right side and then her left, once around in a circle, and set her down. She stooped and tapped Charlotte's nose. "Are you winning?" she signed and motioned toward the girls, who paused in their game of jacks.

Charlotte looked uncertain in the face of Emma's mood change.

"Charlotte is winning," Birdie announced in word and sign.

"Well, good," Emma replied in the same. "Let me see!" She led Charlotte back to the game, drew a chair over and sat beside her.

Behind her Judith left the window and began stirring up a new batch of biscuits on the counter. Within a few minutes a knock came at the door.

"Come in!" Judith called.

Mason stepped in, shut the door behind him and hurried toward the fire.

Charlotte leaped up and ran to him, followed by Birdie. The girls hugged him, one on either side of his waist.

Emma's heart lightened at the sight of their love for their father-brother.

Judith turned from where she'd been rolling out biscuit dough. "Did you see Asa and Colton?"

Mason looked to Judith, holding his hands over the fire.

Emma noted that he avoided looking at her, and that pinched.

"Aren't they back yet from tracking?" he asked.

"No." Judith looked to the window. The sun was nearly down.

Mason followed her gaze. "They may have gone farther afield than they intended. I mean, if they found good tracks."

The three adults fell silent and so did the children.

"I could track them," Mason said finally, pulling his gloves back on.

"Judith," Emma said, rising, "give Mr. Chandler a hot cup of coffee. He's chilled. I'm going to get dressed and go with him."

"That's not necessary—"

"Yes, it is." Emma went to the pegs by the door and began putting on her layers of outerwear. Perhaps they could finally discuss Charlotte.

Mason tried to object once more.

Irritated with his trying to push her aside, Emma silenced him with a stiff and heated look.

Soon they were outside in the dim, cold light.

"You don't have to come," he began again.

"What if you find them in a bad situation?" Emma asked in a low tone, setting a quick pace out of the yard. "You can send me for help." The more he wanted to be rid of her, the more she was determined to stick with him. She tried to ignore the pull to be near him. She quickened her pace.

"I don't think—"

"We don't know what has happened, if anything," she said sharply, as if scolding a student. "Now, where did they head into the woods?"

He sent her a look that showed he was as surprised by her brusqueness as she was. "Here." He pointed to the tracks entering the tree line.

Soon they were walking near each other, threading their way through the thick forest, making the dry leaves crunch beneath their feet. As they navigated around the trees, she tried not to accidentally bump against him. But something inside her hummed because he was near.

"Just because they left this way doesn't mean they're coming back this way," Mason grumbled.

Ducking her head against the sharp wind, Emma considered this. "True. But we need to start somewhere." Then she lifted her chin and called, "Asa! Colton!" She repeated this every few feet. This went on for nearly a mile. Finally the words she didn't want to say but must say popped out, "What are we going to do about what Charlotte said? It got out. People are talking."

* * *

Mason jerked as if she'd struck him. Why had she come out and spoken aloud what he didn't want to think about yet had been thinking of constantly? He'd tried to banish the question from his mind. It wouldn't budge.

"Well?" she prompted after several moments when the only sounds were their footfalls on leaves and twigs and the wind rattling the dried oak leaves clinging to branches above them.

"I don't know what you want me to say." Mason looked everywhere but at her.

A pause. "Asa! Colton!" she called and then said, "I don't know what I want you to say. What you could say. We can't ignore this."

He threw his hands skyward. "I do my best with Charlotte, but…"

Halting, she touched his shoulder. "I know. I know. I do my best, too."

The two of them gazed at each other. Mason felt shaken and couldn't look away from her large eyes glistening in the sparse light.

Mason's reluctance to talk about Charlotte's demand gave way like sand to a wave. "But it's not—"

"Hey!" Asa's voice penetrated the forest. "What are you two doing out taking a stroll in this weather?"

Ahead and to the right, Asa and Colton appeared in the dim light. "Got a lantern?" Asa asked.

"Yes." Mason lifted the one he carried.

"Well, light it, then. It's almost night," Asa ordered. "We were tracking and then decided not to come home empty-handed." He hefted the tom turkey high. "Judith will be happy even if it's a bit too early to save for Thanksgiving."

Mason lit the lantern, and the four of them turned around and headed back to the Brants' cabin, Mason's mind a muddle of thoughts and feelings. He felt like an animal caught in a trap with no way out. He knew he had feelings for Emma. He knew Charlotte and Birdie would be blessed to have her for a mother.

Nonetheless, he couldn't court her without telling her the truth, and if he told her the truth about his father, that would be the end of hope. And still, the fear that his bad blood would come out in the end left him reeling. *I'm not worthy of her. God, I don't know what to do. Help me, us.*

On a cold, clear Wednesday morning, Mason walked into town to the jail. After school yesterday, Colton had brought him the message that Sheriff Merriday wanted to see him. Though Mason knew he had done nothing wrong, he wondered exactly what Merriday wanted. He met the sheriff on the porch in front of the jail.

"Mornin', Chandler." The sheriff nodded to him as he continued to pound nails into a poster on a board on the outside wall of the jail. One of three Wanted posters.

Mason recalled in the past seeing his own father's face and name sought on the charge of bank robbing on such posters in Missouri. Wanted Dead or Alive was nothing a son ever wanted to see about a father. His stomach did a sharp dip and roll. He swallowed down his reaction. "What can I do for you, Sheriff?"

"Well, two things—one for you to tell Asa—save me a trip—and one I want to talk about with you."

Mason nodded once, still tense.

"I finally heard back from the sheriff in Illinois."

Mason had to think what this was about.

"He wrote me that Mrs. Waggoner lived there all her life except for a few years in Chicago. And he gave her a good character reference. She's respected and people were sad to see her go."

"Well, that makes sense from what I've seen of her." Two dogs trotted down the street, frisking and yipping happily to each other. He suddenly wondered if a pup might be good for the girls.

"Yeah, the sheriff said, though, that she's buried all her family back there. Probably why she came north. Lily and Colton are about her only family left—except for their daddy's brother, who went West some time ago."

Mason watched his breath turn white as he said, "I'll tell Asa this quietly—on the side, away from the kids. Let him and Judith handle it."

"Good. Now, what I want from you." Merriday pounded in the last nail on the final poster. "I need to leave someone in charge here when I head off on patrol tomorrow. Be gone 'bout a week. I know you got your girls to care for, but when they're in school, could you stop in and open the jail for those hours? I like to have someone people here can go to if they have a problem."

Mason said the first words that came to mind. "Why me?"

The sheriff chuckled. "That's what I said when the state congressman approached me to run for county sheriff."

A boat was churning its way to the dock. Turning

to watch, Mason used the distraction to try to come up with a response. Him? Sitting in for the sheriff? If Merriday only knew who his father was…

The boat docked and the sheriff, along with everyone else on Main Street, paused to see who got off. Fewer boats were coming now. People were settling in for the winter. Ashford bustled out of his store, headed for the boat. No doubt he was expecting another delivery of winter supplies. Asa and Mason had fixed the storage room so that no critter could get in and start eating his inventory of staples.

One passenger got off and loped up the pier. Then he stopped and scanned the street.

Beside him, Mason sensed the sheriff's interest increase. Mason knew immediately why. Here in Wisconsin, men didn't go around armed, and most owned only rifles for hunting. But this stranger had a six-gun strapped to his leg. Mason had seen this practice, one common in parts of Missouri, and then turbulent eastern Kansas but not here.

The stranger began striding up the street toward them.

The sheriff moved down the porch onto the street and met the stranger. "Hello. I'm Sheriff Merriday. Welcome to Pepin. What brings ya'll to our fair town?"

The stranger stared at the sheriff and then glanced up at Mason.

Mason returned the attention. He didn't know this man.

But the stranger gazed at him a few moments longer than Mason would have expected. Why?

"Just passing through," the man said. Seagulls circling over the river squawked.

The sheriff studied him. "It's getting near winter. The Mississippi's about to freeze."

"Is it?" The man's tone edged just south of sarcastic.

"Yep. So if ya'll got business, better take care of it sooner than later or you'll be spending the winter here."

"Don't worry. I won't be staying long." The man touched his hat brim, but in a mocking way, and then headed toward the saloon.

The sheriff stayed in the middle of the street, watching the man walk away. Finally he rejoined Mason on the jail porch. "Now I definitely want you to be at the jail every day while I'm away. Mark my words—that man's trouble."

"What could he want here?" Mason asked the obvious question.

"Nothing good, nothing honest." The sheriff waved Mason toward the door. "Let's go in and I'll deputize you."

Mason hesitated.

"The county pays an active deputy two dollars a day." Merriday stared at him.

At this inducement, Mason conceded and went toward the door, though the idea of Jedediah Chandler's son being a deputy was some kind of joke, one Mason hoped no one here would ever know.

He glanced up the street once more and found the stranger gazing back at him from outside the door of the saloon. Why? Did a guilty conscience prompt the stranger to look at the sheriff? Why had a man with a six-gun come to this little town? No bank to rob here. Mason stepped inside to become a deputy. He could only hope that while the sheriff was away, no trouble would arise.

Chapter Twelve

Though his girls wanted him to walk them all the way to school, Mason stopped at the jail, where he'd serve his first day as deputy sheriff. Under a sky layered with gray clouds, he sent them on their way with Lily and Colton. He did not need to see Emma today. He was feeling too lonely as it was.

New to town, the two young dogs, some mixed breed of terrier with coats of patches of warm brown and white and floppy and velvety-looking ears, were rolling in the dirt on Main Street, play-fighting. Mason watched the girls skirt way around them, though Birdie kept glancing over her shoulder at the two. Whom did the dogs belong to? Too many people here wanted dogs for them to be strays.

Looking in the direction of the school, he found his errant mind bringing up Emma's face. He forced the image away.

As he unlocked the jail door, he turned to look in the opposite direction, toward the far end of the street, where the saloon sat. He wondered where the stranger had found a bed last night. He did not look like a man with friends here. And there was no hotel in town. No boardinghouse, either.

Mason shoved this aside and entered the jail. The stranger could take care of himself. Mason was here to earn two dollars a day and help out the sheriff and town.

The next few minutes were spent firing up the stove and trying to keep warm doing it. Images of Emma tried to filter into his mind and he began reciting a poem he'd had to memorize in school long ago, something about wandering lonely as a cloud. But Emma's lips, her golden hair, insisted on pushing in between the stanzas about daffodils and stars.

When he went outside to gather another armload of wood, he noted the barkeep out back of the saloon, doing the same. He waved to the man—just being friendly.

Then the bowlegged and nearly bald man did something unexpected. He hurried down the long alley behind the high-side stores to Mason. When he reached the jail, he motioned Mason to go around and inside.

Inside, the stove was barely warming the air near it, but Mason could still see his breath. They both bellied up to the stove, holding up their hands in hope of warmth. The idea of Emma standing at the front of her classroom intruded in Mason's mind. Shivering, he looked to the man. "You're Sam, right?"

"Yeah." Sam paused to catch his breath. "You're Chandler. You have those two little girls and you were supposed to have married Asa Brant's sister-in-law."

Well, word certainly got around—all the way to the saloon, which Mason had not entered for months. He'd occasionally longed for the minutes of jovial companionship he could find there, but with his girls, he was never free to go. "That's me."

"You taking over for the sheriff?"

"Just deputized recently." Mason folded open his jacket collar and showed the star on his shirt. "Merriday is away on patrol this week."

Sam clapped his rough and chapped hands together to warm them and edged closer to the stove. "He see that new man come to town yesterday?"

"The one with the six-gun?" Mason nodded in reply.

"Yeah. Calls himself Smith," the man's tone was disbelieving. "Anyway he come in to my place yesterday… and stayed."

Mason lifted an eyebrow in silent question.

"He didn't threaten or nothing, but when I was closing up, he said he'd just make himself comfortable in the back room on his bedroll."

Mason studied Sam's face. "I see." He did. Potbellied and short of breath, Sam must be in his late sixties at least, and he wasn't going to argue with a man half his age with a gun strapped to his thigh.

"I took the evening's income into my room, which is also in the back, and slept with it under my mattress and my sidearm under my pillow." Sam's forehead furrowed. "He gives off a feelin'… I don't know."

Mason drew in a deep breath. "I understand." He did.

"Anyway, I'd like it if you and the sheriff would keep an eye out and drop in once in a while. I got a bad feelin'. And…" Sam reached into his jacket and pulled out a worn leather pouch with a buckled flap. "We don't have a bank in this little town and I don't want all my ready cash on the premises. So…" Silence reigned as Sam stared at him.

"We have a secret spot for valuables," Mason admitted. "I can't show you—"

Sam held up a hand. "Fine with me." Then he handed Mason the pouch.

"I'll give you a receipt—"

Same hand went up again. "Not necessary—"

"Yes, it is. What if something happened to me—"

"God forbid," Sam said, quoting a verse in Romans.

Mason walked over to the desk, pulled out a pad of paper, scribbled a note and signed and dated it. "Here's your receipt. When you want your funds back, just bring it in."

"Thanks." Sam shoved the receipt into an inner pocket.

"Glad to help."

Sam hurried out and back down the alley.

Mason followed him to gather one more armload of firewood. An eagle swooped over Mason, toward the river. The conversation with the barkeep had driven Emma out of his mind, but now the image of her holding Charlotte flitted back. He forced himself to concentrate on the rough split logs he was loading into his arms.

Emma stood at the front of her classroom, trying to keep her mind on school, not Mason Chandler. An enlarged paper calendar of December and January, tacked onto a board which her older students had spent yesterday making, had been posted onto the wall near the front. The tallest boy, Johann

Lang, stood with a pencil, inscribing each student's name on the day they guessed as when the Mississippi River would freeze over. Though she tried not to, she couldn't stop her thoughts from bringing up Mason.

"Dorcas," Johann asked, "what is your guess?"

"Christmas!" the girl piped up from her bench in the middle.

Emma tried to keep her mind on the present and failed. What about Mason had embedded him in her heart and mind so completely that she couldn't go many hours without thinking of him? Yes, he was good-looking and of very good character. But she'd known many men who were both good-looking and good. Jonathan, for instance. That thought brought her up short. How long had it been since she had recalled her late fiancé?

Johann continued going from student to student and writing down the names on the dates given.

Emma stood, appearing to follow this process, but actually her thoughts carried her back into the past. All through the war Jonathan had been daily on her mind and sometimes, when a battle raged, hourly. After he'd died, memories of him, their childhood together and their sweet courtship had entered her thoughts often. In the worst days of her sister-in-law's vindictive campaign to be rid of her and Judith, the longing for what might have been had often overwhelmed her.

"Miss Jones, what day do you guess?" Jacque, the sheriff's son, asked.

With a start she came back to the present and saw that all her students were staring at her. Gathering her wits, she glanced at the calendar. Evidently all the students had guessed already. She surveyed the remaining dates. "I will choose December 7."

The boy wrote Miss Jones in the square and then turned to her.

"Thank you, Johann. Please be seated. We need to start on our reading today." *And I need to keep my mind here.*

Near the end of the afternoon, Mason tried not to think of all he could have accomplished today at his place. This job had been a godsend. Hard money was difficult to come by, and sitting in this office and walking through town a few times might be boring, but it was paid boredom.

Then he heard a yelp of pain. The sound galvanized him in a way he couldn't have predicted. Grabbing his jacket off the peg, he burst out the door and headed toward the sound. He saw the stranger kick at one of the new dogs in town. An obviously injured pup already lay on the ground. Had the stranger landed one kick already? The uninjured dog growled menacingly, baring its teeth. The stranger reached for his gun.

"Don't!" Mason called out as he ran toward the man. "Put that away!" He heard rapid footsteps behind him.

The stranger, who called himself "Smith," did not put the gun away, but he stilled.

Mason halted in front of the stranger. Unwilling to have a gunfight on Main Street, he did let his hand slip down near his sidearm, a warning. "What's going on here?"

"Yes!" Emma's voice seconded his. "I saw you!

What do you mean by kicking a dog like that? He wasn't menacing you!"

Mason's heart sank. He did not want Emma involved with anything around this man. And with one gun already drawn. Another woman stepped out onto her porch, clutching a shawl around her shoulders, and frowning. Mason's hand slid closer to his gun.

"Just getting rid of a couple of curs." Smith looked past Mason toward Emma.

She barreled up to Mason's side. "God's creatures deserve our protection, not abuse."

Smith stared at Emma appraisingly and then twitched the brim of his battered hat in a mockery of politeness. The woman on the porch went back inside.

Emma's fearless defense did not surprise Mason, but he took a step forward, putting himself between her and the man. "We only shoot rabid dogs here. And how do you know these two don't belong to someone?" Mason propped his hands at his waist, aware that not only Emma but also his girls had reached him. His concern for them spiked.

Smith glared. "What business is this of yours?"

"I'm the deputy—"

Emma at his side was busy holding back Birdie and Charlotte, who were straining to go to help the pup.

"He hurt that doggie," Birdie said. "We saw him."

Mason forged on, "I'm charged with protecting the people who live here and their possessions, including dogs."

"You're the deputy?" Smith burst into raucous and insulting laughter. He turned away, laughing, mocking Mason.

The sound chilled Mason but he couldn't figure out why.

The pup at his feet whimpered.

First Emma instructed the girls to stand back, and then Mason knelt beside the dog on the ground and held out a hand for him to sniff. The other pup approached cautiously. "Who do you two fellas belong to?" he asked.

"He hurt the doggie," Birdie repeated.

The wounded pup struggled to get on his feet and Mason gently helped him up. The pup moaned, and the sound pierced Mason like a needle to the quick. Mason pet both furry heads. Emma's presence beside him unsettled him, his heartbeat speeding up even more than from just running.

Emma murmured to the hurt pup and then pet the other one, too. "It's good that he is able to stand, but he might have a...bruised rib."

Mason thought she had substituted "bruised" for "broken" for Birdie's sake. "Come on." He motioned them all toward the jail. He hoped Emma would excuse herself and leave, and at the same time he intensely wanted her to stay with them. The wind nearly took off his hat. "Let's all go in where it's warm."

The wounded pup walked slowly by Mason, and his obvious sibling stayed close by his side. Birdie was talking to them, reassuring them, "You be all right. We take care of you. Pa won't let that bad man hurt you again."

These words streamed through Mason's mind, but mostly he was aware of how glad he was to have Emma near. He felt alive for the first time that day. Yet he should not be so glad to have her here. They trooped into the jail. Mason helped Emma shed her winter coat, intensely aware of each breath she took. He then hung everyone's coats on the high pegs. Soon the girls sat on the floor by the pups, petting the hurt one and playing with the well one.

Emma sat down in the chair at the side of the sheriff's desk. "Who is that man?" she murmured without preamble.

He leaned forward so only she could hear him. "I don't know who he is. He arrived yesterday and spent the night at the saloon."

"He doesn't look like a homesteader."

Mason grimaced. "You're right. He doesn't."

She stared at him. He stared back, then shrugged. The wind rattled the west window.

"I'm glad you're on duty here."

Mason had not enjoyed the boring part of his day. But meeting the stranger again and protecting the pup had ratcheted up his tension. Merriday would be gone for a week, so Mason was the one who'd have to keep the peace, and he reckoned a law-abiding man would not have kicked a pup on Main Street.

"I'd already observed the pups hanging around town, and today I asked the children at school about them," Emma said, interrupting him as he brooded on Smith. "No one claimed the pups." She looked at him as if expecting something.

"Good!" Birdie chirped from near the stove. "Then we can take them home."

Mason tried to object but couldn't muster the words. He'd loved his childhood pet, Lawrence, an old hound. Why he'd named him Lawrence, he didn't recall, but he'd loved that dog. "I still need to find out if someone brought them to town, Birdie. It's not right to take someone's dog." He rested a hand on the desk. He felt himself reaching for Emma, but kept his hand where it lay.

"That's stealin'," Birdie said, looking stern. "We don't steal. That gets you put in jail and God said, 'Do not steal.'"

"Exactly," Emma agreed. "But I don't think anybody will object to the new deputy taking care of them while he tries to find out if they do belong to someone."

Signing all this, Birdie nodded vigorously, and Charlotte sent Mason one of her rare smiles. And then Emma laid a hand over his.

His heart thumped so hard he felt it in his throat. Her soft hand captured his full attention. He imagined drawing it to his lips and kissing it.

"Well," Emma said, withdrawing her hand abruptly, "I best be getting on. I promised to help Mr. Ashford in the store this afternoon. He's busy storing away more winter supplies." She rose.

Mason jumped to his feet and hurried to help her on with her coat—anything to be near her. An image of the girls, the pups and Emma in his cabin with him, all sitting together by the fire, warmed him. And then left him cold. Why did he keep torturing himself? And then he recalled the stranger's mocking laugh and casual cruelty. *I better keep my mind on my job.* Nothing bad was going to happen while he was on duty.

Birdie and Charlotte put on their coats and hats to go home, too. He stepped outside into the cold. Colton and Lily, who had stopped to visit Dan at the forge, had come to the jail so they could all walk home together. The girls would play with them till he walked home later. He watched the four children till they disappeared around the bend, out of town. But he still worried. Why had a dangerous man come to their quiet little river town? There was nothing here for a man like him.

"I don't want to put myself forward," Eb said, standing in Ashford's store to the far side of the stove. A few hours later, at the end of the workday, Mason had stopped in to warn the storekeeper about the stranger. After a lonely day at the jail, the homey setting here helped him breathe easy again.

The pups waiting in the jail had lessened his loneliness some, but he wanted human companionship. He wondered if Emma was upstairs with Mrs. Ashford and if she might come down. He glanced at the rear entrance and scolded himself.

Dan, with vociferous encouragement from his cohorts, drew Eb over to the chalkboard chart with the dates. "We're asking, so how could that be putting yourself forward?"

Eb glanced around as if assessing public opinion.

"Sure," Ashford from behind the counter urged, "take a guess. What have you got to lose?"

The others sitting by the stove echoed this sentiment with enthusiasm.

Eb folded one arm over his chest, rested his other elbow on it and then propped his chin on his hand. He studied the remaining blank dates. "Hmm."

While everyone was distracted, Mason leaned against the counter and nodded for Ashford to come near.

Ashford bustled over. "What can I do for you?" he asked quietly, as if sensing Mason's mood.

"You seen the stranger that came to town yesterday?" Mason asked in a low voice.

"No." The doorbell jangled as another customer, a woman with a shopping basket over her arm, entered. Cold air rushed in. After exchanging nods with Ashford, she went toward the display of notions.

Mason frowned at Ashford. "The stranger struck the sheriff and me as troublesome. He's wearing a six-gun."

Ashford's eyes widened.

"I don't want to start rumors or anything, but I think it would be wise for the storekeepers to keep very little cash in their tills during the day and none at night."

Ashford's eyebrows rose, nearly touching his graying hairline. They lowered and he said, "Does that make sense, though? We had some thieves come a few years back, but they had a small boat they were going to use to get away."

"I know. I mean, he can't ride away very well without a horse. I can't figure out what he's here for…" Mason shrugged.

"I'll pass the word anyway. Best to be alert for anything."

Mason straightened. "You do that."

Across the room, Eb picked up the chalk. "I just write my name on the date I choose?"

"That's right," Dan encouraged him. "You got it."

Eb paused and then wrote "Eb" on the square for December 16. "That's my choice."

"Oh, Eb," Ashford said, "you got a letter today."

The storekeeper-postmaster pulled a letter from the mail pouch.

Eb hurried over. When he read the front of the letter, his smile nearly split his face.

Mason turned to him, trying to figure out who would be writing to Eb. "Good news?"

"You might say that," Eb walked over to him. "That surprise is still comin'." Eb smirked.

Mason grimaced. "You headed home?"

"Yes, sir, Deputy!" Eb mock-saluted him.

Mason glanced once more at the rear entrance, searching for a glimpse of Emma. Disgusted with himself, he waved Eb on. "Come. I have a couple of friends who will join us on our walk home."

Eb arched an eyebrow and continued to smirk. That was genuine Eb, always the teaser.

Mason led him to the jail and unlocked the door. The two pups met him there.

"Pups!" Eb crowed. "Where'd they come from?"

"I haven't found anybody who claims them, but I've only asked around town. Help me with this one. I think his ribs were hurt."

So as gently as he could, Eb scooped up the injured pup.

The other pup stood on his hind legs and pawed Mason's shins. Mason tied a rope around the pup's neck and then shut and locked the door again. "Let's head homeward." He had to pick up his girls from the Brants'.

As they walked, Mason filled Eb in on how the one pup had been hurt. Mason was glad that he didn't see the stranger on the street. He still burned at the man's cruelty. A man who would threaten to shoot two healthy pups might do anything. And he hadn't appreciated how the man had looked at Emma.

Before long, Eb and Mason parted ways as Eb headed farther north toward his homestead. So Mason led one pup and carried the other toward Asa's cabin. He came to the spot where that night Emma had rested against him, and he stood there till the dog on the rope pulled at him. Longing to see Emma, to touch her hand, swelled within. The wind at his back pushed him. He forced himself to go on.

When, in the early winter twilight, he first glimpsed the white smoke from Asa's fireplace and then the lamplight shining in the window, his heart lurched with longing. Asa had it all, a homestead, children, a wife...

Mason beat down the envy. He had the girls and friends and his own place. He only wished... He stopped that line of thought.

He paused at the door, suddenly cautious. The Brants had two cats who had the run of the house. He couldn't just barge in with two dogs. He turned toward the barn.

"Hey!" Asa hailed him, coming out of the barn and securing the door behind himself. "What you got there?"

"Two orphans."

Asa met him in the yard. "You taking them home?"

"For now—till I find out if anybody owns them."

"Why you carrying that one?"

Mason explained.

Asa frowned. "I'll warn Judith we have canine company. I'll keep the lead to this one." Asa claimed the rope. "And you keep that one in your arms till we see if it will be peace in the valley or open war."

Mason followed Asa to the door and waited there with the pups. Then Asa let them in and held the rope on one pup.

Across the room, near the fire, the gray-and-white cats stood up and arched their backs. The pups gazed at them as if they hadn't seen a cat before. The well pup woofed. The cats hissed. But that was about it.

After a few moments the cats cast nasty looks at the intruders and, still eyeing them, they reclaimed their places on the warm hearth. Then the children gathered around Mason as he sat on the bench with the pups, one in his arms and one at his feet.

All through their comments and petting, Mason kept thinking of only one thing—how Emma had rested a hand over his at the jail. He ached with wanting to say all the words he held in around her. He wanted to tell her how beautiful she was, how kind and good, and how much he wanted to court her. All words he could never say.

Then he felt her gentle touch on his hand once again, a phantom touch. Would time passing help? Would there ever be a day when he could say all these words? He doubted it, and his heart squeezed tightly. Oh, what might have been.

On the cold, clear Thursday, Thanksgiving Day, Emma sat beside Judith on the wagon bench, both swathed in layers of warm wool clothing. Ahead lay the Caruthers family's place. Lavina had invited a few families to the holiday dinner, which would double as a wedding reception for her son Isaiah and his Chippewa bride, who had arrived a few days ago.

Emma knew that Mason might be there and that stressed her, but she hoped she was hiding her inner upset, which unfortunately had been added to. On the way out of town, walking to Judith's, the stranger with the side holster had stepped out of the saloon and started talking to her.

Her father had fortunately been right beside her. And he had told the stranger that his daughter was a respectable woman and then led her away. The man had laughed in a very unpleasant way. That laugh lingered in her mind—no matter how she tried to banish it. And recalling that he'd kicked the pup still stirred her. She found herself clenching her fists.

"What is it?" Judith whispered in her ear.

Emma shook her head and relaxed her hands. "Not now."

And then they were pulling up among a few other wagons. Dan helped her down as Asa helped Judith down. Lily claimed Judith's hand and Colton drifted to Dan's side, as usual.

Tall, smiling, Lavina opened the door and called out, "Welcome!"

Through the sharp wind, they hurried inside and found their friends the Whitmores, Mason and the girls, and Eb, who was the Caruthers' closest neighbor now. Evidently surmising that many in the local congregation would not welcome an Indian bride, Lavina had chosen to hold a private reception at home, not at the schoolhouse. The fragrance of sage and roasting wild turkey greeted them.

Emma tried not to look at Mason immediately and

failed. She could not stop herself from seeking him out. "Is the sheriff back, then?"

"Yes, came home last night. I'm off duty," Mason replied.

Emma felt relieved. The stranger had loitered around town and no one could figure out why he'd come. He'd made everyone nervous.

Wearing crooked hair ribbons as usual, Birdie and Charlotte greeted her. As usual, she had to stop herself from straightening the ribbons Mason had tied for them. That was not her job. She talked in word and sign with them.

"I'm so glad you are learning sign," Lavina said. "A blessing to this child."

Emma merely smiled. Mason stood right behind Lavina and was gazing at Emma in a way that triggered her pulse to jump and skip. Why couldn't she break away from this attraction? Mason rarely if ever made any movement toward her. She couldn't believe she had put her hand on his at the jail that day they'd rescued the pups. Why did she keep reaching for him?

As the introductions proceeded, Emma turned her attention to Isaiah, Lavina's oldest son, who proved to be a tall, lanky young man who looked to be around twenty. He wore a combination of clothing—regular trousers and plaid shirt under a buckskin jacket, beaded and fringed.

"And here is our daughter-in-law," Lavina said, drawing the young woman closer. "Her name is Abeque."

Emma said all that was polite and drank in the young Indian woman's unusual appearance. She was tall and slender like Isaiah. Her hair was braided and her buckskin dress was elaborately beaded. She wore high moccasins, also beaded.

"I am so happy to meet you," Abeque said in a voice low and rich. She smiled then, revealing a true sweetness.

Emma said, "I was wondering before you leave if you and Isaiah would have time to speak to my school-children. I'd like them to hear about the far north of our state and the people who live there."

Abeque glanced to Isaiah.

"We'll try," he said, reluctance evident.

"I think you should," Noah murmured.

Isaiah bent his head in acknowledgment. "Any particular time or day?"

"School's from nine o'clock to four. Any day will be fine," Emma said.

Soon, at Lavina's invitation, everyone found a place around the table and the feast began. Somehow, and Emma didn't know how, she and Mason ended up sitting side by side. Loath to touch him, she sat stiffly and sensed that Mason did, too.

"Isaiah, I wish your grandfather could be here," Lavina said.

Emma had heard of Lavina's late father-in-law, Old Saul, who had started the church in Pepin. The conversation swirled around Emma as she ate the roast turkey, sage dressing, mashed potatoes, glazed carrots and cornbread. She tried not to keep glancing at Mason to her right. She realized then that she was worried for him. He was a deputy now and the man Smith openly taunted Mason whenever they met. She'd witnessed it herself and heard others speak of it.

The meal ended and soon everyone was saying

their goodbyes. On this coming Sunday, Isaiah would also attend church to accept the gifts the women had knitted and sewn for him to take north. Emma tried not to draw near Mason, but somehow they ended up right next to each other at the door. He pointedly ignored her. The cut sliced her to the heart.

As a young girl, she had fallen in love with a boy who became a man who'd gone to war and never returned. Now it appeared she was coming to care for a man who didn't want her. Foolish beyond measure.

Then, at the point of leaving for home, Charlotte turned from the door, where she and Birdie were. She ran to Emma and clung to her waist. Emma looked at Mason, witnessing his pain. She didn't know what to do. She stood there, frozen by indecision.

"Why don't you let Emma ride to our place in your wagon? It's on your way home," Judith suggested.

Emma didn't even look at Mason to see what his opinion might be. She did not want an emotional scene to end this pleasant occasion. "Good idea." She tapped Charlotte on her head. The girl looked up, anxious and tearful. Emma signed, "I'm coming with you. Let's go. Wave goodbye."

With that, Emma led the girls into the chill, gloomy day and onto Mason's wagon. Without a word, Mason helped Emma up onto the bench. She tried not to look directly into his eyes for that moment, only a moment, but failed. She tingled as if he'd touched more than her gloved hand.

Then he moved and lifted Birdie, who then stood behind the bench, holding onto the back while Charlotte still clung to Emma's waist. The Brant wagon headed out, rocking over the ruts, and Mason's followed. Emma tried to come up with a way to leave without sending Charlotte into a spiral of distress. But no thought occurred. She began praying.

Chapter Thirteen

On the way home, with Emma so near him on the wagon bench, Mason racked his brain trying to come up with some solution to Charlotte's clinging to Emma. *This can't go on.*

"Mason," Emma said in a low voice as if she didn't want those in the wagon ahead to overhear, "we need to figure out how to handle Charlotte when…she has these…spells."

Didn't she think he knew that? He gripped the reins, holding in his irritation, a burning in his midsection. Then she touched his shoulder.

Oh, the comfort of her touch. He couldn't stop himself. He reached over and pressed her hand on his shoulder. "I don't know… I can't think…" A deer, almost invisible in its winter coat, paused at the edge of the wood, watching them pass by, the fading light making its large brown eyes glisten.

"I don't either, but God will show us the way." Emma's low voice caused the deer's ears to twitch and Mason to press her hand more tightly.

"He hasn't so far," he said with audible rancor.

"If she were a normal child, we would discipline her and that would be the end of it. But she has a wounded heart and needs special understanding." The deer turned back into the trees.

"But she wants you…" His voice faltered. *She wants you to be her mother.*

"I know." She drew in a long breath. "Father, show us the way."

He glanced at her then. She was stroking Charlotte's hair and she'd lifted her face to the night sky. He would never—even if he lived to be a hundred—forget how she looked in this moment as she prayed and loved his little sister. Emotion flooded him. *I love you, Emma.* The words bubbled up from deep within. He'd tried to hide from them but now, in this moment of stress, he couldn't deny their truth.

"Miz Hawkins at the orphans' home would just pray over her, ask God to heal her," Birdie said from her stance behind them as she rocked with the wagon, gripping the top of the bench. "Sometime she would carry Charlotte, walk back and forth and pray over her out loud. And we children would pray too. We all worried about Charlotte."

Mason's heart clenched.

"Why don't you pray now, Birdie?" Emma said.

"Oh, God," Birdie said, her voice rising, "my Charlotte be hurting. She want Miss Emma for her mama. But Pa don't want to marry her."

Yes, I do. I'd give anything, Lord, to be worthy of her. He swallowed down his distress, blinking his eyes.

Birdie continued to pray aloud. He drove on in the deepening darkness and his mind repeated Birdie's words. Finally the Brant cabin came into view. Now the scene would happen. Emma would try to leave and Charlotte would be inconsolable. His stomach twisted into knots. What could he do?

Asa drove his wagon to the barn, helped his wife down and then turned to Mason, who moved to tie up the reins, then get down to help Emma.

She held up a hand, stopping him. "Judith, I'm going on ahead with Mason. Could I spend the night at your place, please?"

Asa and Judith exchanged glances. "Of course, you're always welcome," Asa replied.

Emma turned to Mason, her golden hair gleaming in the low light. "Mason, after we get the girls settled for the night, will you walk me back here?"

"Of course." He stared at her. What did she have in mind?

"Father, you can go on home," Emma said. "I'll see you at church."

After gazing at Emma for a moment, Dan waved and started down the road before the early winter darkness completely closed in.

"Let's head home, Mason," Emma said.

Confused but willing, he slapped the reins and started up the track to his place. She'd said, *"Let's head home, Mason."* How much he wanted her in his home. Then he realized— *She said my given name.* He recalled now that she had she used his given name in the letter when she had agreed to marry him and accepted the fare for the trip to Pepin. *Emma.* He wanted to say her name aloud, but all the dark past he kept secret within clogged his throat.

Then he pulled up in front of his cabin. He came

around and helped her down—her touch flowing up his arms—and then he swung Birdie down. "I'll be right in after I settle the horses. The fire is banked low—"

"We'll stir it up, won't we, Birdie?" Emma turned and held out a hand to Charlotte, who climbed down without any fuss.

Mason couldn't help himself. He paused to watch Emma shepherd the girls into the cabin. Emotions shivered through him—powerful and rich. This coming home like a family was what had been meant to happen. But hadn't.

He drove the team to the barn and got them settled for the night. His barn's thick log walls and half-log roof held in the cows' body heat, warming the structure. He latched the door and hurried through the gathering night to the cabin.

When he stepped inside, he found both girls had already donned their long flannel nightgowns and stood in stocking feet before the fire that burned brightly again. The pups ran to him, yipping. He bent to pet them and then he let them outside one more time. In the cold, they quickly finished and hurried back inside to the warmth by the fire.

Mason stayed by the door, captured by the sight of Emma. Her back to him, Emma was sitting in the chair by the fire, behind Charlotte, brushing her long, golden brown hair. He stood mute, observing the image of mother and children. The homey scene took away his words. But what could he say in any event?

He forced himself to shed his coat and hat, and he approached the group with caution, not wanting to disturb the peace of the trio.

"Draw up a chair, Mason," Emma said.

For her, he wished he had better furniture, more comfortable than straight-back chairs. But he obeyed her request and drew his chair toward the fire.

"I thought it best just to begin the girls' nightly routine. Birdie told me that you brush Charlotte's hair and then braid it every night. " Emma said.

He nodded, swallowing to get his dry throat ready for words. Finally he managed, "It gets tangled and hard to comb by morning."

She smiled at him. "I know."

He nearly hit himself on the forehead. Of course she knew. Her hair was longer and thicker than Charlotte's. She hadn't had to learn about how to manage long, thick hair as he had.

"My hair is already braided. It stays better than Charlotte's does," Birdie commented, and then she climbed onto Mason's lap and made herself comfortable. He folded his arms around the small, warm body of this sweet child. He kissed her right ear and she giggled.

And with that sound, his tension began to leak out of his body. He watched the orange-gold flames dance in the hearth, and occasionally he allowed himself to glance at Emma, who was still brushing Charlotte's hair. Finally she braided the light brown hair and then drew Charlotte onto her lap. The little girl let out a long sigh and snuggled against Emma.

Emma had averted another dreadful tantrum. Mason let himself drink in the moment.

Finally, when both girls had fallen asleep in their respective laps, Emma motioned for him to carry Birdie to the loft. Then he returned for Charlotte, and Emma followed him to the base of the ladder. He came back down and Emma surprised him. She had not moved to the door to don her coat but instead had returned to her place by the fire.

She patted the chair next to her. "I think it's time we talked. Honestly."

Talked? Honestly? Like a tornado, all the things he could not say to her or anyone but Eb swirled through him, ripping, clawing at his resistance. He swallowed and then approached the chair as if it were an unexploded shell. He sat.

"I have feelings for you, Mason." She said this but trained her gaze on the fire. "I didn't think I ever could have feelings for a man again. I told you in my letters that I had been engaged to a man... Jonathan... who was killed in the war."

"I remember," he managed, though his voice came out rough.

"I promised to marry you, but I never thought I'd be able to love again. I don't know if what I feel for you is love. It's different but somehow the same. I can't explain. I know I'm being very forward, but..."

"...honest," he said. "You're being honest." *I wish I could be.*

"Something is holding you back. What is it?" Then she did look him straight in the eye.

He had trouble breathing. "I... I..."

"Whatever it is...you can trust me. I will tell no one."

"I know that," he said with force.

"Then?" she prompted. A log gave way to the fire and fell apart, sending up red-gold sparks in the dim light.

Wishing his reluctance could fall apart in the same way, he tried to speak. He couldn't. He could not tell her the truth. It wasn't just about the past, his past, but his father's. What if it held some danger for the future? What if his bad blood did appear? And for some reason, the stranger came to mind. His father had congregated with that kind of man.

"From Eb's story, I take it that you and your father fought on opposite sides in the war?" She reached over and claimed his hand.

Her touch shuddered through him like waves lapping a shore. He nodded.

"But there's more than that, isn't there?" She stroked the top of his hand, soothing him as she had Charlotte. A humbling thought.

So much more. Betrayal. Outlawry. Murder. The words unsaid wanted to pour from his lips.

"Don't you trust me?" Her hand paused.

"With my life." The declaration rushed out. He clasped her hand in both of his. "Emma...you're too good, too fine for me."

"Nonsense." She returned his pressure within his grip. "You're a fine man. You've proved that over and over."

He squeezed his eyes shut, trying to keep from shedding tears.

"Oh, Mason." Emma drew out one hand, cupped his cheek and smoothed away the moisture with her thumb. "Trust me."

Her touch heightened his longing to be free, to be worthy of her. He tried to speak but a dam had formed in his throat. He wished one had formed in his eyes. Tears wet his face, unmanning him.

"I can see that you want to trust me but just can't," Emma murmured. She sighed, then pressed his hands to her cheek once and rose. "You best walk me partway to Judith's. She'll be waiting up for me."

He wanted to shout his need for her, to tell her how much her presence in his life meant. He could say nothing, not a word. He rose mutely and did as she asked.

The cold wrapped around them as they walked the path toward the Brants'. When the cabin came into sight in the half-moon light, Emma paused. "You can go back now. I can see my way."

She started on without him.

"Emma," he said.

She paused and turned back.

His voice died and he could only stare at her.

She started walking again. "You will tell me, Mason. I'm not going anywhere. Whatever it is, it will come out."

Her final words shook him to the core. He watched till she disappeared around the corner of Asa's cabin. Then he turned and walked home—alone, humbled by Miss Emma Jones's courage. Why did he have to carry his father's sins? Her final sentence shook him. *"Whatever it is, it will come out."* If she were right, then he'd be forced to leave—without her.

Past the leafless maples and birches among the thick firs, Emma walked to church the next morning with her sister's family. She'd heard Mason and the girls pass Judith's cabin earlier than usual. Was Mason intending to try to distance himself from her? She drew in a cold breath, warming the air in her nose and preparing herself to face Mason today after all she'd revealed last night.

Part of her felt as brave as she had been last night in that firelit cabin; part of her trembled over her audacity. How would he behave toward her today in front of the whole town? Her sister said something to Lily and as they walked in the bright, cold morning sunlight, Emma recalled arriving at Judith's after leaving Mason.

In her night robe, Judith had met Emma at the door and ushered her inside. The fire had still burned brightly on the hearth, the only light in the room. After Emma had shed her outerwear on the pegs, her sister led her to the rocking chairs by the fire. For the first few moments, they'd merely rocked side by side.

With a shout in the cool morning, Eb hailed them from the trail to the north, calling Emma back to the present. The five of them paused to let him join them on their way. When he greeted them, Eb seemed happier than usual. Emma again tried to gauge her own unruly emotions, lingering from last night.

Last night Judith had turned her head to face Emma. "So?" she'd whispered.

Again, Emma felt herself rest her head against the high back of the chair and come clean with her sister. "I told him I care about him."

"And?"

"And he's got something locked inside him that holds him back."

Judith had nodded. "I understand." But though Emma felt that there was a wealth of experience in those words, that was all her sister had said.

Now Emma shivered in the cold, shivered over

what that something might be. She tried to remember the early months of Judith's marriage to Asa, but her mind rebelled. Mason dominated her thoughts.

The six of them crested the final rise into town. Ahead the saloon was dark and all the shops were closed for the day. But many townspeople turned and waved and greeted them as most of Pepin headed toward church. Dan came out of the forge and Colton ran to him. All these things were the same as they were every Sunday. *But I'm different. I've been changing. Has Mason?*

Then Emma heard a wagon approaching behind her and turned to see the Caruthers family, including Isaiah and Abeque. That's right. Today the ladies would present their gifts to Isaiah. Emma hoped Mrs. Stanley would be able to contain herself, contain her characteristic rudeness—not insult or hurt the young couple.

They all entered the school yard. With a wave, Emma separated from them and walked into her quarters to shed her coat and scarf and don her Sunday hat. Then, taking a deep breath and whispering a prayer for wisdom, she entered the schoolroom from the connecting door.

From the rear, Charlotte flew down the front aisle and ran straight into Emma. The child clasped her arms around Emma's waist, capturing her. Many turned to look. Emma smiled. What else could she do?

She began walking toward her sister, drawing Charlotte along with her. Emma moved to sit beside her sister. Charlotte would not stand for that. She butted Emma's midsection with her head. Emma sighed and walked to the rear, where Mason sat with Birdie.

"I'm sorry," Mason murmured, rising politely.

She cast him a gentle glance as she sat down beside him. "Perhaps this will pass if Charlotte can learn to trust." *Will you learn to trust, Mason?* If he didn't, where would that leave them—all of them?

Emma glanced around and received a variety of responses. Some faces—smug. Others surprised. Some disapproving. Emma smiled at all of them serenely. They had no idea what was really happening—just saw the outside. Charlotte settled on the bench beside her, sitting up and swinging her legs back and forth. Content. *And that's all I care about.* Or it was all she cared about at this moment.

The faces that had been looking at her and Mason suddenly swung to the doorway. She didn't have to turn to know that Isaiah and his bride had entered. The faces revealed a variety of responses: shock, surprise, interest, disapproval and a few even outrage. Emma shut her eyes and began praying for the young couple who had dared to bridge the chasm between cultures.

Noah Whitmore surged up the aisle. "Isaiah, welcome!" Noah clasped the young man's hand and then turned to greet Abeque. He drew the couple forward to the Caruthers' usual bench. Once again she thanked God for Noah Whitmore, a man of courage and compassion.

The service began as usual. Emma ignored or tried to ignore the unusual stiffness or wariness that shrouded the room. And she continued to pray for the young couple as Noah prayed and Lavina led the singing. Then, before his sermon, Noah motioned for Isaiah and Mrs. Ashford to come forward. Isaiah stood on one side of Noah and the storekeeper's wife on the other.

"The ladies of our congregation have been knitting and quilting and sewing gifts for the northern tribe," Noah began. "Today we welcome our brother Isaiah Caruthers, who is serving in a mission in Lac du Flambeau among the Chippewa, or some say Ojibwa. Welcome, Isaiah. Mrs. Ashford?"

Mrs. Ashford handed Isaiah a basket of colorful mittens, scarves and hats. "This is just a bit of what we've made and collected to send home with you."

Isaiah received the gift. "Thank you."

"We were happy to do it." Mrs. Ashford beamed. "We know how the winter can be. We wouldn't want any child or anyone to face it without warm things."

As Mrs. Ashford continued, Mason studied the young man. He wished he didn't know how it felt to be front and center, under everyone's eye. Charlotte's troubles and her predilection for Miss Emma guaranteed that he would remain an object of interest. Emma's words last night, her warning, repeated in his mind—*"Whatever it is, it will come out."* No.

Isaiah smiled at Mrs. Ashford and turned to the congregation. "Our thanks. These are desperately needed and will show that people far away care about the tribe, a lesson in Christ's love."

"On behalf of the ladies of Pepin, you're welcome." Mrs. Ashford shook his hand and returned to her husband's side amid polite applause.

Isaiah moved to return to his family, but Noah

stopped him. "I'd like you to share a few words about your work in the north."

Mason hurt for the young man. *Just let him sit down, Noah. Not many here are interested.*

Isaiah paused and then stepped forward. "As you wish. I am happy to be here with family and so many people I know. Many of you recall my grandfather, Old Saul, who started this church preaching on the steps of the Ashford's store."

Many in the congregation nodded, and Mason wished he'd known Old Saul, a man people still recalled with great respect and affection.

"I never thought," Isaiah continued, "I would be engaged in mission work, but my grandfather started me off when I took the Ojibwa woman and her son home. Some of you recall her time here."

Heads around the room nodded.

"She is now a member of our infant church there. The fact that the people of Pepin helped her was not ignored. You, this town, are held in respect by the Ojibwa. The Ojibwa have weathered over a hundred years of white people who only wanted what they could take from them, so no kindness is overlooked or forgotten."

Isaiah shook his head. "That makes the mission work hard. Again, your gifts will be physical proof that not all white people are out for themselves. Yet the need in the north is not just for the wonderful gifts you have just presented us. We need most of all your prayers. That God will no longer be termed *Gitchee Manitou*, the Great Mystery, by the Ojibwa, but that He will become known to them. Thank you." Isaiah returned to his family, sitting down by his wife.

To his surprise, Mason sensed an easing of the tension in the room. Isaiah had struck just the right note, and his respect for the young man rose. *Well done.* He tried not to glance sideways at Emma but could not resist. Her goodness radiated like sunlight in the simple room. He recalled her asking him to trust her. *Oh, Emma, I do trust you, but it's not you. It's me.*

On Tuesday, one of the last days of November, Mason walked the girls to town on their way to school. The sheriff had told him to drop by to pick up his pay for the days he'd served as active deputy. Treetops swayed with the strong western wind. On the brisk walk into town, Eb had joined the threesome. Eb did not look like this was an everyday trip to town. Mason wanted to demand an explanation of why Eb was spit-shined this weekday morning as if he was bound for church.

As soon as the girls left them, heading to school, Mason looked to Eb. "Okay? What?"

Eb laughed out loud. "I tole you a surprise comin'. Today's the day."

With that Mason shook his head. As he turned to enter the jail, he glimpsed the stranger stride out of the saloon. Alert, Mason entered the jail and moved to the window. Eb walked to the forge and went inside while the stranger headed to the store.

"Mornin'," the sheriff greeted Mason. "I got your pay right here." He drew out an envelope and tapped it on the desktop.

Mason loped over to the desk and received the envelope with gratitude. "Just saw the stranger head to the store."

"That's not illegal." Merriday grinned.

Mason sank into the chair by the desk. "I know. He hasn't done anything, but—"

A boat whistle interrupted him. Eb's last words repeated in Mason's mind. He rose and walked to the window.

"What is it?"

"Just curious," Mason hedged. "There was a skim of ice on the creek we passed this morning."

"Yeah, I didn't put my name on the store calendar but I think the river will close well before January." Merriday joined Mason by the front window.

Eb hurried out of the forge and down to the pier. At the same time the stranger sauntered out of the store and…headed toward the boat.

"Is he leavin'?" the sheriff asked beside Mason's ear.

The stranger walked down the pier and boarded the boat.

"Looks like it." Mason thought he should feel relief but for some unknown reason, he felt none. The stranger's effect lingered like a sour taste in his mouth.

Then Eb hurried forward and, on the dock, met a buxom black woman with a valise. Eb swept her up off her feet into a hug and kissed her right there in front of everyone watching on Main Street.

"Well, that's interestin'," Merriday commented, a smile in his voice.

Mason felt his jaw drop. Without a word, he moved outside and down the steps, hurrying toward Eb.

With one arm around the woman and her valise

in the other hand, Eb drew her from the dock up the street toward the store.

"Eb!" Mason called.

Eb paused. "Come on. I'm aiming to introduce my…bride-to-be to the town." Eb hurried forward, shepherding the woman through the brisk wind. And then snow began falling.

The boat whistled, announcing it would soon depart.

Mason halted, the snow flying into his face. He turned for one last look at the boat. As the crew cast off the ropes, the stranger tipped his hat. Mason couldn't see the man's face, but he knew the man must be smirking at him. Why had he come to town? Mason stared as the boat moved out into the rapid current. Again, at the stranger's departure, he waited for the relief to come. It didn't.

"Hey! Mr. Mason!" Eb called. "Come on!"

Mason turned and headed toward his friend. He drew up a smile and plastered it over his face. "So what did you tell this poor woman to make her come to marry you, Eb?"

Eb chortled. "I asked her the same question, but she took pity on me."

The three of them moved into the store and drew toward the stove. The older men there rose, making Mason proud of Dan and his friends.

"Gentlemen," Eb announced, "I'd like to introduce you to my bride-to-be, Miss Kizzie Fremont. Soon to be Mrs. Ebenezer Mason."

The older gentlemen clapped Eb on the back and bowed over the lady's hand.

"So you found yourself a bride," Dan said when

all the congratulations had been exhausted. "He who findeth a wife findeth a good thing," he said, para-phrasing scripture.

Mason's stomach clenched at the fact he hadn't found one and wouldn't. But this was Eb's happy day. He forced himself forward to meet Eb's bride-to-be. "Miss, I don't know if Eb deserves you, but we're so glad you've come."

"Thank you, sir. Ebenezer has told me all about you. I am happy to make your acquaintance." Her round face possessed a deep serenity.

Mason continued smiling, but inside he rioted. Was everyone going to marry while he soldiered on alone? And was the stranger gone for good? Why had he come in the first place?

Chapter Fourteen

At her door, as she gazed at Eb and a plump black woman in a simple blue cambric dress, Emma couldn't hide her surprise. "Your fiancée, Eb? I didn't know… I…"

"Yes, Miss Emma. This is Miss Kizzie Fremont. She arrived as arranged on the boat today." Eb's face lit up like the dawn.

Still processing, Emma managed, "Welcome!" And then realized she was blocking their way. "Come in. Come in. You just surprised me." They stepped inside and she closed the door behind them, shutting out much of the late afternoon daylight.

They went straight to the fire she had just stirred up after school. The connecting door stood open, letting the warmth from the schoolroom stove take the chill off the room. Though happy to meet Eb's fiancée, Emma wondered why they had come to her door.

"Eb, would you draw my desk chair in here?" Emma asked. That would provide enough seats and give her a moment to digest the fact that Eb was marrying and to this stranger. She was, of course, happy for them, but her own heart felt as if it were being beaten with a rod. Would everyone marry and she remain alone, bereft again? *I shouldn't have fallen in love with Mason.* But hearts evidently had minds of their own. Emma pulled her thoughts back to the present while Eb carried the chair in, and soon the three of them sat around the fire, waiting for teakettle to boil.

"Now tell me how you two met," Emma said the usual phrase asked of couples in love.

"After the war I left my home in Tennessee," Kizzie began. "I began looking for family."

Emma nodded.

"And I was doing the same," Eb said.

"We didn't find any family," Kizzie continued, looking suddenly somber.

"But we found each other," Eb said, grinning, and claimed Kizzie's hand. Kizzie smiled and squeezed his hand in return.

"And now you two will make a new family," Emma finished, another tug at her heart. A family. Her mind conjured up an image of Mason, Birdie and Charlotte.

"Yes." Kizzie blinked away tears.

The pot boiled, bubbling insistently, and Emma busied herself making tea on the table behind them. And she set out a plate of sugar cookies from her sister.

"So, that's how the two of you met?" Emma prompted the conversation to continue.

"Yes. I knew right away that Eb was the man for me, a good man."

Emma nodded and a genuine smile lifted her face. "Your fiancé has already gained a good reputation in his short time here." She poured three cups of tea.

"It doesn't hurt that I can play the harmonica," Eb said modestly.

"Miss Emma, you were supposed to marry Eb's friend, Mr. Mason," Kizzie said.

A needle to Emma's heart. "Yes, I was." She sat again and lifted her tea cup, hiding her lower face. "Now, when will you two marry?"

"Well, I didn't want to wait till next Saturday, when the schoolroom would be available for the wedding. But Mr. Ashford has invited us to use his store for our wedding after closing," Eb said.

Emma smiled at his surprised tone. The Ashfords liked the store to be the center of activity. "I think that's a wonderful idea. When will the wedding be?"

"Tomorrow I'm going to drive us out to Noah Whitmore's and talk to him. I hope he'll come in to perform the weddin' the next afternoon."

"I see." As she gazed at them and once again at Kizzie's valise, she realized why they had come to her. "And of course, Miss Fremont, you must stay with me until your wedding."

Both Eb and Kizzie tried to politely decline.

But Emma insisted. "I'm about the only woman in town who isn't married and has room for you. Of course you'll stay with me."

The couple looked relieved. "It will only be for a couple of nights," Eb said.

"As long as Miss Fremont doesn't mind a pallet by the fire," Emma replied. She rose to add another log to the fire. But Eb motioned her to sit and did it himself.

"That be fine," Kizzie said.

"We've been invited to eat supper with Mason,"

Eb said, relieving Emma's mind of how to feed them. "I'll bring Kizzie back by dark."

The poker hung nearest her on a hook in the masonry and she lifted it down to stir the fire. "Excellent. I'll be taking my supper at the Ashfords', as usual. If you get here before I do, just let yourself in. I rarely lock the door." She hung the poker back in place.

After a few more words, the couple rose and left for Mason's. Emma wished she could follow them, go to Mason's, but of course, she had not been invited. How would she endure Mason pushing her away time after time? She sighed and gathered up the few dishes to wash.

She was the maiden lady schoolteacher, and Kizzie staying with her before the wedding would protect Kizzie's reputation. She gazed around her quarters. She had been so happy to have a place of her own, but now she saw years, lonely years in this room, and before long people would start calling her a spinster. Or an old maid schoolteacher.

She poured the last of the hot kettle water into the small basin on the table and began washing the dishes, trying to stop thinking of Mason.

If only Mason would trust her. She turned the thought away, finished the tea things and wrapped up in her coat, hat and gloves to walk to the store to help out and eat supper there. Gratitude to the Ashfords and their always warm welcome and cheerful chatter filled her. At least she wouldn't be left here sitting alone, thinking of Mason and the girls.

Late Thursday afternoon Mason, dressed in his Sunday clothes, bundled against the cold December wind, walked toward the store. The sunlight was already thin as the early twilight advanced. He felt as gloomy as the gray sky above. Today he would stand as Eb's best man. And since Kizzie had stayed two nights with Emma, she'd been asked to stand as Kizzie's maid of honor. Mason's heart felt like an ingot of lead. At times the weight of it caused him to have trouble breathing. How could how he felt make it hard to breathe?

He walked down Main Street, trying to prepare himself to face another wedding, knowing he'd never have one of his own. And to make everything harder, Emma would be there, looking lovely as usual. *"Trust me,"* she'd said.

He did trust her. The sticking point remained—he didn't trust himself. And what if anybody else found out about his father's horrible crimes and his dying in prison? He couldn't bear to let that mar Emma's reputation by association. And worse what if his father's blood in his veins finally came to the fore? Could that happen?

He walked up the two steps to the store, trying to drag up a smile for the happy occasion. Eb had already arrived in town to help the Ashfords prepare the store for the wedding, moving furnishings around. Kizzie had spent the morning visiting at school, speaking to the children about being a former slave. Leave it to Emma to take every opportunity to teach her students and to help engender sympathy for Eb and Kizzie.

Eb, alone, met Mason at the door. "Kizzie is at Miss Emma's, dressing for the wedding."

Shedding his coat, Mason managed to nod and give something of a smile. His lips felt frozen. And not from the cold. The store's counters had been pushed back closer to the walls, clearing space around the stove. A few more benches ringed the room. Mason's emotions simmered just under the surface. Could he keep everything in, not reveal what he was feeling? And what was he feeling?

"Where are Birdie and Charlotte?" he asked. The girls had been told to come to the store after school and wait for him.

"They are helping get the bride ready," Mr. Ashford said. "My wife is at Miss Jones's quarters, too." The storekeeper looked excited. What about weddings made everyone but Mason happy?

"You men, stay in the store," Mrs. Ashford called. She'd opened the rear entrance just a crack. "I'm taking the ladies upstairs until the preacher arrives!"

Dan Jones entered the store's front door, wearing his Sunday best, and soon a few others joined the gathering—every face smiling, everyone dressed for the occasion. Eb's hand was pumped vigorously by the older men. Mason's lead ingot somehow weighed more and more. But he forged on, showing a happy face.

Then Noah and his family arrived by wagon. The preacher strode inside, greeting everyone. Soon he and his family had shed their outerwear and looked around. "Well," he asked Eb, "is your bride here?"

"Upstairs, sir," Eb replied. "We were just waiting for you to arrive."

Noah rubbed his hands together. "Sunny, would you go upstairs and bring the ladies down?" Their toddler son wrapped his arms around one of Noah's thighs.

"Of course." Sunny let Dan take the baby, and she and little Dawn hurried out the rear.

"I think you two should stand over here." Ashford positioned Eb and Mason near the front to get the best of the lowering daylight. Noah took his place with his back to the front windows and just out of the way of the door. Then Ashford flipped the Open sign to the Closed side and bustled to the rear.

Asa and Judith and the children opened the front door. "Are we too late?"

"No," Noah replied, "come in. The bride will be down in a minute."

The Brants greeted and were greeted. Around a dozen people had come to witness the wedding. Sitting on one of the benches near Dan, Mrs. Waggoner kept wiping her eyes. "I'm sorry but I always cry at weddings."

Then Sunny peeked in from the rear door. "Are we ready?"

"Yes!" Noah replied with cheerful gusto.

Sunny and Mrs. Ashford with Birdie and Charlotte by the hand entered and joined the group who'd settled on the benches. A pause.

Then Emma entered the store, carrying a dried bouquet that was a little worn but elegant. After she stepped farther inside, Kizzie entered. She also carried a dried bouquet. She wore a purple dress in the latest style with a bustle and white lace at the throat.

Mason heard the low spontaneous growl of joy from deep in Eb's throat. Mason had glanced at the bride but he could not look away from Emma in her Sunday dress of rose-pink with ivory lace at the high neck. His heart pounded as he wished, wished that today he were the groom and she the bride. Torture.

The ceremony lasted only moments and Mason was grateful for the brevity. He tried not to stare at Emma but knew he was. At the right moment, he drew out the simple gold band Eb had given him to hold. Eb slipped it onto Kizzie's finger and then, at Noah's command, Eb bent and tenderly kissed his bride.

Applause broke out and Mason glanced at Emma. A single tear slid from her right eye, and the sight pierced him. *Don't cry, Emma. Please.*

Fortunately society accepted—in fact, encouraged—women to weep at a wedding. However Emma held in her real tears, the tears that would reveal the depth of her anguish. *I love Mason Chandler but he won't let himself admit his feelings for me.*

Emma trained her gaze toward the happy couple, not at Mason, not at her sister, who could read her so easily. *Dear Father in heaven, please show me the way. Help me. Is Mason going to shut me out forever? If he does, how will I bear it?*

Throwing herself on God's mercy let her keep breathing, keep smiling, but doing so demanded such faith. She felt as if she were climbing a mountain so high she couldn't glimpse the summit. How long? How high must she climb for relief, for peace?

A verse she'd memorized as a child, Psalms 121:1-2, returned to her—"I will lift up mine eyes unto the hills, from whence cometh my help. My help cometh from the Lord, which made heaven and earth." She added a ragged plea—*Lord, help now.*

But to Emma's dismay, Mason resisted God's help throughout the wedding party. After the vows had been exchanged, Mrs. Ashford with the help of many brought down a huge, fragrant brown-sugar-baked ham, bowls of pureed acorn squash, baskets of buttery cornbread. And then the Merridays arrived, bringing a vast sheet cake iced in white with fancy pink rosettes. At the sight of one of Miss Rachel's special cakes, spontaneous applause broke out.

After the meal, which the guests sat on benches or leaned against the walls to eat, Eb pulled out his harmonica and began playing "Oh, Susanna." Everyone clapped and then cheered when the Ashfords began to do-si-do around the stove to the lively tune. Emma kept her place on the bench between her sister and her father. Her face had frozen into a cheerful expression completely at odds with the agony within, sawing away at her peace.

She couldn't stop herself from glancing at Mason. For only one moment their gazes met. Then he broke the connection, turning away. Her heart clenched with pain.

As the night shadows lengthened and the half moon rose, the guests began to bundle up and leave with thanks and best wishes to the happy couple. Many guests had spoken to the storekeeper quietly, and an assortment of practical gifts waited for the young couple on the store counter. Emma had donated a mixing bowl set of sturdy pottery. The wedding had been bittersweet for her.

Finally all but a few remained. Emma donned her winter clothing by rote as she listened to Ashford and Eb. Saying it was the least they could do, Eb and Kizzie insisted on staying to help wash dishes and put the store back in order.

Dumbly Emma watched as Mason followed her sister's family out the door to the wagon that would take them home. Night's curtain had nearly dropped over them. At the last minute, Charlotte insisted that Emma come too. Mason appeared distressed. To avoid another public tantrum, Emma mounted the wagon bench beside her sister. She wanted to go home and cry, but going home with Charlotte must be done for Mason's sake.

The ride through the cold night passed in silence. The drowsy children sat in the back with Mason. Emma tried to think of a way to avoid the tantrum that would come. When the wagon stopped in front of Asa's barn, she glanced over her shoulder and saw that Charlotte had fallen asleep.

She pressed her index finger to her lips and then hurried down without help and into the barn and hid. Perhaps if Charlotte woke and didn't see her, she would go on home without a fuss.

After Emma hurried out of sight, Mason did not let himself look toward the barn. As Emma had sensed, Charlotte woke and, not seeing Emma and still drowsy, let him lead her with Birdie up the trail on their short walk home in the half moonlight. He was relieved not to have to face a tantrum on the heels of the ordeal of suffering through Eb's wedding, suffering because he knew that he loved Emma yet would never have her.

Birdie, as usual, led the three of them. They turned the last bend toward home.

Birdie cried out in surprise.

The stranger rushed her. Grabbed her up by the waist. Clamped a hand over her mouth.

"What?" Mason yelled.

"Quiet. Or I'll snap her neck," the man growled. "Now I want it."

"Want—"

Charlotte slipped from Mason's slack grip and ran back into the trees. "Charlotte!"

"Quiet," the stranger snapped, pulling Birdie tighter and closer. "Do what I say or I'll snap her neck and shoot you before you get ten feet."

Mason froze. *Stay away, Charlotte.* "How did you get here?"

"Just got off the boat a few miles down." The man grinned at his own cleverness. "They let me off and I walked back. Been living in an old shack I found. Now give me what I want."

"What do you want?" Mason's hoarse voice sounded odd to his own ears.

"I want the gold, my gold. I've waited long enough. Now, where is it?"

Mason's mind whirled. "Gold? What gold?"

"I'm out of patience," the man growled. "I'm Houghton. I rode with your dad with Quantrill and the James brothers. I was in on your dad's last bank job. He was wounded but he got away with the gold. We were supposed to meet and divide it up. He never showed."

"He'd been arrested," Mason blurted and wished he'd remained silent.

The man grinned, taking this as some kind of admission. "Now I don't need to kill anyone. Give me the gold and I'm gone. Your half-bit sheriff don't scare me."

Mason nearly let out the truth. He had no gold, but would the man believe him? *God, help. God, help us.* Mason shook inside, fear for Birdie ricocheting around inside him. "The cabin," he gasped. If he could get the man moving, he might have a chance to rush him.

"Glad you see reason. All I want is the gold."

Mason didn't believe him for a moment. If the man had run with his father's gang, he was a murderer.

"Now move. You take the lead. I'll follow, and remember, I can snap her neck in one second."

Bile rose in Mason's throat. Why hadn't he brought his gun along? Why hadn't he realized this man, Houghton, was not done with them? *God, help. God, show me what to do.* His mind brought up Emma's face and Charlotte's. Would he ever see them again?

"Walk!" Houghton barked.

Mason turned toward his cabin, tingling with apprehension. *God, help.*

He began walking as slowly as he could without making the man angrier. His mind tried to drag him into frozen fear but he fought through it. If the man had just come at him, he would know what to do.

But Birdie, sweet and loving, Birdie was gripped in the arms of a killer. Charlotte had run. Would she know enough to run to Asa? But if Emma had already set out for home, how would she tell them what happened? And did he want to put Asa in danger?

"Move along," Houghton growled. "And don't

think I won't kill this little chit and you if I don't get what I came for."

Keep him talking. "How did you find me? I mean, my pa and I hadn't seen each other in years till…" The image of the prison shook Mason.

"I seen you in Jeff City. I was tryin' to figure out how to get inside to see Jed. But I'm wanted so I couldn't just stroll in for a visit. I saw you going in every day and I asked around. Thought I could pay you to go in and take a message to Jed. I found out you were his son. Who knew Jed Chandler had a honest man for a son?"

"It happens." A gust of wind rattled the dry leaves on the trees, somehow mimicking Mason's desolate feelings.

Houghton ground out something like a chuckle.

Mason's cabin came into sight. He did not want to go into that cabin. Outside there was a better chance of overpowering him.

"Don't get any ideas," Houghton warned, gripping Birdie so tightly that she moaned.

Mason had no choice. He had to obey. *God, send help.* But who could come and why? Charlotte was probably lost in the forest. Mason's despair churned inside him. What would happen to Charlotte if Houghton killed him and Birdie tonight?

Emma had just gone around the bend on the road toward home when she heard a child scream. Shock iced her spine. The sound came from behind her, from Judith's. She whipped around and raced back.

Ahead in the yard in the moonlight, she saw Judith stooped and Charlotte gripping Judith's arms.

"Bad...man!" Charlotte's voice sounded odd, strangled, hysterical. "Hurt... Birdie!" The little girl gulped for air. "Help!"

For a second everyone froze. Charlotte speaking! And the words!

Leaving the horses he'd just unharnessed, Asa dropped to his knees beside Judith and reached for Charlotte. "A bad man is hurting Birdie?"

Charlotte nodded frantically. "Help!"

Asa sprang to his feet. "Judith, get into the house with Lily and Charlotte!" he ordered. "Colton, ride bareback for the sheriff! Tell him what you heard! Tell him come ready for anything!"

Colton turned, ran to the nearest horse and, using the wagon steps, mounted the horse. Holding the mane, he kicked the horse and it started off. "Yah!"

Asa lifted Judith to her feet. "Go inside and bar the door behind you!" Asa turned and saw Emma. "Get inside and don't come out! I need to help Mason. And I can't if you two and the girls aren't safe."

Asa raced to the wagon. He swatted the other horse, sending it into the barn, grabbed the rifle from under the wagon bench and ran flat out toward Mason's.

Thunderstruck, Emma watched, unmoving, till Judith grabbed her arm.

"Come!" Judith dragged her toward the cabin. Charlotte clung to Judith and Lily was crying in fear.

Emma felt tears washing her face. "Oh, Father in heaven, help!"

Then Judith shoved them all inside and dropped the bar in place against the door. In the dimly lit room, Emma felt Charlotte slam into her. She knelt and wrapped her arms around the weeping child. Fear like she'd never known froze her. Mason, Mason, would she ever see him again—alive?

Chapter Fifteen

At Houghton's order, Mason entered his cabin with hands still up and backed away from the door, moving toward the loft side. His mind was frozen on one idea—how to get to the man before Birdie could be harmed.

Houghton entered and moved to the other side, keeping the table between them. "Okay. Where's the gold?"

"Why do you think I have gold?" Mason stalled.

"Why else would you go see your old man? The rumor was he had a son—a turncoat, fought for the Union." He sneered over the last phrase.

"I went to sit with my father as he died," Mason said. "Any son would do that for a father."

Houghton barked something like a laugh. "Real family reunion, huh?"

Mason moved forward, ready to spring for Houghton. He couldn't stall much longer or Birdie would be lost.

"Do you think I won't kill her?" Houghton snapped. "I shot your pa's woman. I'll shoot you."

Aghast, Mason jerked up straighter. "You shot... Charlotte's mother?"

"I wouldn't have but she pulled a gun on me. A man has a right to defend himself. I didn't kill the little girl, did I?" The man sounded defensive.

"You didn't shoot Charlotte!" Mason roared, incensed, rocking forward. His hands itched to circle the man's throat and squeeze. A man shooting a woman? Only the lowest of the low did this. And Houghton knew it. "You caused her to go deaf and mute!"

The man shrugged. "This talkin' is over. Now where is the gold? I'll do whatever it takes to get what's mine. I'm counting to three and then your little black girl dies. One—"

A shot. Window glass exploded. Mason lunged forward, grabbed the frying pan left on the counter. He swung. Connected with Houghton's head. The man dropped to the floor.

Mason swept a sobbing Birdie into his arms.

The door burst open and Asa entered, rifle in hand. "Did I get him?"

Mason looked down. "No, I don't think so, but I got him with the cast iron skillet."

Asa advanced, his rifle at the ready. He looked down. "He's out cold, but for how long? Get some rope."

Mason hurried out to his barn, still carrying Birdie, who clung to him. Back inside, he handed the rope to Asa.

Asa made quick work of hog-tying Houghton's hands and feet and connecting them so the man would be helpless. Then Asa dragged the man into the center of the room. "Stir up the fire and light a lamp. I've sent Colton for the sheriff."

"How did you know I needed help?" Mason asked as he set Birdie down and did as Asa instructed. Birdie shadowed him.

"Charlotte came and told us. She spoke."

"What?" Mason halted with the poker in hand.

"She came and said something about a bad man hurting Birdie and yelled for help. We were all stunned, but then we got busy."

"Charlotte, my Charlotte talked?" Birdie said, moving toward Asa, staring up.

Mason echoed her words inwardly, stunned.

A horse neighed in the distance and then silence.

Asa walked to the door. "Sheriff, we got him hogtied and out cold! Come on in!"

Merriday's face loomed in the broken window. "Good. You got him." The sheriff turned and called over his shoulder, "It's safe, boy. You can come on!" Within moments, Merriday and Colton entered. "I wasn't going to take any chances and just barge in."

"Good thinking," Asa said, shaking Merriday's hand. Then he motioned for Colton, who ran to him and hugged his waist. "You did good, Colton. Real good."

"I just did what you told me," Colton said, his voice muffled against Asa's shirt.

"I knew I could count on you to be brave," Asa said, patting the boy on the back. "You will be a fine man, Colton."

The tender exchange loosened shock's hold on Mason. His knees became mush and he sat down on the nearest chair. Birdie clambered up onto his lap. "We gotta go get Charlotte," the little girl stated.

Mason nodded, his heart thumping and his breath coming in gasps. He felt like he'd sprinted a mile or ten. "As soon as... I catch my breath."

"I'm going to take this one to our new jail," Merriday said with satisfaction. "Our first tenant. You find out anythin' about him, Chandler?"

"His name is Houghton. He rode with Quantrill and the James gang."

"Whoa!" Merriday exclaimed and took a step back. "What's he doin' in Pepin?"

Mason stared at the sheriff. The moment of truth had come. But he needed to tell Emma first. Still, he had to start. "He knew my father. I'll come to the jail tomorrow and tell you everything." He motioned toward the broken window. "Now I need to board up this window or I'll have bats in tonight. Then I've got to get Charlotte and comfort her." Worried over his little sister, Mason rose and steadied himself. He must do what he must and reveal what could no longer be hidden. But to Emma first to hear it all.

Soon Asa was helping pound nails to board up the gap. "Sorry about the window," Asa said.

"It's a small price to pay for Birdie's life." *And mine.*

Inside the cabin again, Mason added a log to the fire and set the fender in place. He led Birdie outside where Asa waited and shut the door firmly behind himself.

They started walking in the moonlight, back to Asa's, back to Emma, who waited there with Charlotte.

Then he knew he must tell Asa the bare truth. The man had saved their lives. He'd been a friend…until now.

"My father had doings with Houghton. He died in prison. That's where I was in Jefferson City, at the prison there."

Asa paused in midstep and then started up again. "That's hard."

Mason couldn't yet reveal his father's connection with Quantrill and the James gang. What he'd revealed was all he could say now until he made a clean breast of everything to the woman he loved. Tomorrow he'd have to face the sheriff and tonight Emma. What would Emma say, do? Emma. Emma.

Emma paced, drawing a distraught Charlotte along back and forth over the half-log floor of Judith's cabin. Judith sat in the rocking chair with Lily in her lap, praying sometimes aloud. "Father, protect those we love."

"Father, protect those we love," Emma repeated silently.

Charlotte bumped her head against Emma once again. A thought occurred to Emma. Above the child's head, she spread wide her hands. And slapped them together sharply.

Charlotte jumped and looked up.

"You can hear now, Charlotte," Judith spoke clearly and distinctly.

The child stared up at her and finally nodded.

"And you can talk." Emma gazed down at her and stroked her cheek. She must take advantage of these moments to keep Charlotte moving forward. "Say,

'Yes, I can,'" Emma prompted and gestured to her as if she were calling on her in school.

Charlotte's lips moved and her throat swallowed. "I…can…Pa?"

"He will be here soon," Emma promised, hoping and praying to be proved correct.

"Yes," Judith added, "we are praying and the sheriff went with Colton—"

"Judith! We're safe!" Asa's voice boomed through the night—muffled only slightly by the shut door and windows.

"Asa!" Judith sprang up with Lily. They ran to the door and threw it open wide. "Asa! Colton!"

Within moments the two men, Colton and Birdie crowded into the cabin. Exclamations of joy, unrestrained hugging and weeping ensued.

Finally Asa and Judith settled side by side on one bench with their children, and Emma and Mason sat opposite with Birdie and Charlotte. Emma's relief and joy were equally matched.

"Where…" Charlotte began, "bad…man?"

"You talked." Mason stared at her and then lifted her onto his lap and kissed her.

"Where…bad…man?" Charlotte insisted in spite of her halting speech.

"The sheriff took him to jail," Mason said, stroking her soft hair.

Birdie leaned around Mason and touched Charlotte's mouth. "You can talk now. You can hear," she said, wonder in her voice.

Charlotte gripped Birdie's hand. "My…friend."

Tears sprang into Birdie's eyes. "My friend."

Emma wiped away happy tears. But she could not

let this moment pass, either, without the truth. "I was so frightened," she admitted.

"We all were," Asa said. "I hope I never have to face an outlaw like that again. When I peered into Mason's window, I couldn't believe my eyes. The outlaw had Birdie by the throat."

Colton shivered and Asa put an arm around him.

"But why was an outlaw here and why Mason?" Judith asked. "I don't understand."

Asa looked to Mason.

Emma looked to Mason, too.

All in the room awaited his reply.

Mason cleared his throat. "Miss Emma, will you come with us and help me get the girls settled down for the night?"

Emma gazed at him, assessing. He appeared ready to tell her the truth. At last. "Yes." She glanced across the table. "Judith, I don't think I should walk home tonight—"

"I'll have the pallet by the fire ready for you," Judith said, eyeing both of them. "Just let yourself back in."

And with that, Mason watched as Emma donned her coat and scarf. Still keyed up, he tried to gather his thoughts and prepare, but he couldn't. He'd just have to do the best he could with the truth. Then she and Mason with the girls walked out into the frigid night. Charlotte linked Emma and Mason by holding a hand of each, and Birdie clung to Mason's other hand. The moonlight provided cool light, silvering everything in sight.

"Bad man in…jail?" Charlotte asked.

"Yes, I knocked him unconscious. Then Mr. Brant and I hog-tied him and the sheriff took him away on the Brants' horse."

"And he not gonna get outta that jail?" Birdie pursued. Unseen, a barred owl hooted quietly nearby.

"Not till the sheriff takes him away to court," Emma said. "I think that's what he'll do."

"The sheriff will handle it, Birdie," Mason reassured her, glancing down. "We don't have to worry anymore. Are you all right? Did he hurt you?"

"He hurt me when he was holdin' me, but I'm okay. I was praying to God to save us."

"We all were praying," Emma said.

"Yes," Mason agreed.

"Thank you, Jesus," Birdie pronounced and skipped once, showing a bit of her usual cheerful self.

The cold urged them to walk briskly, and soon they stepped into the cabin. Mason stirred up the fire and added another two logs while Emma lit the oil lamp on the table. "What happened to the window?" she asked.

"Asa shot through it. I don't think he had a hope to hit the outlaw, but it startled Houghton and I was able to grab the skillet and knock him out."

Emma shook her head and then drew in a deep breath. "Let's get you girls, ready to sleep."

The getting ready for bed process went more smoothly than Mason expected. The girls appeared exhausted. Sitting in front of the fire, getting warm, he and Emma held and comforted Birdie and Charlotte respectively. Finally both girls fell deeply asleep. Mason carried Birdie and then Charlotte up to their pallets in the loft. Then he faced her.

From her chair in front of the fire, she looked up at him "Tell me," she said simply.

He gazed at her, grateful somehow for the low light. Nonetheless, no more hiding. He must speak the truth now. He tried to take a breath and found his lungs constricted, tense. He paused by the chair beside her. "You already guessed that my father fought for the Confederacy. I wish he'd just enlisted in the regular Confederate Army like I enlisted in the Union Army. That would have been honest, at least." Mason fought for some air, bracing himself. "Instead he rode with Quantrill's Raiders during the war."

At the name "Quantrill," Emma's mouth formed a perfect oval. Still, she patted the chair beside her.

He slumped into it, overwhelmed by the shame of a father who had killed not in battle but in raids, burning honest people out of their homes, attacking unarmed soldiers on leave, doing terrible things he didn't even want to think of.

Emma began, "Is that how this man—"

"There's more. After the war, Quantrill and his raiders did not go back to normal life." He paused as his face twisted with something like mental pain. These thoughts hurt. "Or I guess their normal life had become outlawry. My father joined the James gang."

Emma gasped.

Mason wasn't surprised. It was like saying his father had gone over to the evil one. He went on, just wanting to get through this. "My father was wounded in a bank robbery and then was captured. He wrote to me in late February that he was dying in Missouri State Prison. As soon as the river opened, I headed south—" *And missed meeting you as planned and marrying.* "I thought his death was imminent and I hoped...for reconciliation."

Emma sat very still. "He did not repent?"

"No, and he lingered for months. And then he finally told me the real reason he'd summoned me. He wanted me to find Charlotte and care for her." He forced himself to go on. "He and her mother were not married. He'd heard of her mother's death, her murder." He did not want to say more, but this was the time to tell it all, let it all out. "Houghton, the outlaw, killed Charlotte's mother."

"Oh, no," she gasped again. She reached for him and claimed his hand. "How awful. But why?"

Her touching him, reaching for him, lent him strength. "He thought she knew where the gold from my father's last bank robbery had been stashed."

"And," Emma continued, "he thought you had it."

And what more did Mason have to tell?

Emma sat very still, going over everything that had been revealed in these dark moments. No wonder Mason had held her at arm's length for months. The truth had been much more dreadful than she could have imagined. How awful for this good man. She hazarded a sideways glance at his starkly suffering expression. "I understand now why you keep pushing me away. But why didn't you trust me? You are not your father—"

"How do I know that?" Mason's voice vibrated with pain, sounding tortured. "He was an honest man once, too. How do I know I won't turn out just like him?"

Mason's voice wrenched her heart. She couldn't

hold back the words. "What do you mean? You're one of the finest men I've ever known."

Mason leaped up from the chair. "The sins of the father—"

"Are his sins, not yours." Emma rose, facing him.

He turned away, toward the fire. "He wasn't a bad man when I was a boy—"

"People can change for the better or for the worse. Your father chose the wrong direction. Was it the issue of slavery? The war?"

Mason pressed his hands to the mantel, staring down into the fire, looking defeated. "No, he went off the rails after my mother died."

Emma moved to stand behind him, gripping his shirt and resting her cheek on the back of Mason's shoulders, his soft flannel shirt. "I never knew your father, but I do know people can take a wrong turn. My own brother came back from the war a different man, bitter, angry and given over to drink. That's why Judith and I left home. It was too painful to witness."

Mason shrugged as if dismissing her words.

"Don't take what I say lightly," she said with force. "This is your future, our future we're talking about. Now I know why you've held back from me. I know your secret, or your father's, now. And I'm not frightened of it. You are a good man. Everyone knows that—"

He tried to interrupt.

"Do you think the sheriff would have deputized a man he didn't trust?" she demanded. "Stop it." She hit his shoulder with her open hand. "Now. You're wallowing in your pain. I get that. I can't imagine being ashamed of my father, of seeing him die in prison.

But," she said, emphasizing each word, "*it has nothing to do with the kind of man you are.*"

Mason stilled under her cheek and hands.

"It has nothing to do with us. Now are you going to hold back because of another man's wrongdoing and thus lose me, lose what we could have together?"

Still Mason didn't move.

"You proposed to me once as a stranger and then you released me. Are you going to make me—"

He turned and drew her into his arms. "Emma, my sweet Emma." He buried his face against her right ear. "I don't deserve you—"

"Mason—"

"But I'm going to claim you." He gazed down into her eyes. "If you will consent—once again—to be my wife."

She let the smile claim her face slowly. "At last." She stroked the hair back from his forehead. "Yes, Mason, I love you and will be your wife."

Emma's words sang through Mason's every fiber. Joy sprang up and flooded him. "Emma."

She stood on tiptoe and tilted her head. "Mason?"

Recognizing her invitation, he chuckled deep in his throat. "Emma." Then he lowered his mouth to hers. The kiss began tentatively as he explored her lips. Then he turned serious and claimed her mouth for his own. Finally he breathed, "Emma, my sweet Emma. I love you so."

She snuggled closer, resting against him. The warmth of the fire behind him and Emma soft against him lifted him up. After all this dreadful year, this dreadful night, he felt reclaimed, blessed and fearless.

Emma loved him. They would make a family. He'd have all he ever wanted.

He growled with pleasure and tugged her more tightly into his embrace. She sighed, and the sound released every last shred of his tension. *Thank you, God, for saving us tonight and for this special woman.*

By midmorning the next day, news of the outlaw in the jail swept through town. People were flocking toward the jail to see the outlaw who'd invaded their peaceful and law-abiding town. Mason walked to town and halted at sight of the crowd. He paused— then greeted everyone, and they all wore question marks on their faces. He wished the town had a newspaper. The crowd gathered around him, clamoring for information about the prisoner, and he didn't know what to say.

"We seen the sheriff bring him in last night after dark. Sheriff said he tried to hurt one of your girls," the saloon barkeep said from the edge of the crowd.

Heads turned to the man. Many voices demanded, "Hurt one of Chandler's girls?"

"Why?"

"How?"

"Who is he?"

Mason could not speak. The day he'd dreaded had come.

The sheriff hailed him from the jail porch, "Come on in! I want to hear it all, too."

Mason excused himself, or tried to. But the crowd followed him. He didn't blame them. He'd want to know the truth, too. Then he realized that yesterday he would have been devastated to reveal the truth, but

Emma's sweet kisses the night before and her bene-
diction that he was not his father was healing him.
He could face this.

The townspeople filled the room inside the jail.
Mason and Merriday stood by his desk. "Morning,
Sheriff," Mason said, not knowing how to begin.

"I can hardly believe that your little mute sister
sounded the alarm about this outlaw holding Birdie
hostage," the sheriff said.

People around let out sounds of surprise.

Mason prepared himself to say what he must. "This
is all about my father. I never wanted anybody to
know, but my father died in prison."

A few around him gasped.

Mason ignored it and went on, just wanting to get
through this. "Losing my ma and then the war did
something to him. He was once a law-abiding farmer
but he became an outlaw. This Houghton—" he nodded toward the closed door to the cell "—rode with
him, and they did a bank robbery together."

More gasps and then silence.

Mason forged on. "My father carried away the gold
but never gave Houghton his share. My father was
wounded and then arrested. Houghton thought I'd vis-
ited my father in prison as he lay dying just to get the
gold. Houghton saw me around the prison and found
out who I was. He came after me. That's all I know."

The people around remained silent, evidently unwilling to miss a word.

The sheriff shook his head. "A sorry business.
Sorry you lost your father in such a way. That's hard."

A few around murmured in agreement. The others
watched and waited for more.

"Well, the good thing that came of it was that my father told me about Charlotte so I could get her from the orphans' home."

"I can't quite believe she talked last night."

At the sheriff's statement, a babble of questions broke out around them.

Mason turned to face the crowd that quieted again so they would hear every word. "Charlotte had what the doctor in Illinois called hysterical deafness. Her ears could hear but she had sustained a shock that brought on deafness. I'd never heard of anything like that, but the doc maintained there were cases."

"Oh, my," said Mrs. Ashford, who'd come in late and stood near the door. "The poor child. What was the shock?"

Mason's face fell into grim lines—he felt it droop and harden. He had to work to bring up words. "Last night Houghton admitted to me that he…murdered Charlotte's mother in front of her."

More gasps, more words of outrage. In fact, the crowd surged as if going to the cell to get Houghton.

"Hold up," the sheriff ordered, his hand held high. "The man's in custody, and a deputy and I will be transporting him to Madison to face trial as soon as possible. He will be tried in a court of law for his crimes. Never fear."

The crowd halted and began nodding.

"That's the right way," Mrs. Ashford agreed. "No jury will let a man like that off."

"Any more questions?" the sheriff asked.

The crowd milled around as if waiting to see if anybody would ask one.

"Did your little sister really speak?" Mrs. Ashford asked.

"Yes," Mason replied, hoping this public interrogation would soon end. "She was behind me when Houghton grabbed Birdie and threatened her." The memory still shook him. "Charlotte ran away, straight to Asa and Judith's cabin, and gave the alarm."

"That was brave of such a little girl," the storekeeper's wife pronounced.

The crowd softened at this. "Poor child," some murmured.

The sheriff summarized the rest of the events and then began shooing people out. "I need to take down a formal statement from Mason. And then I'm riding out to Asa's to deputize him. I just want to get this outlaw out of town. Winter's closin' in."

People filed out, all talking.

At the end, Mrs. Ashford hurried inside and surprised Mason with a hug. "I'm going home to bake cookies for your girls. What a terrible thing to happen to them. Poor Birdie." The woman was still talking and she left, closing the door behind her.

"Sit down," Merriday invited.

Mason sank into the chair by the desk.

"I know you'd have rather said all that private-like, but this way you won't have to repeat it. At least, not till the court date. You'll have to appear as a witness and bring your girls."

"I don't want Birdie to have to testify—"

"Just seeing her sweet little face will do the trick. That child could charm the birds from the trees. Houghton doesn't have a chance of beating this charge. Asa will have to testify too."

"I hate this."

"I hate it, too. I'd hoped this jail would remain empty. But we built it for a purpose. Pepin's a great little town with a lot of good people, but we aren't immune to the evil in this world."

Mason nodded. Soon he'd written down his formal statement and signed it. Now all he wanted to do was see Emma. He'd debated about sending the girls to school today, but Emma had arrived at his door that morning and insisted it was best for them to have as normal a day as possible. She'd brought them with her to school earlier. He'd had to take care of the stock before he could leave.

As he stepped out once again, he wished he could be invisible. But people had heard everything and had returned to their normal business. However, everyone waved to him as he passed, which surprised him. He'd thought that after hearing the truth about his father, they'd reject him. *I shouldn't have doubted them, doubted Emma.*

He found himself nearly running as he headed for the schoolhouse. When he reached it, common sense stopped him from going inside and disturbing her while she taught. And what could he say to her in front of a classroom of children?

Still he couldn't make himself not gaze at her through one of the tall windows. He still couldn't believe that everything had come right. He had Birdie and Charlotte, who could now talk, and soon Emma would be his wife. He'd have a whole family once more.

Then Emma, the woman he loved, glanced out the window. Their gazes connected them. She smiled and he felt it go straight to his heart. He mouthed, "I love you."

She returned the words and then a child rose, his hand raised, blocking Mason's view and the moment was broken.

Mason turned away, suddenly aware of the chill again. What a woman. What a gift from God.

Chapter Sixteen

The stove in the Ashfords' store was sending out heat, but most who'd come to town on this early December Saturday kept on their coats. As if it were a prearranged social occasion, people from the surrounding homesteads crowded the store.

And from behind the fabric counter, Emma, who'd been asked to help out on this busy pre-Christmas shopping day, supposed it was a special day. Everyone—even those who lived far from town—had by now heard about the prisoner in the jail and wanted to discuss the events leading up to it. And something else of note had happened. The Mississippi had frozen over two days before.

The chalkboard calendar stood propped up and everyone kept glancing at it. Mr. Ashford had circled the winning day—December 7, and the winning name. And while most of the people here were waiting for the winner, she tried not to let her excitement show, for she was keyed for more than that. She was waiting for the man she loved. The days since their first kiss had passed as a blur of happiness to Emma.

The doorbell jingled. Her father, followed by a grinning Eb, entered. Everyone turned and applauded. Her father was followed in by Judith's family, all grinning. Dan bowed his head, modestly acknowledging the accolade.

Ashford bustled around the counter. "The winner of the competition over the date of the Mississippi freezing over is, of course, our friend Dan Jones!"

More applause and some whistles and some foot-stamping greeted this.

"Speech! Speech!" someone called out.

Dan chuckled. "Nothing much to say, friends." He spread his hands wide, palms up. "I just chose a date and it happened to be the right one. However…" He paused dramatically. "I intend to milk this reputation for wisdom for the next ten years! At least!"

Everyone chuckled. Dan's special friends slapped him on the back and shook his hand. The fact that her father had already made a place for himself in this town, now their hometown, pleased her.

The doorbell jingled and Charlotte ran in. "Mama!" she called out, running straight for Emma.

Instant silence. Every face turned toward her and then to Mason, who entered with Birdie in hand. Emma and Mason had tried to stop Charlotte from addressing Emma as "Mama," but the little girl refused. And they were so happy she was talking, they'd given up. Birdie ran to Emma and hugged her, too.

"Mason," Dan said loudly, "I won!"

Mason paused on his way toward Emma. "No, I won."

Everyone looked confused.

"Yes, folks," Dan said even more proudly, rocking

back on his heels, "Mason Chandler has asked permission to marry my daughter Emma…come spring. And I've given my blessing."

A shocked moment of silence and then more applause. All the women gathered around Emma, kissing her cheek and patting her back, voicing their happiness for her.

Emma gazed across the crowded room and exchanged tender glances with the man she loved and whom she'd marry come spring. She had decided to finish the school year and to enjoy being courted.

"But who will teach school next year?" Mrs. Ashford asked above the hubbub.

Mrs. Waggoner stepped away from Emma. "Well, I never mentioned it, but in the years before I married, I taught school. I may have silver in my hair, but I don't think I'm too old to take over our small school. I'd like to apply."

Another shocked moment of silence, followed by a buzz of voices.

Mr. Ashford held up his hands. "The school board will of course consider you as a candidate, Mrs. Waggoner. But right now let's celebrate—Dan's success and the engagement of our deputy and charming schoolmarm!" Turning toward the counter, he swept off a cloth, revealing a heaping tray of cookies. "On the house!" he announced.

More applause.

Mason finally managed to escape those congratulating him and reached Emma. He slipped an arm around her waist. Birdie and Charlotte held Mason's and Emma's hands respectively. Emma saw her own happiness reflected in their faces and in Mason's. Two years ago she'd begun writing to a lonely stranger in faraway Wisconsin. She'd been convinced she could never love again but had been compelled to find a better place for her and her sister.

Now she glanced at Judith, who was just beginning to show her delicate condition and who was holding hands with Asa, surrounded by Lily and Colton. And she glanced down at Birdie's bright, happy face and Charlotte, who was healing day by day. Mason leaned over and kissed her cheek, and her heart sang a wordless song of praise to God, who'd worked everything out for their good.

* * * * *

Don't miss these other
WILDERNESS BRIDES *stories from Lyn Cote:*

*THEIR FRONTIER FAMILY
THE BABY BEQUEST
HEARTLAND COURTSHIP
FRONTIER WANT AD BRIDE*

Available now from Love Inspired Historical!

Find more great reads at www.LoveInspired.com

Dear Reader,

Well, my stories of the twin mail-order brides comes to an end, a happy one. Mason discovered that his father's past sins were not his own and Emma learned that her heart had not died with her first love. And sweet little Birdie and Charlotte have a real family at last.

This is the fifth story set in Pepin, Wisconsin. I've enjoyed researching and writing about this town so rich in history, beginning with the birth there of Laura Ingalls Wilder. If you recall, Pepin was the setting for *Little House in the Big Woods*, the first of the Little House stories.

The romances of Sunny and Noah (*Their Frontier Family*), Ellen and Kurt (*The Baby Bequest*), Rachel and Brennan (*Heartland Courtship*), Judith and Asa (*Frontier Want Ad Bride*) and finally Emma and Mason (*Suddenly a Frontier Father*) have been delightful stories to write. I've enjoyed each one and hope you have, too.

If you'd like to keep up with my next book or check on older titles, drop by my website: www.LynCote.com. I maintain a printable booklist there. Also you can sign up for my newsletter so you don't miss what I'll be doing. Hope you'll keep in touch.

Blessings,
Lyn Cote

COMING NEXT MONTH FROM
Love Inspired® Historical

Available March 6, 2018

FRONTIER MATCHMAKER BRIDE

Frontier Bachelors • by Regina Scott

When the most influential women in Seattle ask successful matchmaker Beth Wallin to find a wife for Deputy Sheriff Hart McCormick, she can't turn them down...even if the handsome lawman once refused her love. But when she realizes *she's* his best match, will she be able to convince him?

THE AMISH NANNY'S SWEETHEART

Amish Country Brides • by Jan Drexler

After moving in with her sister to act as nanny for her nieces and nephew, Judith Lapp doesn't expect to teach Pennsylvania Dutch to the *Englischer* across the road...or to fall for him. But will he put his past aside to embrace Amish life—and their love?

ACCIDENTAL FAMILY

The Bachelors of Aspen Valley • by Lisa Bingham

After newborn twins are left on his doorstep—along with a note begging him to protect them—Pastor Charles Wanlass marries mail-order bride Willow Granger to keep the babies safe. But can their temporary arrangement blossom into the forever family they both hope for?

HUSBAND BY ARRANGEMENT

by Angel Moore

Pregnant and abandoned by the man who promised to marry her, Rena Livingston must enter a marriage of convenience with Sheriff Scott Braden to save her reputation. The more time they spend together, though, the more she wishes theirs could be a true marriage...

LOOK FOR THESE AND OTHER LOVE INSPIRED BOOKS WHEREVER BOOKS ARE SOLD, INCLUDING MOST BOOKSTORES, SUPERMARKETS, DISCOUNT STORES AND DRUGSTORES.

Get 2 Free Books,
Plus 2 Free Gifts—
just for trying the Reader Service!

YES! Please send me 2 FREE Love Inspired® Romance novels and my 2 FREE mystery gifts (gifts are worth about $10 retail). After receiving them, if I don't wish to receive any more books, I can return the shipping statement marked "cancel." If I don't cancel, I will receive 6 brand-new novels every month and be billed just $5.24 for the regular-print edition or $5.74 each for the larger-print edition in the U.S., or $5.74 each for the regular-print edition or $6.24 each for the larger-print edition in Canada. That's a saving of at least 13% off the cover price. It's quite a bargain! Shipping and handling is just 50¢ per book in the U.S. and 75¢ per book in Canada.* I understand that accepting the 2 free books and gifts places me under no obligation to buy anything. I can always return a shipment and cancel at any time. The free books and gifts are mine to keep no matter what I decide.

Please check one:
- ☐ Love Inspired Romance Regular-Print
  (105/305 IDN GMWU)
- ☐ Love Inspired Romance Larger-Print
  (122/322 IDN GMWU)

Name _____ (PLEASE PRINT)

Address _____ Apt. # _____

City _____ State/Province _____ Zip/Postal Code _____

Signature (if under 18, a parent or guardian must sign)

Mail to the **Reader Service:**
IN U.S.A.: P.O. Box 1341, Buffalo, NY 14240-8531
IN CANADA: P.O. Box 603, Fort Erie, Ontario L2A 5X3

Want to try two free books from another line?
Call 1-800-873-8635 today or visit www.ReaderService.com.

*Terms and prices subject to change without notice. Prices do not include applicable taxes. Sales tax applicable in N.Y. Canadian residents will be charged applicable taxes. Offer not valid in Quebec. This offer is limited to one order per household. Books received may not be as shown. Not valid for current subscribers to Love Inspired Romance books. All orders subject to approval. Credit or debit balances in a customer's account(s) may be offset by any other outstanding balance owed by or to the customer. Please allow 4 to 6 weeks for delivery. Offer available while quantities last.

Your Privacy—The Reader Service is committed to protecting your privacy. Our Privacy Policy is available online at www.ReaderService.com or upon request from the Reader Service.

We make a portion of our mailing list available to reputable third parties that offer products we believe may interest you. If you prefer that we not exchange your name with third parties, or if you wish to clarify or modify your communication preferences, please visit us at www.ReaderService.com/consumerschoice or write to us at Reader Service Preference Service, P.O. Box 9062, Buffalo, NY 14240-9062. Include your complete name and address.

LI17R3

If you loved this story from
Love Inspired® Historical
be sure to discover more inspirational
stories to warm your heart from
Love Inspired® and
Love Inspired® Suspense!

Love Inspired stories show that
faith, forgiveness and hope have the power
to lift spirits and change lives—always.

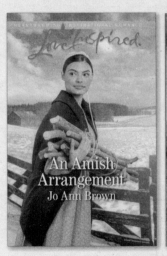

Look for six new romances every month
from **Love Inspired®** and
Love Inspired® Suspense!

"Beth, stay away from the docks. There are some rough
sorts down there."

The two workers hadn't seemed all that rough to her.
"You forget. I have five brothers."

"Your brothers are gentlemen. Some of those workers
aren't."

She really shouldn't take Hart's statements as anything
more than his duty as a lawman. "Very well. I'll be careful."

His gaze moved to the wharves, as if he saw a gang of
marauding pirates rather than busy longshoremen. "Good. I
wouldn't want anything to happen to you."

Beth stared at him.

"I'd hate to have to explain to your brothers," he added.

Well! She was about to tell him exactly what she thought
of the idea when she noticed a light in his eyes. Was that a
twinkle in the gray?

Beth tossed her head. "Oh, they'll take your side. You

know they will. They always say I have more enthusiasm than sense."

He shrugged. "I know a few women who match that description."

Beth grinned. "But none as pretty as me."

"That's the truth." His gaze warmed, and she caught her breath. Hart McCormick, flirting with her? It couldn't be!

Fingers fumbling, she untied the horses and hurried for the bench. "I should go. Lots to do before two. See you at the Emporium."

He followed her around. Before she knew what he was about, he'd placed his hands on her waist. For one moment, she stood in his embrace. Her stomach fluttered.

He lifted her easily onto the bench and stepped back, face impassive as if he hadn't been affected in the slightest. "Until two, Miss Wallin."

Her heart didn't slow until she'd rounded the corner.

Silly! Why did she keep reacting that way? He wasn't interested in her. He'd told her so himself.

She was not about to offer him her heart. There was no reason to behave like a giddy schoolgirl on her first infatuation.

Even if he had been her schoolgirl infatuation.

She was a woman now, with opportunities, plans, dreams for a future. And she wasn't about to allow herself to take a chance on love again, especially not with Hart McCormick.

For now, the important thing was to find the perfect woman for him, and she knew just where to look.

Don't miss
FRONTIER MATCHMAKER BRIDE by Regina Scott,
available March 2018 wherever
Love Inspired® Historical books and ebooks are sold.

www.LoveInspired.com